Praise for

THE APPRENTICE WITCH

"A pleasant trip back to a simpler age."
—*The New York Times Book Review*

"As cozy as a teapot and as comfy as old slippers."
—*Kirkus Reviews*

"Magical. . . . Readers will love this fast-paced fantasy read and won't be able to put it down."
—*B&N Kids Blog*

"One of those rare, unputdownable gems. . . . Reminiscent of J.K. Rowling's
Fantastic Beasts and Where to Find Them."
—*School Library Journal*

"*The Apprentice Witch* will at once open a new and imaginative world and feel
like the book you have loved forever."
—**Jennifer A. Nielsen, author of** *The False Prince*

"*The Apprentice Witch* is entirely more charming, adventurous, and full of heart than
a book has any right to be."
—**Trenton Lee Stewart, author of** *The Mysterious Benedict Society*

"While adorned with funny and charming details, Arianwyn's story is primarily
one of personal growth and discovery that will gratify fantasy readers. . ."
—*Booklist*

"At once fresh and familiar . . ."
—*Shelf Awareness*

"Readers who enjoy fantasy and challenging predicaments will appreciate Arianwyn's
transformation from a failure to a competent and valued sorcerer."
—*School Library Connection*

"Arianwyn Gribble learns of the power that comes with knowing one's
self-worth and conquering the darkness within."
—*Publishers Weekly*

A WITCH ALONE

JAMES NICOL

Chicken House

SCHOLASTIC INC. / NEW YORK

Library of Congress Cataloging-in-Publication Data available

ISBN 978-1-338-18851-6

10 9 8 7 6 5 4 3 2 1   18 19 20 21 22

Printed in the U.S.A.   23

First edition, October 2018

Book design by Maeve Norton

For Julian, who brings music,
laughter, and sunshine into my life.

A WITCH ALONE: A MANUAL FOR THE NEWLY QUALIFIED WITCH

✦ ✦ ✦

EXCERPT FROM THE MANUAL

Before setting out as a fully fledged witch and taking up your new position, wherever that may be, be sure to ask yourself these three key questions:

1. What do you hope to achieve as a witch?
2. What do you have to offer the community you will serve in the months and years ahead of you?
3. How will you build on your strengths and remedy any weaknesses?

As you embark on this new chapter in your career, remember that you are no longer an apprentice. Others will now look to you for advice and guidance and support. Are you ready for the task at hand?

CHAPTER ONE

BREAKFAST

The kitchen was littered with the remains of breakfast. Plates and bowls were discarded on the table, eggshells sat cracked and empty in their cups, crusts of toast lay abandoned on plates. The tablecloth was sprinkled with crumbs and smeared here and there with rich orange marmalade, butter, or bright raspberry jam. The radio burbled in the background.

Arianwyn took a sip from her cup of tea, looking up from the charm recipe she had been working on to gaze out through the window across the rooftops of Kingsport. Ribbons of smoke snaked high into the bright, cool sky. The leaves of a nearby tree were beginning to fade dusty and pale, and the air through the open window had the crisp, cool feeling of autumn.

She felt wonderfully relaxed. She really had needed a vacation after all the goings-on back in Lull over the summer.

Salle, her best friend in the whole world, gave a squeal of excitement and thrust a crumpled newspaper in her face. "Look! There's going to be a parade from the palace this afternoon." She beamed. "Can we go, Wyn? Please?" she asked, her eyes wide, lashes fluttering.

"But don't you have an audition today?" Arianwyn asked. This would be Salle's fourth audition since they had arrived a week and a half ago. She had her heart set on becoming a great actress.

"Oh, I did." Salle smiled and glanced away for a moment. "But it's a silly part, boring, hardly any lines—I'd much rather go and see the king, wouldn't you? *Pleeeeease*, Arianwyn?"

Arianwyn laughed. "I suppose so. We could go to the Museum of Hylund too; it's just around the corner from the Royal Palace."

Salle nodded enthusiastically, stuffing the last piece of toast into her mouth and beaming again. "I still need to visit Leighton & Dennison's to get Aunt Grace a present," she said.

It was Salle's first visit to Kingsport and they had been making the most of it. They'd explored the city on foot and by bus, visited parks, galleries, and the harbor market—and, in between, they'd hurried to theaters all over the capital in hopes of Salle finally securing her first part in a proper play, show, or revue. She really didn't seem to mind what it was at this point, as long as it was in a real theater.

From out in the hallway, they heard the front door of the apartment open quietly, followed by the clatter of shoes being kicked off in the hall and the sound of keys being dropped into the bowl that stood on the hall table. "Girls?" Arianwyn's grandmother called. "Are you still home?"

"In here!" Salle called cheerfully, spraying a few more crumbs across the table. Grandmother appeared at the door. She leaned on the frame and yawned.

"Late meeting?" Arianwyn asked.

"Or early, I'm not entirely sure!" Grandmother replied as she dropped into her armchair next to the kitchen fireplace. She sighed contentedly, stretching her legs out and resting her head back against the seat. "I had no idea when I agreed to rejoin the Council of Elders that there would be quite so many meetings."

"I guess there's a lot going on at the moment with the war. Is there still a shortage of trained witches?" Salle asked.

Grandmother nodded wearily.

The war against the Urisians in the northern kingdom of Veersland and the increasing magical activity across the Four Kingdoms in the last few years required skilled witches. There just didn't seem to be enough of them.

"I'll make you some fresh tea," Arianwyn said, getting to her feet. She moved quickly across the kitchen. "Do you want some breakfast as well?" she asked, putting the kettle back on the stove and then arranging a cup and saucer ready for the tea.

"Well, actually, I think it's nearly lunchtime. What on earth have you girls been doing all morning? You're still in your dressing gowns!" Grandmother chuckled.

"We're planning to go and see the parade at the palace and then maybe go to the museum," Salle said brightly.

"That does sound very lovely," Grandmother said, closing her eyes for just a moment.

"Why don't you come with us?" Salle asked. "Have the day off?"

"If only." Grandmother sighed. "But I've got reports to read." She reached for her bag, which bulged with folders and papers. "And I've got to meet with some members of the Royal Senate. Why the High Elder asked me, I have no idea, as the last thing I want to be doing is dealing with a load of politicians. I can't be doing with all their bluster and nonsense."

"Perhaps that's why she asked *you,* then." Arianwyn handed her the cup of tea.

Grandmother rolled her eyes and groaned, but she smiled as she settled back into her seat and sipped gently on the tea.

"We should go and get ready—we don't want to miss the parade," Salle said as she darted out of the kitchen. Arianwyn scooped up some of the breakfast things and carried them to the sink.

"I can sort those things out for you. Off you go and get ready." Grandmother smiled.

Arianwyn skipped to the door and then paused, her hand held on the frame.

"Everything okay?" Grandmother asked, the teacup hovering near her lips.

"I . . ." The question had been gnawing at the back of Arianwyn's mind since they arrived in Kingsport. "I wanted to know what had happened about the . . ." She felt a chill just thinking about the night ghast they had encountered in Lull. She didn't dare to say the words, worried that this most terrible of dark spirits might suddenly appear before them in all its horrifying darkness.

Grandmother sighed and placed the teacup carefully down. "The night ghast?" she said, rising to her feet. She was tall, her long silver hair pinned tidily away. She put her hand on Arianwyn's shoulder. "I keep telling you there's nothing to worry about. The council has reviewed all the reports. Mine, yours, Mayor Belcher's, even the Alverston girl's—"

"Gimma?" Arianwyn asked. A name that she also hadn't dared say for weeks.

Grandmother smiled. "That's all done now, all behind you. You don't need to be worrying about anything, Arianwyn. You did everything you could. There is no blame."

Arianwyn smiled, Grandmother's words soothing the worry. She always knew how to make things right again. Then Salle came barreling along the hallway, pulling on her jacket and at the same time fixing a hair clip into place. "Hurry up, Wyn, or we'll be late . . . unless you're planning on going to the royal parade like that?"

Arianwyn smiled and did a quick spin on the spot, flapping her dressing gown around her like a cloak. "But I hear it's all the rage in Highbridge!" she laughed, her dark thoughts briefly chased away.

Salle and Arianwyn hurried along the sidewalk. The streets were packed with people waving small paper flags and jostling toward the palace.

"Hylund flags! Two for a shilling!" a man called from the street corner. He held a bunch of flags tight in his hand like a bouquet of flowers. "Flags, ladies?" he called as Salle and Arianwyn approached.

"No thank you!" Arianwyn called. Salle looked crestfallen. "You don't want to miss the parade, do you?" Arianwyn asked, dragging Salle along as she gazed forlornly back at the flag seller.

They turned off the main street and onto a smaller, quieter avenue full of dazzling white Highbridge houses, each identical to the last, finished with clipped hedges and high metal railings, with ebony front doors and gleaming brass handles. "We can cut down to the Royal Circle this way," Arianwyn explained, recalling so many trips with her grandmother to look at the palace or visit the nearby parks.

The sidewalks in Highbridge were spotlessly clean—not even the first few scatterings of autumn leaves littered the paving stones. They passed a pristine nanny pushing a vast stroller with huge silver wheels that flashed in the warm afternoon sun.

"Well, it's certainly the swankiest bit of Kingsport, isn't it?" Salle said, twirling on the spot just as an impeccably dressed woman emerged from her front yard. Salle's clumsy pirouette forced the lady to dodge aside, almost tumbling into her neatly trimmed hedge. She muttered something under her breath in a biting, crisp Highbridge accent.

"Sorry!" Arianwyn offered quickly, but the woman only glared at them both and carried on without another word, a bit of hedge stuck to her bottom.

"Snob!" Salle called, with no effort to lower her voice, then imitating the woman's very stiff upright walk farther down the street.

Arianwyn chuckled and ran to catch her up. Just ahead, the avenue widened, the buildings curving off to the left and right, opening onto the Royal Crescent, which was already packed with people. As they passed the last house, they were swept giggling into the crowd like paper boats on a river.

CHAPTER TWO

A GLIMPSE OF THE KING

Arianwyn reached for Salle's hand as she was pulled forward by the overenthusiastic spectators. Her fingers tightened around Salle's and they held on tight.

"Wow—this is mad!" Salle laughed. "I LOVE it!"

They clung to each other and were jostled along with the flow of the crowd, everyone calling and cheering merrily.

"Don't let go," Arianwyn shouted. "Or we'll never find each other again!"

Salle nodded. They were suddenly and miraculously shoved to the edge of the sidewalk, and the scene of the parade opened wide before them. The Royal Crescent stood at the heart of Kingsport, the actual "crescent" being a huge oval park that had once been a rose garden for the palace but was now a public space full of trees, fountains, and brightly colored flowers. A broad road circled the park. Usually clogged with Kingsport traffic, today it was empty of cars and buses and swept spotlessly clean. The sidewalks were stuffed full of well-wishers, all kept in place behind strings of bright bunting and a line of soldiers and policemen. It was a sea of fluttering flags, bright camera flashes, and smiles.

"Oh, Wyn, this is amazing!" Salle beamed.

"I think we'd get a better view from farther up." Arianwyn gestured ahead of them.

"My goodness, that's the Royal Palace!" Salle said, tugging on Arianwyn's coat and dragging her along. "I didn't know we'd get so close. Aunt Grace would love this."

Soon, the flowing crowd of people became an immovable wall. "Will this do?" Arianwyn asked. If she stood on tiptoes and wobbled slightly to the right, she could just see the broad steps that led up to the palace gates.

Salle smiled.

"Oh, and here," Arianwyn said, reaching into her satchel. "I didn't think we could do without these!" She pulled out two small Hylund paper flags. She handed one to Salle and gave her own a little wave.

"Oh, Wyn! Thank you!" Salle grinned in delight and swished her flag this way and that with more enthusiasm than Arianwyn had thought physically possible. From the steps of the palace came the blasting sound of trumpets, which brought a sudden hush to the crowd. "I can see the king!" Salle squealed, tugging at Arianwyn's coat sleeve. "Look. *Look!*"

A figure appeared, walking steadily down the steps of the palace, flanked by courtiers in shining top hats and long flapping tailcoats, or elegant dresses and hats that looked like very fancy cakes. The king waved gently, and the crowd responded with a loud cheer that became a roar. There was a small surge forward, and as Arianwyn tried to stay upright, she stood on someone's foot.

"Oh my word!" Salle gaped, her eyes wide. Then in a mock cheery voice she said, "Goodness, look who it is." She nudged Arianwyn hard in the ribs.

"Sorry," Arianwyn said, looking quickly up and coming face-to-face with Gimma Alverston. "Oh, heavens!"

"Arianwyn?" Gimma's perfect blonde hair, impeccably styled, was swept over one shoulder in a tumble of white gold. Her eyes, usually bright blue, looked dull and red-rimmed, and her skin was pale, as though she had been shut up inside for too long. The effect on anyone else would have been awful, but it just seemed to make Gimma more beautiful than ever.

"Gimma?" Arianwyn asked, thinking for a moment she was hallucinating. But no. She tugged at the sleeve of her thrift store dress. It was too short for her long arms, her wrists sticking out inelegantly. Gimma's was perfect, pristine white—handmade in the best fashion houses in Kingsport, of that you could be certain.

"What are *you* doing here?" Gimma asked, taking the smallest but most definite step away from them.

"Salle wanted to see the parade," Arianwyn explained. Half of Kingsport was here—what an odd question!

"Exciting, isn't it?" Salle said, fixing Gimma with a hard glare and flicking her flag back and forth.

"If you like that sort of thing," Gimma said, stifling a little yawn and studying her hands. She was wearing pink suede gloves, despite the warm afternoon.

"Well, I think it's amazing!" Salle said, undeterred, waving her flag twice as fast. "It's nearly as good as the Flaxsham parade in the summer, don't you think?"

Gimma's head snapped around. She glowered at Salle. The Flaxsham witches' parade had been a massive disaster, thanks to Gimma.

"Anyway," Arianwyn said brightly, trying to change the subject, "what brings you here, Gimma?"

"Oh, my father's in the parade with some of the Royal Senate." Gimma flicked her hand as though she wasn't really bothered.

Just then, a lady and her small daughter edged their way carefully to the front of the crowd beside Gimma. The daughter was busily eating a bright pink ice cream. The mother smiled at the three girls and then pointed across the wide street. "Can you see Papa?" A soldier nearby blushed and briefly raised a hand in greeting.

"Been doing anything interesting with your stay, then?" Gimma asked, but she only sounded bored.

"Salle's been for some auditions, haven't you?" Arianwyn said.

Salle nodded, but didn't look at Gimma; her flag-flapping became rather less enthusiastic.

"Oh . . . ," Gimma replied, flicking her hair back across her shoulder. "Of course you probably know that I'm on probation, pending further investigation or something like that," she added, as though it was quite an everyday sort of thing to open a rift and let a night ghast through from the void, placing a whole town at risk. "And I have to go back to dreary old Lull. To retrain with dotty old Delafield and . . . oh, *you*, Arianwyn."

Arianwyn nearly choked. Someone was having a great deal of fun at her expense, it would seem. "What? Is that a . . . good idea?" she asked carefully, trying not to sound unkind.

"Precisely what my mother said," Gimma answered. "But the director was having none of it, so back to Lull it is. Wretched little place!"

Arianwyn looked at Salle, who rolled her eyes. Near the palace, the royal party were finally seated in several carriages, which were now moving slowly away. At the head of the parade, a pair of guards sat astride two huge white horses. The horses held their heads as though the parade was for them alone.

"Are you ready to wave your flag?" Salle asked the small girl, who smiled up at her shyly. She handed her ice cream to her mother and flicked her flag this way and that.

"You can do better than that!" the girl's mother encouraged her, and Salle gave her flag a sudden crazy swoosh and whooped with delight.

The girl giggled and tried to match Salle's movement. But she was a little too haphazard. As the girl moved her flag back and forth, she knocked her mother's hand. The pink ice cream flicked from the sugar cone and splodged onto Gimma's pristine white dress before sliding to the ground, leaving a gooey pink trail.

"Watch it! You clumsy idiots!" Gimma roared. She spun around, towering over the small child and the mother, who both shrank back a little. The girl burst into tears.

Arianwyn rushed forward. "Gimma, it's just a little bit of—"

"I'm so sorry. I didn't mean to—" The mother tried to apologize.

"Oh, be quiet, you fool!" Gimma spat.

"Gimma!" Arianwyn gasped. She turned to the mother. "I am so sorry, she's—" Arianwyn started to apologize on Gimma's behalf, but what could she say? *She's not usually like this*? That wasn't entirely the truth. But even so, this seemed more than usually unkind, even for Gimma Alverston.

The mother looked quickly at the three girls, grabbed up her daughter and her basket, and hurried away into the crowd as fast as she could.

"What was all that about?" Arianwyn asked, turning to Gimma.

Gimma, pale and blinking, gazed up at Arianwyn as though she had just woken from a dream. "I . . ." she faltered.

"Do you want us to help you home?" Salle asked, stepping forward and reaching out a hand toward Gimma.

"Just boggin well leave me alone!" Gimma snapped. She pulled away from Arianwyn and turned, crashing into a gentleman behind her.

"Watch it, love!" he said merrily, but shrank back when Gimma glowered at him.

"Gimma!" Arianwyn called.

She turned and her eyes suddenly looked dark and blurry, locking with Arianwyn's for a second. She looked quite unlike herself. Her gloved hand came up to brush her hair from her face, and then she was swallowed up in the mass of people.

Gone.

CHAPTER THREE

ROYAL PANDEMONIUM

"That was a bit weird, wasn't it?" Salle sighed. Arianwyn looked off into the crowd, rather stunned. "What on earth do you think is wrong with her?"

"Who knows. Just Gimma being . . . *Gimma*. But she seems to be worse than ever, don't you think? Are you okay, Wyn?" she asked, placing her hand on Arianwyn's back.

Arianwyn looked off in the direction Gimma had gone. "I guess people don't ever really change, do they?" she said, distracted and unnerved by the outburst. Was that actually true, though? She felt *she* had perhaps changed a little in the last nine months.

"Is that what you really think?" Salle asked. She looked rather cross.

"What?" Arianwyn asked. "Well, I don't know. But look at Gimma."

"Never mind her," Salle grumbled. "Just forget I said anything. Don't let her spoil the day entirely—oh, look, here they come!"

First came the royal guards mounted on their huge white

horses. The guards were dressed from top to toe in red and gold, silver breastplates gleaming in the afternoon sun like brilliant mirrors. They kept their eyes fixed on the road ahead as the music from the band played on farther around the crescent. There was a small break, and then came a gleaming, maroon, open-topped carriage. It moved slowly along the crescent, stately and elegant, pulled by eight dark horses, their manes and tails twisted in tight braids entwined with ribbons in the colors of the Hylund flag: yellow, blue, and red.

"Oh, it's him!" Salle cheered. "It's the king!"

There was a loud cheer from the crowd as the carriage drew closer. And then Arianwyn saw him, the king himself, waving and smiling from the carriage.

Salle started to wave her flag again as the cheers grew louder and the carriage drew nearer. "This is so exciting, Wyn. I can't believe it!"

There was a flash of light. And the sky was suddenly full of fluttering, falling shapes. The crowd cooed. Was it some sort of firework? Or perhaps flowers or streamers, shot into the sky from somewhere nearby?

But for Arianwyn the surprise and excitement were speedily, hurriedly, replaced with a tug of fear. She felt the urgent prickle of magic around her. And she looked up at the sky again. Whatever it was that filled the air above them now was not confetti or flowers or fireworks, of that she was certain. And now the things began to move, to twist in the air, to dive and swoop.

"Oh no," she breathed.

"What is it?" Salle asked as the oohs and aahs turned to low, uncertain murmurs.

Flying just a few feet or so above their heads was a flock of spirit creatures, each one no larger than a cat but with wide, batlike wings, tusked mouths, and four legs that ended in grabbing, snatching, many-fingered hands.

"Jinxing-jiggery!" Arianwyn groaned. "Where did they boggin well come from?"

"What are they?" Salle asked, her eyes now fixed on the airborne swarm.

"Winged grippets!"

"Is that . . . bad?" Salle asked.

"Well, it's not good." Arianwyn reached for Salle and pulled her back, away from the edge of the street. "They're not *entirely* dangerous, but with so many of them, they could cause—"

At that very moment a small portion of the swarm nosedived into the crowd a little farther along the sidewalk, and chaos erupted around them. There were shrieks and agitated cries as the winged grippets snatched at anything and everything they could get their many grabbing hands on. Flags, hats, ice creams, purses, parasols, and shawls were wrenched from their owners and carried speedily aloft before being hurled or dropped back down just moments later.

Then another group broke away from the flock and spiraled down over the mounted guards, who were now about three buildings along from Arianwyn and Salle, seemingly oblivious to what was going on. Before Arianwyn could react, it was already too late, and the guards were taken by surprise as the winged grippets fell upon them and then lifted them from their horses and up a few yards into the air. Legs and arms kicking wildly, all guardly composure fled in the face of this magical menace. Their swords were snatched away and sent shooting across the street as people darted for cover. The shouts of confusion were now changing to screams of fear.

. The horses—spooked by the chattering, snorting cries of the winged grippets and the frantic shouts from their riders—charged off along the road, three of them mounting the sidewalk as bystanders leapt out of their way into shop doorways and alleyways. One lady even jumped into a garbage can as one of the out-of-control horses raced past as though it were about to win first place at the Kingsport Derby.

"Stay here!" Arianwyn called to Salle as she ducked under the bunting that was strung up as a cordon for the crowds on the sidewalk. She ran forward and aimed a swift kick at a nearby winged-grippet that was running to rejoin the others. It went tumbling across the street and she quickly stunned it with a spell orb. It twitched against the curb and then fell still. There was a small cheer from the crowd that watched nearby.

But this was followed by a scream. Someone pointed up to the winged grippets, who had just released the guards they had lifted from the horses. And the men were suddenly dropping through the air, like huge red-and-gold rag dolls.

"Briå!" Arianwyn called loudly, her instincts taking over.

Her hands sketched the air glyph at the same time. She felt a rush of magic, stronger than it would usually be in the city, but she was thankful for it as it connected with the glyph and she formed the spell. It was crude and rushed, far from fancy, but it would have to do. She sent a rush of air straight at the falling guards, hoping to cushion them against the hard road. It didn't quite work like that, but thankfully the spell slowed them enough so that although they hit the ground—swords, breastplates, and helmets clattering against the road as they landed—it looked like she'd saved them from the worst.

"Oh, please be okay," Arianwyn muttered, hurrying toward the guards, who lay worryingly still. But then one of them sat up, shaking his head in disbelief. He saw Arianwyn, his eyes falling on her silver star badge. He smiled and raised a hand.

"Look out!" Arianwyn turned at Salle's frantic cry just as another two carriages, empty of their passengers, raced toward her, winged grippets sitting astride the horses. Arianwyn leapt aside just in time, monkeylike chatter filling the air as the carriages hurtled past. Her eyes scrunched tightly closed, she felt the rush of wind as the carriages sped past, just inches from her.

A smaller group of winged grippets flew behind the carriages. Arianwyn moved to the middle of the street, where the guards were still helping one another to their feet. She readied her spell orb and waited until the winged grippets were close enough before launching the popping, fizzing ball of energy toward them. There was a gasp of surprise from the assembled crowd as the spell orb flew up into the air and among the creatures. But they were faster than Arianwyn's spell and they shot off in every direction as the orb flashed in the air, raining down a shower of fizzing sparks, like rather disappointing fireworks.

Arianwyn glanced quickly back at Salle, who gave a supportive shrug that more or less said, *That wasn't brilliant, but you can do better!*

Farther along the street, she saw another carriage was under attack by yet more of the winged grippets, and the sole occupant was calling for help as they tried to drag him feetfirst up into the air. The carriage appeared to have lost one whole wheel and part of another, and as a result it wobbled, threatening to topple over.

Arianwyn ran along the crescent, dodging a horse that was making a break for freedom, reins dangling behind it as it charged past. She hurled another spell orb toward the winged grippets, smacking one squarely as it tugged on the boot of the man in the carriage. The force helped the boot loosen, and the winged-grippet went tumbling through the air briefly before landing amid the watching crowd on the sidewalk. "Sorry!" Arianwyn called as she neared the carriage, the man still bravely resisting the creatures, their quick hands grasping and grabbing for his trousers, jacket, and occasionally his hair.

She was just about to launch another spell when a burst of magic arced over her head and stunned another two winged grippets. The man was freed, and fell with a crash back into the carriage, which then tipped onto its side. She heard quick feet on the road behind and, turning, saw two other witches racing toward her, hurling spell orbs this way and that as the winged grippets crashed to the ground, stunned. Arianwyn felt a moment of relief at the reinforcements, despite the number of winged grippets still swooping about.

"All right over here?" one of the witches asked Arianwyn as they drew level with her. She was tall and had warm golden hair that brushed her shoulders. The other was shorter, her hair tied up in a series of twists and braids. They stepped elegantly around the stunned grippets and debris on the road.

Arianwyn glanced at their badges and saw the golden edge to their silver stars. They were elder witches, and more than that, they served on the Council of Elders, just like her grandmother. She bowed her head in respect.

"We saw all the commotion from the other side of the crescent. Came as soon as we could," the witch with braids explained.

"I tried to do what I could. I'm Arianwyn Gribble," Arianwyn explained, suddenly worrying she was in trouble. She felt herself blush.

"Well done, Miss Gribble." The blonde witch smiled, but then her brow creased for a second and she said, "Oh, wait, you're Madame Stronelli's granddaughter, aren't you?"

Arianwyn nodded.

"Well, excellent work. Look, we'd best go and deal with the rest of these winged grippets. Can you stay here and keep an eye out for any more of them? Reinforcements are on the way."

Arianwyn nodded silently again, thrilled to have been asked by the council elders for *her* help.

"I say, I think that chap might need a hand." The other witch pointed to the upturned carriage, and they both smiled as they dashed off toward the sounds of more shouts farther along the crescent.

Arianwyn could feel her own smile stretching across her face, pride making her feel six feet tall. Then she heard a muffled squeak from behind her. She turned just as one of the wheels from the carriage fell with a loud crack onto the ground. She saw a hand waving from behind the carriage and heard another muffled call for help. The man the elder had asked her to help—she'd already forgotten! She winced, her momentary pride deflating. She crossed to the carriage, which lay on its side, the fine dark wood all smashed and scraped now. "Hello?" Arianwyn said tentatively as she reached the carriage.

She walked slowly around it. The man lay on the road, his leg pinned under the toppled carriage. He glanced up at Arianwyn—uncertainly at first—but then smiled with a slight grimace. "Rather gone and bashed up my leg, I think." He winced.

"Oh dear!"

"Can you help me out, please? I'd rather not lie here like

this." The man smiled, his face marked with dust and filth from the road, his hair ruffled and sweaty.

"Yes—right—of course." Arianwyn stood, thinking for a moment. Then she moved quickly around the side of the carriage and knelt by the man's side. On the dusty road she sketched Er̲te, the earth glyph, and waited for a seam of magic to connect with it.

She felt the magic pulse around the glyph and then she moved her hands, making the street buckle and wobble a little, creating a small earthquake under the overturned carriage. It shifted, and the man managed to quickly pull his leg free. He gave a small cry of pain and at the same moment a winged grippet that must have also been trapped under the carriage shot out straight at the man.

With the spell still working under the carriage, Arianwyn didn't think about summoning another glyph; she used the magic that was at hand already, which was a mistake. The Er̲te spell was already strong, and the hurried, clumsy spell she threw toward the winged grippet sent it rushing back against the carriage, where it then burst open like a balloon filled with putrid purple jelly! The grippet slime splashed back at Arianwyn, who managed to cover her face just in time. But as she lowered her hands she saw that the man had not fared so well.

"Oh—I am so sorry," Arianwyn said.

"That's quite all right," the man replied, wiping the slime from his face.

"That does seem to happen to me quite a lot . . . ," Arianwyn smiled.

"There's really no need to explain—"

There was the sound of more hurried feet, and a small group of guards and smartly dressed attendants rushed past her, toward the man. They paused and eyed the purple slime with suspicion.

"Oh, it's not dangerous," Arianwyn explained. "In fact, winged-grippet slime was once used to treat burns. Some people think it's quite good for rashes as well," she added, as a large dollop of slime fell off the man's nose. He laughed loudly and smiled at Arianwyn, but everyone else looked rather . . . horrified.

"Well, Your Majesty. We had best get you back to the palace and have the royal physician take a look at your leg," one of the finely dressed people said.

Your Majesty? Arianwyn swallowed hard. It couldn't be, could it? And then she saw one of the guards retrieve the crown from the other side of the carriage, where it must have fallen off when the man, the king, was attacked.

She looked up at the king, who just laughed gently again and smiled. "Thank you for your assistance. It was most . . . interesting!"

Unsure what else to do, Arianwyn waved as the king— THE KING, who she had just covered in grippet slime— was led away toward the Royal Palace.

"I'm sure it's not that bad," Salle said, her words mixed with bright laughter as Arianwyn explained what had happened.

"I'm going to go down in history as the witch who slimed the king!" Arianwyn wailed as they crossed back toward the sidewalk. The crowds were dispersing, the excitement of the afternoon over at last.

"Miss Gribble, wasn't it?" a voice called from behind them, and Arianwyn turned, expecting to be summoned before the king now. Was sliming the monarch an act of high treason? she wondered.

But thankfully it was the tall elder witch from earlier.

"Hi . . . ," Arianwyn said uncertainly.

The elder witch smiled. "You handled that all very well."

"I don't know . . ." Should she mention the bursting grippet?

"Not everyone would have rushed in to help like that."

"She's always doing stuff like that," Salle said proudly.

Arianwyn felt her cheeks warm. It felt as though everyone was looking right at her.

The elder witch smiled. "Well, it was nice to meet you. I can see you have picked up your grandmother's talents."

A car drew up a few feet away and the horn sounded twice quickly. "I'm sorry, I have to go—we're recalling the council to discuss where the winged grippets came from. It looks as though there may have been a rift open in the park."

Arianwyn felt a spike of fear jab at her.

"But don't worry, we managed to catch all the grippets, we think, thanks to you as well."

The elder smiled and turned to walk back to the car. Arianwyn watched her go. As the car door opened, she caught a glimpse of someone in the back, a flash of white robe and midnight-blue talma, a broad, lined face half hidden in shadow.

It couldn't be, could it?

There was a hurried exchange and something was passed to the tall elder, who turned and walked quickly back to Arianwyn and Salle, her hand extended. She held a small white card.

"For you, Miss Gribble. From the High Elder."

Arianwyn swallowed and suddenly felt entirely conspicuous standing there in the middle of the street.

"She was very impressed to hear about your assistance." The tall elder gestured back to the car. Photographs of the High Elder were rare, appearances in public like snow in July—but there she was. Arianwyn could now see the large gold-and-silver star glinting in the shadows of the car.

The High Elder nodded once, a small smile on her lips.

Arianwyn flipped the card over, and on it in straight bold letters was written:

Tomorrow morning, 11 o'clock

Arianwyn had been summoned by the High Elder.

CHAPTER FOUR

LETTERS

"More hot chocolate, girls?" Grandmother asked, crossing back through the bookshop carrying a tray with three steaming mugs and a plate piled high with scones. The delicious smell of chocolate and baking mingled with the smell of the books. It was Arianwyn's idea of heaven.

Beyond the windows, the sky was darkening, and people hurried home for the evening.

"That'll be my third mug!" Arianwyn giggled.

"Well, it's good for shock, I think." Grandmother smiled as she placed the tray down on her desk in between towering stacks of books. "What are you doing there?"

"Writing to Dad," Arianwyn replied, glancing down at the start of her letter. Her father was still off with the army fighting against the Urisians in the north of Veersland. Arianwyn's letter was long overdue.

Dear Dad,

I'm worried that you've not written for a
while but I know how difficult it must be

to find time so I thought I'd write to you
instead.

Salle and I are in Kingsport, staying with
Grandma. I thought I'd feel at home again
coming back to the city but it doesn't feel like
that really and I sort of miss Lull. I certainly
miss the space, the meadows and river and the
trees. I might even miss Mayor Belcher!!! (In a
roundabout way!)

Scrap that—I DO miss Lull. I can't wait to show
you, though I'm sure you'll think it's just a tiny
little place in the middle of nowhere—not as
exciting as Kingsport—well, not exciting in the
same way as Kingsport!

I met the king today—sort of! It was the oddest
afternoon...But, well, I'll save all that for
another letter.

Salle has been busy going to lots of auditions to
various theaters in the city. She's so excited and
I really hope she does get one of the parts, but...
Well, I'd miss her so much if she wasn't in Lull,
she's the truest friend I think I've ever had.
We've got another week in the city and
then I have to get back to Lull. We've still got

lots of the museums and galleries to visit and
Salle is desperate to go and look around
Leighton & Dennison's to find a present for
Aunt Grace...

"Don't forget to tell him about meeting the king!" Salle beamed, and then sipped from her mug.

"I'm not sure sliming the king is the same as meeting him," Arianwyn said, the shame hitting her again in a wave that made her clammy. She shook the thought away.

"Stop worrying. You didn't do anything wrong," Grandmother said gently. "And who knows what might have happened if you hadn't been there. Oh, Salle, I forgot: The postman brought you these." Grandma reached forward with a small pile of letters. "Hopefully some good news from your auditions!"

Salle took them eagerly. "Do you mind if I go and read these now?" she asked, unable to hide the excitement or anxiety from her voice.

"Go for it!" Arianwyn smiled.

Salle grabbed her mug of hot chocolate and the letters. With a scone held in between her teeth, she disappeared into a nearby alcove of bookcases.

"So, I suppose you don't get to spend much time down here in the bookshop these days," Arianwyn asked, desperate to change the subject from the parade, the king, and the slime.

Grandmother sat in the armchair Salle had vacated and flicked through the first book that caught her eye. "Well, Mr. Lomax keeps most things in order and I have my council duties to attend to as well now. I hadn't thought returning to the council would result in quite so much work. But it seems there's lots going on in the world that involves us these days. The war, the increase in dark spirits. Miss Alverston's mishap with the rift in the Great Wood was just the tip of the iceberg, it would seem . . . and then the winged grippets appearing in the midst of the royal parade like that—"

"Oh, don't mention it," Arianwyn groaned, burying her face in her hands again.

Grandmother reached out and took Arianwyn's hand. "I told you, it was fine. They're more concerned with how the rift was opened in the first place in the park and why no one spotted it. Besides, everyone agreed you did *wonderfully*!" She raised her chin, pride flashing in her eyes.

Arianwyn felt bolstered by her grandmother's words. But then another nagging worry replaced the first. "But why does the High Elder want to see me, then?" she asked. "Is it about the night ghast in Lull? About Gimma? She was acting strangely this afternoon."

"You saw Gimma today?" Grandmother asked.

"Just briefly. Did you know she was being sent back to Lull?"

"Yes. Actually, I thought it might be a good idea."

"What? You didn't really, Grandma?"

"Oh, calm down now. You've overcome so much over this last year." Grandmother fixed Arianwyn with a level gaze. She still held Arianwyn's hand, her grip warm and gentle but strong. "You've faced more than most witches face in their whole lives. Gimma should be lucky to have you and Miss Delafield supporting her. Jucasta is one of the finest district supervisors we have! She's been offered countless other postings, you know, but always refuses them. And now it's not like you not to want to help." Grandma peered hard at her.

She was right, of course. Had she written Gimma off too soon? Arianwyn wondered. Maybe she did deserve a second chance. Or was it a third chance?

"She was just so weird, though; ask Salle—" She stopped talking as her grandmother flashed her a look, a look she knew too well.

"Well, that's as may be. Now, remember it is a huge honor to be asked to see the High Elder, but don't go agreeing to anything foolish. I know what you're like."

"Yes, all right," Arianwyn said, and then sipped noisily on her hot chocolate, which she knew annoyed her grandmother more than anything.

Grandmother silently studied the spine of a book. "Aha! I was looking for this for you." She handed a blue cloth-bound book to Arianwyn:

A Witch Alone: A Manual for the Newly
Qualified Witch
by Agnes Brackett
4th Edition

"I thought you might find it useful or interesting!" Grandmother smiled. "Another of my old books."

Arianwyn flipped through it, her eyes skimming the pages. She saw chapters entitled "Setting up the Spellorium," "Magic and Local Politics," and "Magical Plagues: What to Do When One Strikes."

"I'm certain you'll know most of this already, of course," Grandmother said, "but perhaps it will reassure you just how much you *do* know now, my clever girl!"

"Thank you." Arianwyn smiled back at Grandmother. She felt suddenly bad for giving her a hard time. She squashed into the armchair beside her and allowed herself to be folded into a tight hug. She could smell her grandmother's favorite perfume, a scent like roses and cool summer evenings. Sitting there, the day dissolved away: Gimma, the king, the slime! If only every problem could be so easily fixed.

Everything was quiet now except for the ticktock of the shop clock and the occasional sound from the street of a passing car or someone calling across the evening traffic. The calm was fractured by the sudden sound of hurried feet across the floorboards and rugs of the bookshop. The front door rattled open and the bell charm sang out.

"Salle?" Arianwyn sat up and called into the bookcases. "Salle, are you there?"

She got out of the chair and went quickly to the front of the shop. Strewn across the floor were the letters Grandmother had given Salle just fifteen minutes before. But now Salle was nowhere to be seen.

A cool breeze blew through the open door. Arianwyn bent, scooped up the discarded mail, and dashed out into the street.

CHAPTER FIVE

THE ALHAMBRA

It was raining, and the air was full of that delicious smell of rain after a warm day—fresh and cool and green. The sidewalks were already shiny and wet. People hurried past, finding cover and glancing every few seconds at the ominous gray sky above. Thunder rumbled somewhere far away, beyond the city.

Salle stood at the edge of the sidewalk, staring over at the buildings opposite, but something made Arianwyn think that her friend wasn't really looking at them: Her mind was elsewhere. "Salle!" she said softly, placing her hand on Salle's already damp arm. "What's the matter? Is everything okay?"

Salle turned and saw the letters Arianwyn held in her hand. She looked quickly away again. "I didn't get the part," she said sadly, still not turning to look at Arianwyn. A car that was just a little too close to the sidewalk splashed them as it drove past. Arianwyn leapt back, but Salle stayed put.

"Which part?" Arianwyn asked.

Salle said nothing for the longest moment as the rain carried on falling. She was going to be soaked through very soon, Arianwyn thought. "I didn't get *any* of the parts. Not one," she said. Her voice wasn't angry, or hurt. She sounded lost, confused, like someone who had been speaking in a different language all her life and had only just discovered that nobody understood her.

For Arianwyn it felt a bit like a blow to the stomach. How could it be that Salle hadn't managed to get one single part? She was so talented! She knew every line for every part in *Consequence and Courage*, possibly the most boring play Arianwyn had been forced to read at school. And she could replicate just about any accent from across the Four Kingdoms.

"Surely it's a mistake?" Arianwyn said, lifting the now damp letters as though they might reveal something of use.

"No mistake, Wyn. I'm obviously just not good enough."

"No. That's not true—you're amazing, Salle."

"Thank you. But you're my friend and so you have to say things like that." Salle turned and smiled a little, though Arianwyn could see tears on her face. "All those auditions, Wyn . . . and not one bit of interest. Not even for a part that didn't actually have any blasted lines."

"Oh, Salle!" Arianwyn reached out a hand. "I'm sorry."

"Girls, you're going to get soaked out there." Grandma hurried toward them carrying a large black umbrella, which she handed to Arianwyn. "Is everything okay? Won't you come back inside?"

Salle didn't move, but carried on staring at nothing in particular.

"I think we'll wait here for just a bit," Arianwyn replied, raising her eyebrows at Grandmother. Thankfully she took the hint and went back inside the bookshop, where she watched the girls from the large window.

After a few minutes Salle spoke, her voice quiet, difficult to hear over the traffic. "All I've ever wanted to do, Wyn, and now it turns out I'm not really any good at it." She sniffed.

"That's not true. Don't say that, Salle. You're a great actress. So, these parts weren't the right ones for you. There'll be other parts, other chances." Arianwyn felt certain of this, but she knew it would just sound like friendly hot air to Salle.

"Perhaps I'm just wasting my time. I should be doing something useful . . . like you."

"But all you've ever wanted to do was act. You can't just give up on your dreams like that."

"Can't I?" Salle asked sadly, before falling silent again.

Arianwyn looked along the street, waiting for her friend to say something more. If she decided to stand there all night long, Arianwyn would stand right beside her.

But perhaps she wouldn't need to. Farther along the street from the bookshop, Arianwyn saw the bright lights from the Alhambra movie theater. A plan blossomed in her mind. "Shall we walk a little way along the street, Salle?" she asked, and she was rewarded with Salle taking her arm and allowing herself to be led slowly away from the side of the road.

The rain started to fall more heavily, a huge gust of wind driving it faster. The umbrella shook and wobbled.

"Let's take cover in here," Arianwyn suggested, leading Salle through the doors of the movie theater. They skidded a little on the wet marble floor. As Arianwyn lowered the umbrella Salle took in the sights around her: the huge movie posters, the sweeping staircase, the uniformed staff waiting by doors or handing out tickets or boxes of sweet-smelling popcorn.

"Fancy seeing the new Pearl Perkins film? I know you're a huge fan." Arianwyn gestured up at the poster high above the gleaming glass counter. Salle's eyes were already fixed on Pearl Perkins, swathed in exotic clothes and veils and staring out of the poster with a look of determination. *Desert Queen* was written in huge sloping letters across the top. Salle turned and, finally, smiled.

"Two tickets, please," Arianwyn told the young man behind the counter.

Salle and Arianwyn sat in their seats, wrapped in darkness and companionable silence.

The pictures on the screen wobbled and blurred a few times. A crisp Kingsport accent boomed out through the theater: "The latest news across the Four Kingdoms, brought to you by the Hylund News Broadcasting Service."

The flickering light of the screen illuminated the faces of the people around them. They were all expectant, their eyes wide and fixed ahead, waiting for the magic to unfurl before them.

Arianwyn glanced quickly at Salle. Her face was relaxed, a small smile on her lips.

The screen flickered again and showed the familiar view of the Royal Palace in Kingsport. Arianwyn felt a lurch in her stomach, thinking they might be about to show footage of today's disastrous parade. But thankfully it was a series of sleek black motorcars that passed through the gates. Not carriages!

Elegant, uniformed men clambered out and were greeted by the king of Hylund. The news anchor continued: "The prime minister of Dannis arrives in Kingsport for the latest in a round of talks about the ongoing Urisian attacks with the king and the Grunnean ambassador. Key members of the Royal Senate were also part of the conference."

The scene changed and a procession of robed figures marched toward the doors of the palace. Then the screen flickered and displayed the heading of the next news item:

A Fine Example of a Witch!

"Oh, snotlings!" Arianwyn moaned, and sank a little lower in her seat.

The announcer started again, his voice full of enthusiasm. "Out across the country our wondrous witches are doing *their* bit. Just watch them go!"

A witch zoomed past the camera on her broom, waving and smiling like a maniac.

The announcer continued, "Lord Cowley recently paid tribute to the eleven thousand qualified witches of

Hylund and the vital work they are doing in service to the country and the crown. As well as to the Civil Witchcraft Authority, who have been allocating the recently qualified witches to their new posts throughout Hylund, as sightings of dark spirit creatures see an unprecedented fifteen percent increase."

The screen flickered again, and this time they saw a battlefield, all churned-up earth and twisted metal. The announcer's voice took on a grave tone. "In the north of Veersland, the combined forces of the Four Kingdoms have seen small successes pushing the Urisian attackers back across the border for the first time in nine months. But even with the fighting temporarily on hold there is still work to do."

"Isn't that where your dad is?" Salle whispered to Arianwyn.

Across the screen ran several medical staff, displaying the green cross on their sleeves. Two bore a wounded soldier on a stretcher between them. Arianwyn felt a flutter of fear in her chest. The war always felt so far away, but recently it had started to feel frighteningly close. Wherever you went these days there seemed to be soldiers around.

The next shot was of a young woman, a medic judging from her uniform, ripping in half a piece of bandage quickly and calmly, and applying it to someone out of shot. She tucked her hair behind her ears, holding a syringe in her teeth as she carried on attending to her patient.

Salle gazed up at the screen in awe. "That's the sort of useful thing I should be doing, don't you think, Wyn?"

Arianwyn glanced at Salle as she continued to watch the screen. Would her friend make a good nurse or medic? She couldn't picture it, somehow, but the thought made her feel spiteful and mean. "I think you can be whatever you put your mind to, Salle," she offered quietly.

Desert Queen began to play to loud cheers and whoops. But no one cheered louder than Salle, whose face was luminous in the flickering light from the screen.

CHAPTER SIX

THE HIGH ELDER

rianwyn glanced up at the high black gates, the official entrance to the Civil Witchcraft Authority building. She was precisely five minutes late! She hurried through, weaving in and out of a group of young apprentices. "Pardon me, can I get through?" she called. The apprentices spotted her silver star badge and moved quickly to one side to let through a fully qualified witch.

Arianwyn felt them all staring up at her as she dashed past. It was a strange feeling. She kept her eyes fixed on the doors ahead and hurried on, pulling her satchel straight, adjusting her jacket, and giving her messy curls a few tugs, attempting to pull them into something that didn't make her resemble a wild brunkun.

This was the first time she had been back to the Civil Witchcraft Authority building since her evaluation in January, but although everything was just as it had been then, Arianwyn felt she was a different person altogether. So much had happened in those nine months, lots of wonderful and strange things and lots of dark and terrible things. And now here she was off to meet the High Elder! Her stomach turned a somersault as she approached the receptionist, who was just finishing a phone call. "How may I help you?" the lady asked brightly, smiling up at Arianwyn.

"I have an appointment with the . . ." She faltered for a second, her anxiety bubbling to the surface. "The High Elder," she said quietly.

"Oh, I'm sorry, did you say the Office of Clairvoyance?" the receptionist said.

Arianwyn blushed and shook her head. She could feel the line forming behind her and she felt a little sweaty. "No, the, um . . . the *High Elder*." She managed to say it a little louder and the woman responded at once, sitting suddenly straighter, her pen poised.

"Oops, yes, of course. Sorry! Name, please?"

"Gribble. Arianwyn Gribble. From Lull." She handed over her witch's identity card and the card the High Elder had given her the day before.

"Just a moment, please." The receptionist lifted the heavy receiver of the telephone and quickly dialed. She smiled at Arianwyn while waiting for the call to be answered. "Hello? It's the reception hall here. I have a Miss Gribble from . . . Dull?" She looked up in panic.

"Lull," Arianwyn said.

"Sorry—Miss Gribble from Lull here to see—yes, of course. Thank you." She replaced the receiver and smiled again at Arianwyn. "Just a moment, Miss Gribble. If you could wait here . . ." She handed back Arianwyn's card.

"Thank you," Arianwyn replied, but the receptionist was already helping the next person in the line, a young apprentice clearly late for her evaluation ceremony.

Had it really only been nine months since she had been in that position? It felt like a lifetime ago, but at the same time it felt like it could have been just yesterday. Arianwyn could almost hear the gasps of shock at her evaluation ceremony as the gauge had fizzed and issued forth a cloud of smoke, and all power to the whole CWA building had suddenly been lost. It had been the shadow glyph and Arianwyn's connection to it—and indeed her own high magical level—that had caused the blackout that day. She hoped none of today's apprentices got off to such an inauspicious start.

"Miss Gribble?" It was the receptionist again. "The High Elder is ready to see you now. If you'd like to take an elevator to the fourth floor, someone will meet you there." She gestured across the lobby to the elevators.

"Thank you," Arianwyn said again. She moved toward the elevators, suddenly aware that she was hurrying. She paused and took a deep, steadying breath. "Just keep calm, Wyn," she told herself.

The elevator doors slid open and a narrow corridor opened before Arianwyn. A small bell rang somewhere nearby. Leaning against the wall opposite, flicking through a folder, was a young man just a little older than herself, with thick brown hair falling into his dark eyes.

"COLIN!" Arianwyn called as she charged out of the elevator toward him, startling a man who was walking past. "Oh my goodness, it's so wonderful to see you! Where've you been? What've you been up to? Do you work up here now? You didn't reply to my letter. Did you know Salle was in Kingsport too?" she asked all at once, her words tumbling into one another. She felt a sudden tightening of her throat.

"I'm sorry I've not been in touch." Colin blushed and stared at the floor. "I've been quite busy. You can probably guess I've been moved from Miss Newam's evaluation department and I'm now working for the Council of Elders."

"Oh, Colin, that's amazing!" Arianwyn smiled. "I bet you're pleased not to be working for Miss Newam anymore." She shuddered, thinking about the spidery, vicious little woman.

"Well, your grandmother recommended me for it, didn't she tell you?"

Arianwyn shook her head. "I've not seen much of Grandmother really, she's so busy. She must have forgotten."

"The council have been meeting a lot just recently," Colin explained. "Well, shall we go? Don't want to keep the High Elder waiting, do we?"

They headed along the corridor, Colin leading the way. Arianwyn saw glimpses of offices, banks of people sitting at typewriters or answering telephones. There were doors that led into rooms filled with books and folders, and even one holding a huge prototype of the spirit lanterns that the witches were using to catalog spirit creatures across the whole of Hylund.

Colin suddenly turned right and headed through two massive open doors into a vast room that was flooded with bright autumn light. "This is the council chamber," he said quietly.

Long windows, the full height of the room, filled the space with sunshine. To one side a vast table waited, covered with various maps and charts. Beside the table stood the High Elder and, rather surprisingly, Grandmother, who kept her eyes fixed ahead. She hadn't said that she was going to be here, Arianwyn thought. She'd left the house before Arianwyn and Salle had woken up.

"Welcome, Miss Gribble." The High Elder smiled warmly. She had a broad face that was tanned and lined, as though it had been finely carved from oak. Arianwyn guessed she might be about the same age as her grandmother. Her hair was pulled back from her face and tied in a tight bun. In her severe white robes, a midnight-blue talma pinned over one shoulder, she looked like someone you didn't meddle with. The phrase *no-nonsense* stuck in Arianwyn's mind. "Shall we?" The High Elder gestured toward the table. "Mr. Twine, the doors, please."

As Arianwyn crossed to the table, she felt she was being carefully studied by the High Elder, who didn't take her eyes off her once. She heard Colin lock the doors, and then he jogged across the room, reaching the table at the same time as Arianwyn. They peered down at what lay on the surface. A map of Hylund waited to one side with an assortment of blurred pictures strewn across and pinned to it.

The High Elder folded her hands before her and said, "Miss Gribble, I have heard great things about you and your abilities. What you succeeded in doing in Lull over the summer was . . . miraculous!" Her voice was gravelly and steady. "Your assistance during the parade was also greatly appreciated. You acted quickly and decisively and that is a credit to you—and to your grandmother, of course."

Arianwyn noticed Grandma smile a little in her direction.

"I was happy to help, High Elder."

The High Elder pursed her lips and looked toward the windows. "And now I have need of your help again, Miss Gribble." She gestured to the table and the map and photographs. "Do you recognize any of these?"

Arianwyn glanced down, looking more carefully. But the images were poor and blurred, revealing only half of an arm or leg, or the back of something moving away at speed. She started to shake her head but then saw something that made her pause, her skin chilled as though an icy breeze had blown through the room.

She reached out to touch the image, her hand shaking. "That's a night ghast," she said in a small, frightened voice, pulling her hand away again as though it might bring the dark spirit creature into the room. She looked quickly at Grandmother and Colin, who both gave her reassuring smiles.

"Like the one you encountered in Lull?" the High Elder asked.

Arianwyn nodded.

The High Elder leaned on the table, surveying the map and the photographs again. "We have a problem, Miss Gribble. A terrible, frightening problem. You see, each of these photographs, or points on the map here, indicate a separate sighting or report of a dark spirit creature since mid-summer. Far more than have ever been recorded."

The room fell silent. Colin gave a low whistle and scuffed at the floor with his shoe.

"Until recently no human had encountered one of these dark spirits for hundreds of years." The High Elder lifted up one of the photographs and passed it to Arianwyn. It was doglike but winged, and had a huge head with sharp teeth. Its midnight-dark skin stretched tight across its bony frame.

A shudder ran along Arianwyn's spine . . .

CHAPTER SEVEN

THE SUMMONING SPELL

"We believe it to be a razlor," the High Elder said, taking the photograph from Arianwyn.

"And what's that?" Colin asked, leaning across the table and pointing to a photo of a creature that was a jumble of limbs that looked human, but not. It was twisted and awful. It had a huge, bony beak that looked like it could rip things apart easily.

"That was recently identified as a skalk," the High Elder explained. "There have been no recorded sightings of this creature for nearly eight hundred years." The room fell silent for several long minutes as everyone looked at the photographs and the map.

Razlor.

Night ghast.

Skalk.

Arianwyn stared down at the photographs for a moment and then glanced away again, a chill crawling over her skin.

"But all our spells, thus far, remain ineffective. And it is time for new ideas, new spells . . . or maybe old ones," the High Elder said. "We've long suspected that the cardinal glyphs were just the tip of the iceberg as far as magic was concerned. History books and legends indicate that the glyphs are remnants of a far more intricate magical language, long since forgotten. As we face increasing threats from dark spirit creatures and now from countries beyond the Four Kingdoms, we need to understand this forgotten language more than ever."

The flickering film image of the battlefield filled Arianwyn's mind.

"Your grandmother spent quite a lot of her time over the summer searching for anything that alluded to this greater magic." The High Elder moved closer to Arianwyn, until she was just inches away. The closeness felt too much; Arianwyn felt trapped but didn't dare to move. "How ironic that you were the key all along. I, and indeed all the council, have been so very impressed with your control of the shadow glyph." Her voice was full of wonder, and Arianwyn noticed a slight tremble in her hands. "This glyph and others like it could help to ensure our safety, Arianwyn. Perhaps help win—I mean *end*—the war!"

"The new glyphs could also be dangerous, especially if they fall into the wrong hands," Grandmother added. She tapped her fingers on the table, a sure sign of her annoyance.

The High Elder raised her chin. "Then of course I shall ensure *that* does not happen." She winked at Arianwyn. But Arianwyn wasn't sure this made her feel any better. The High Elder was clearly formidable, and Arianwyn felt certain that she could achieve anything and everything she wanted and wasn't used to being told no.

"Don't make promises that you are unable to keep," Grandmother said, a warning edge to her voice now.

The two elder witches looked at each other for a long moment before the High Elder spoke again. "From the reports I have read about the attack in Lull over the summer, the feylings claim to have in their possession a book containing more of these glyphs?"

"Yes," replied Arianwyn. "It's the *Book of Quiet Glyphs*, kept in the demon library in the feyling settlement."

The High Elder's eyes seemed to shine for a moment.

"But we have no proof of that," Grandmother added quickly. "Nor that they will work against these new creatures—"

The High Elder interrupted. "That book could yield a whole new set of spells for the witches of Hylund. Their application could be beyond our imaginations." She turned back to Arianwyn. "You trust the feyling who told you of the book? You have no reason to doubt him?"

Arianwyn's heart warmed as she thought about Estar. "He is certainly curious, mysterious even, but Estar showed me nothing but kindness and friendship." She had followed her heart and instincts and protected him—they had protected each other. She had no reason to doubt him. "I trust him with my life," she added.

The High Elder seemed to consider this for a while before speaking at last. "That will be of great advantage to our work today."

"And what exactly is it, the work?"

The High Elder stepped to one side and gestured to the floor. Arianwyn hadn't noticed it before, but sprawling across the polished wood was a series of lines, markings, and glyphs sketched with brilliant white chalk.

"What's that?" Arianwyn asked, stepping carefully around the lines. She tilted her head this way and that in the hope it might all make sense.

"Looks like a . . . summoning spell?" Grandmother offered, peering closer.

"A what?" Arianwyn asked.

"A summoning spell," said the High Elder. "They're not always reliable, but I thought under the circumstances it was the best hope of reaching your friend."

It took a moment for it to all sink in. "Estar?" Arianwyn asked.

"Indeed. He is our best hope of obtaining this *Book of Quiet Glyphs*."

Can it really be that easy, though? Arianwyn wondered.

"Summoning spells are dangerous, Constance," Grandmother said. "For the caster of the spell as well as the summoned."

"I'm well aware of that," the High Elder replied. "So I will need your help, Maria . . . and that is *not* a request."

The two elder witches stared each other down for a few moments as Arianwyn looked on. She was worried about what this spell might do if it went wrong, but her concerns were swallowed up by excitement at the prospect of seeing her friend Estar again.

"We should try!" she said, looking at her grandmother and immediately feeling like a traitor. "We should do whatever we can to help, shouldn't we, Grandma?"

There was a pause, and then Grandmother said quietly, "Of course." She didn't look at Arianwyn as she spoke.

A few minutes later and the chamber was thrown into semi-gloom as Colin and Arianwyn pulled the curtains half across the long windows.

Crossing back, Arianwyn could see that the two elder witches had positioned themselves amid the network of chalk markings. She felt only the faintest tingle of magic, flowing somewhere outside, far beyond the building. But it was testament to Grandmother's and the High Elder's skills that they could work spells so easily with such a weak pocket of magic to draw upon.

"We use Årdra for its strength," Grandmother explained as she added it to the symbols already on the floor using a piece of chalk.

At the opposite end the High Elder was drawing L'ier, the banishing glyph, but she had drawn it back to front.

The symbols complete, they flared and glowed red and dark purple. Arianwyn could feel the thrum of magic in the room and watched as Grandmother and the High Elder pulled the magic toward the luminous glyphs.

As they connected there was a brilliant, blinding flash; even Colin had to shield his eyes. A gleaming, pulsing circle formed in the center of the room and a rushing wind whipped around the council chamber. Papers from somewhere began to whirl about. Arianwyn had to hold her hair back out of her eyes to see what was happening. In a graceful and speedy movement, Grandmother threw her arms wide and muttered something quietly, over and over again.

Arianwyn stepped forward, straining to hear her grand-mother's words.

"We summon you, we call you forth. Hear us and return to us, creature of the Great Wood. Come forth, feyling. We summon you . . ." Grandmother cast an urgent glance at Arianwyn. "Oh, boil it, what was his name again?" she hissed.

"Estar Sha-Vamirian!" Arianwyn said quickly.

"Come forth, Estar Sha-Vamirian. We summon you!" She repeated the words, and then the High Elder joined the chant.

After several minutes the floorboards of the council chamber started to rattle as if they had broken free of their nails. The spell circle pulsated rapidly, throwing out bright flashes of light. The wind doubled in strength, howling around the room.

"Come forth, Estar Sha-Vamirian. I, Maria Stronelli, witch of the Council of Elders, summon you!"

"Come forth, Estar Sha-Vamirian. I, Constance Braith-waite, High Elder of the witches of Hylund, summon you!"

They repeated the words over and over, their voices merging, combining into a low hum. The wind whooshed around the room wilder than ever, the curtains twisting and the autumn sunlight flashing briefly in bursts and snatches. Arianwyn staggered back under the force of the gale.

In the center of the room the spell circle pulsed with a growing light, once, twice. The light was quite blinding! The wind pulled through scents of the Great Wood, earthy and damp. Arianwyn felt a sudden pang to be back in Lull, unaware until that very moment just how much she was missing her home there.

Suddenly bits of twig, small branches, and leaves were whirling about the room. Arianwyn thought she saw a blue flash. "Estar!" she called, reaching toward the light, her voice snatched away by churning winds.

There was a final burst of brilliance, then a smack of air that felt like a brick wall sent them all skidding across the floor of the chamber.

CRASH!

Arianwyn shielded her eyes and ducked as one of the long windows in the council chamber shattered, sending tiny shards of glass out across the room.

The wind seemed to die as quickly as it had been born. Everything fell silent, the curtains dropping back against the windows, the room returning to semi-darkness. A thick column of smoke rose from the middle of the floor.

Coughing, Grandmother and the High Elder struggled to their feet. Colin hurried toward them. Arianwyn peered curiously at the smoke. It twisted and coiled. Shadows and another flash of blue danced at the center of the rotating column. She thought she heard the snatch of words, a call, a scream?

But then it was gone.

The smoke column collapsed, drifting off throughout the chamber. The circle of light faded.

A wide oval was burned into the floor and at its center sat a rather bemused-looking squirrel, an acorn clamped tightly between its teeth. Its bushy red tail flicked this way and that. It studied them all carefully for a few seconds, obviously trying to figure out where it was, and then it turned and scampered across the floor, passing through the smashed window, its angry chatter fading as it vanished out into the city.

"What . . . what happened?" Colin asked, helping Grandmother to her feet.

"I'm not sure," Grandmother replied. She looked at the High Elder. "We clearly made some sort of opening into the Great Wood, but—"

"Perhaps it was just the wild magic of the wood, or maybe it was too great a distance for the spell," the High Elder said, dusting off her robes. She sounded uncertain and rather annoyed.

Arianwyn's mind retraced her encounters with Estar. He had the ability to transport himself at will. Perhaps that same skill had prevented or protected him from being pulled through by the summoning spell. "Could Estar himself have blocked the spell somehow?" she asked.

"What? I don't know if that's possible," the High Elder blustered. "Do you have any idea how powerful that spell was, Miss Gribble?"

Arianwyn blushed. "It's just . . . the feylings seem to have a different approach to using magic. Well, Estar did anyway," she said softly, suddenly unsure.

"I'm sure that's all very interesting, if not terribly help-ful," the High Elder huffed, and she fixed Arianwyn with a hard stare as though this were all entirely her fault.

CHAPTER EIGHT

PLAN B

"That was rather disappointing, I must say," the High Elder muttered as she stalked back across the council chamber, her white robes billowing behind her. She looked thunderously angry as she reached the map- and photograph-strewn table. Colin poured some hot coffee from the pot that waited there and handed cups to the High Elder, Grandmother, and then Arianwyn. Arianwyn held her cup for a moment, staring out the long windows across the rooftops of Kingsport.

"Is there anything else we can try?" Colin asked as he poured himself a drink.

The High Elder nodded slowly. "There is an alternative."

Arianwyn noticed Grandmother shooting the High Elder a sharp look, but the High Elder was unaware, or chose not to see it.

She continued. "As we have been unable to summon your friend, we will retrieve the book ourselves. We need to send a group into the Great Wood in search of the feyling city." The High Elder leveled her gaze at Arianwyn. "And I need *you* to lead that team, Miss Gribble."

Colin gasped, choking on his mouthful of coffee, which he then spat onto the floor.

Grandmother stepped protectively in front of Arianwyn. "No, absolutely not, Constance. I won't allow it!"

"Maria, you have to understand that Arianwyn is our best hope—"

"I do understand, Constance. But Arianwyn is *my* granddaughter, and I will not allow her to be placed in harm in this way. It's reckless of you, to say the least!"

As the two elder witches bickered, and Colin mopped up the spilled coffee, Arianwyn wandered slowly away from them all, across the council chamber to the long windows. A hundred thoughts rushed through her mind as her shoes crunched over the shattered glass that sprinkled the floor like millions of tiny diamonds. She heard the High Elder say sharply, "And yet we still need the book. It is our highest priority, our duty to find it. This council could go down in history for this discovery, Maria—surely you can see that!"

"I'm more concerned with my granddaughter's safety than history books, Constance. Arianwyn is *my* highest priority!"

"And if I refuse?" Arianwyn interrupted, her voice steady. She glanced back across her shoulder.

The High Elder looked at the floor and sighed. "Then I don't know what else we can do . . . We could perhaps try and send others to search—but no one else has your link with the feylings or your knowledge of the quiet glyphs.

Who knows how long it might take? And all the while the people of Hylund are more and more at risk from the dark spirits coming through from the void."

Arianwyn thought of the night ghast and the photos on the table of the skalk and the razlor. She felt herself go cold. Who knew what else might be out there? She looked out onto the street below. People busy with their own lives rushed from shops and offices, greeting friends for lunch outside cafés and restaurants. Car horns blared out, and then above all the noises of the city came the high cry of a child, and Arianwyn saw a small boy temporarily separated from his mother on the crowded street.

It was just a few seconds and then she was there, wrapping her arms around him, whispering soothing words into his ear and brushing hot tears from his eyes.

If only everything could be made right so easily, so simply.

If she went to find the book, she would see Estar, perhaps. Maybe even see Erraldur, the feyling city. And she couldn't expect others to go in her place. She was the only one able to read from the book, so how could they hope someone else would be able to find it?

"I'll do it," she said quietly without turning, still mesmerized by the scene below.

"What?" the High Elder asked.

"I said I'll do it. I'll find the book." Arianwyn turned back toward the High Elder and her grandmother, who now fidgeted nervously with the collar of her dress, her lips pursed in concern.

The High Elder brought her hands together as though she were about to pray, her fingers tucked under her chin. "Thank you, Arianwyn."

"The mission is to be kept a secret," the High Elder said as they all followed her into her small, almost bare office. "And I do mean SECRET!"

Arianwyn had imagined the High Elder's office would be rather grand, but the reality was quite the opposite. There were no paintings on the wall and the furniture was sturdy and functional: a broad desk, a single chair, a small table by the window, and a glass cabinet in the alcove by the fire that held a collection of jars, bottles, and containers. That was it.

"That looks like hex!" Arianwyn said, peering into the cabinet.

"Yes, some samples I was analyzing along with a report on the outbreaks," the High Elder said, gesturing back toward the desk. "Nobody outside this room is to know of the plan—do I make myself clear? Not your friends, not your families, not even Miss Delafield! If the idea alone of the book was to fall into the wrong hands, we could all be in very real danger, as could anyone else who knew about it!"

They all stood around the High Elder's desk, which was piled high with further charts and maps.

"Now, the Great Wood is not well mapped," Colin explained, pulling some of the papers across the desk for everyone to see. "Despite there being quite a lot of it!"

There were some photographs and prints of paintings showing the wood, even a few with the walled town of Lull in the foreground. They were all very pretty and interesting, but Arianwyn wasn't sure any of them would be of much practical use.

Colin lifted a large roll of thick-looking parchment or canvas. "The last official expedition into the heart of the Great Wood was about eighty years ago. It wasn't a huge success, but the witch who led it did manage to map farther than ever before."

Colin unrolled the map and Arianwyn saw a never-ending swath of green. But crisscrossing this way and that were lines and borders. Each section of the Great Wood had been divided up and named.

"It's amazing!" Arianwyn sighed.

"I know. Impressive, right?" Colin secured the four corners of the map with two books, a mug, and a large chunk of crystal. He ran his hands over the paper, smoothing out the wrinkles and creases.

Arianwyn peered closer to read some of the names on the map: South Copse, Lake Spinney, and Down Wood. The Great Wood was really hundreds, possibly thousands of smaller woods! Also across the map wound the snaking shapes of rivers, rocky outcrops, and canyons. Arianwyn had never thought the Great Wood was anything but trees, but she saw now how wrong she had been.

"We think the old settlements of the feylings were somewhere . . . *here!*" The High Elder stabbed a finger at the bottom of the map, where the woods circled a huge lake.

"Erraldur," Arianwyn murmured quietly.

"What was that?" the High Elder asked, her head whipping around, bright eyes locked on Arianwyn.

"The feyling settlement. Estar said it was called Erraldur."

"And that is your destination." The High Elder smiled. "We will ensure you have copies of this map and all the other relevant detail on the Great Wood before you set off on your expedition."

"I should accompany Arianwyn," Grandmother suggested quickly. She looked at Arianwyn and smiled.

"I suspected you might make that request, Maria." The High Elder's brow furrowed more than usual.

"Then let me go."

Arianwyn looked at the High Elder; she felt certain the answer was going to be no.

"Maria, I'm sorry, but I have need of you—"

"Then I won't allow you to send Arianwyn," Grandmother said, folding her arms across her chest.

"That's not your decision to make, Maria."

Grandmother looked at Arianwyn, her eyes full of worry. Arianwyn moved to her grandmother's side, reaching for her shaking hands. They looked at each other quickly, a hundred unsaid things held in that glance.

"There is work I need you for, Maria, important work! At times like this I need all those I can trust as close to me as possible." The High Elder kept a steady gaze on Grandmother. "Arianwyn is the only witch who has been able to read or see these quiet glyphs, the only witch . . . *so far.*"

Grandmother eyed the High Elder suspiciously for a moment. "You think there might be others who can read from the book? Others like Arianwyn?"

"Not many. But some, I am sure. Witches like Arianwyn. Wasn't Lull's previous witch also able to see the shadow glyph?" She gave Arianwyn a meaningful look.

Miss Delafield's sister! thought Arianwyn. Poor Effie had struggled with the ability. Arianwyn shuddered.

"What is the connection between those two?" the High Elder continued. "We need to find out and find those witches, bring them together. They are our best hope and yet probably too afraid to come forward, misunderstanding what gifts they hold."

Arianwyn remembered her fear at seeing the shadow glyph for all those years, unsure what to do, who to turn to. Could there really be other witches in the world who might be able to read from the book? She felt a small thrill of excitement at the possibility.

"Even so, she is not to go alone, Constance," Grandmother warned.

"It'll be all right, Grandma," Arianwyn said quickly. Her voice sounded far more confident than she felt.

"You will of course have a small team to assist you. Mr. Twine has already expressed interest."

Arianwyn smiled shyly at Colin, who blushed and looked quickly away.

"I assume that will not be an issue!" the High Elder added, with a smile of her own. "I also have my eye on someone from the Magical Research and Science Department. Someone who will not raise suspicion. And they will offer you a suitable excuse to enter the Great Wood, which is still out of bounds to the general public."

"What's our cover story?" asked Colin brightly.

"The Magical Research and Science Department is in need of fresh samples of hex to see exactly how it develops. You will utilize that as your reason for going into the Great Wood. It's not a complete fabrication." The High Elder reached for a pile of papers that were marked with various stamps and seals. She handed these to Arianwyn. "Your authorization from the CWA for your team to pass into the Great Wood to gather the required hex samples."

Arianwyn handed the papers to Colin, who smiled as he accepted them, sliding them into a small card file that was secured with a piece of thin cord. He held the file close.

"For pity's sake, Constance, young Mr. Twine here and some . . . scientist—that's all you're sending with Arianwyn into the Great Wood?" said Grandmother, her voice high and tight with concern.

"We need to keep the party small, minimize the risk of anyone asking too many questions!"

There was a knock on the door.

"I'm afraid that's my next meeting," the High Elder said, looking toward the door. "Are we all in agreement, then? Arianwyn?"

She nodded.

"Mr. Twine?"

Colin smiled across at Arianwyn.

"Maria?"

The room fell uncomfortably quiet. Arianwyn glanced at her grandmother, who looked slightly defeated. Arianwyn reached out and took her grandmother's hands. "Go and find the others like me, if they're out there. They'll need someone like you to help them."

Grandmother offered a small smile. "All right, but you have to promise me you'll take good care of yourself."

Arianwyn nodded.

"Well, if that's all settled then, we will arrange for you to return to Lull tomorrow," the High Elder said, smiling across the office at Arianwyn.

She felt a small thrill of excitement. She was going to be leading an expedition into the Great Wood! Although . . . it was a shame she wouldn't be able to tell Salle or anyone else anything about it. Despite her excitement, a feeling of unease curled in her stomach as she followed Colin and Grandmother out of the High Elder's office.

CHAPTER NINE

HOME TO LULL

"All change at Flaxsham, please! ALL CHANGE!" The train guard's voice cut through Arianwyn's dream, jolting her awake.

She straightened herself in her seat, yawning as the train came to a slow, juddering stop. "I think I nodded off there for a second." She smiled at Salle.

They had been on the train to Flaxsham since first thing that morning and it was now early evening. And they still had to face the long drive back to Lull on the town bus, Beryl, which was possibly the most uncomfortable bus in the whole of Hylund.

"I can't wait to get home!" Salle smiled. "Even though it was rather rotten of the council to cancel the rest of your vacation for . . . what did you say it was again?" she asked, wrestling her suitcase off the luggage rack.

"Hex samples," Arianwyn mumbled. She flushed and was thankful Salle wasn't watching as she pulled her own luggage together in a rather flustered and clumsy way.

Arianwyn's excitement about the mission to find the book was tempered by guilt about her lies to Salle. But it was for her own good. That was what the High Elder had said, wasn't it? Arianwyn hopped down from the train and was hit at once by the driving rain. Salle was ahead, running along the platform, screaming at the top of her voice as the wind and rain swept her toward the station waiting room.

They found Mr. Thorn in the waiting room, fast asleep beside the fire that popped and snapped in the grate. And curled on the floor by his feet was Arianwyn's moon hare, Bob.

Salle had named the moon hare Bob as a temporary measure, but it seemed to have stuck. Its brilliant white body was snuggled into a tight bundle, long ears flat against its back, pearly scales shimmering in the light of the flames. Arianwyn's heart leapt with joy at the sight. She felt as though she might cry with happiness. Bob had become her faithful companion and she now couldn't imagine life without the moon hare. She had missed the moon hare so much while in Kingsport, even though she was certain Aunt Grace and Uncle Mat would have taken the very best care of Bob. And Bob would have loved Aunt Grace's cooking far more than Arianwyn's! At the sound of the closing door, Bob and Mr. Thorn both jumped awake.

"Oh, Miss Gribble! Salle!" Mr. Thorn snorted, his little white mustache wobbling.

Bob dashed across the waiting room. Arianwyn knelt on the cold floor and let Bob happily nuzzle against her cheek, making small noises of excitement as Arianwyn scratched its ears, legs, and back. "Must have nodded off for a second. Thought you'd be pleased to see Bob here. He's a rare old thing, ain't he?"

"Not a *he*, Mr. Thorn." Arianwyn shook her head as the moon hare washed her frantically with its rough tongue.

"Eh?" Mr. Thorn looked puzzled.

"Moon hares aren't male or female, Mr. Thorn," Salle explained. "Like a snail or a . . . worm!"

"Oh, I see . . . ," Mr. Thorn replied, scratching his head and staring quizzically at the moon hare, who paused from its task and stared back at him, large gray-blue eyes blinking.

Just then, the door opened with another gust of wet wind and a small group of soggy people carrying suitcases walked in. "Do you happen to know where we can get a bus to Lull, please?" a gentleman asked, a fancy leather camera case and a pair of binoculars hanging around his neck.

"We're headed for Lull." Arianwyn smiled. She didn't recognize the man—and that was unusual. Lull was so small and ordinary, visitors were rare. She looked at Mr. Thorn, an eyebrow raised.

"Been like this for a few weeks," he said quietly. "Tourists from all over coming to ogle at the wood. Your aunt and uncle are doing a roaring trade, Salle." He picked up their luggage and headed for the door, the tourists following like a herd of sheep. "And did you both have lots of adventures in Kingsport, then? Back sooner than planned, I hear, though?"

"It was lovely to see my grandmother and show Salle the city," Arianwyn said, ignoring the second question to avoid lying again about hex samples.

"And you gonna be a big star now, then, Salle?" Mr. Thorn joked, giving her a nudge.

"I don't think so," Salle said, trying to keep her voice bright.

Mr. Thorn gave Arianwyn a wide-eyed, questioning look. But she just shook her head and mouthed, "Not now." She could see Salle's mood was not quite one of triumphant return.

As Beryl bumped her way over every small pothole and lump in the road, the tourists gave little cries of fright, jostled around in their seats.

"Is this normal?" a lady in thick glasses and a broad straw hat asked Arianwyn.

Arianwyn nodded. "I'm afraid so . . . but you do kind of get used to it!"

"Or after a while your bottom will be so numb you won't feel it," Salle added with a giggle.

Arianwyn watched the countryside flash past and in her mind ran over everything that had happened. She wanted to share everything with Salle—she would be so interested and excited. But Arianwyn knew that she couldn't. Sharing her worries might have helped with the nagging fear that perhaps something had happened to Estar and that was why the summoning spell had failed.

She shook that thought away quickly. However much she wanted Salle's support, she knew she was alone with the secret until Colin arrived: the High Elder had made that clear.

Mr. Thorn called over the roar of Beryl's engine: "Not much changed since you pair went off. Mrs. Ganby had her baby, a little boy called Oscar. Oh, and Dr. Cadbury is looking for some help at the office. Miss Tooly, the last assistant, upped and left without a by-your-leave. Apparently she signed up with the army medical division."

"Heavens!" Arianwyn said.

"We've not seen much of Miss Delafield—reckon her poor leg must still be causing her problems, eh?"

Miss Delafield had broken her leg during the fight with the night ghast. "I had a letter from her when I was in Kingsport. Her leg's nearly better, but she's not allowed to drive yet," Arianwyn explained.

"Well, everyone will be right pleased to have you back home!" Mr. Thorn smiled.

Arianwyn smiled too. She realized that all the way back she had felt like she *was* coming home, not like when she had left Kingsport nearly a year before to start her posting. Then, Lull had been an alien place. Now, as each bridge, church, or tree whizzed past, she felt a little closer to home—and to new adventures. She hugged Bob, who gazed out the window. Across a wide, open field, a tractor was dragging a plow in the far corner, turning golden stubble over to reveal velvety brown earth.

"I don't suppose anyone has really noticed I've gone!" Salle laughed, but something in her voice told Arianwyn that her friend felt this might be true. She reached for Salle's hand and squeezed it, smiling.

"I'm sure your aunt and uncle will be right pleased you're back, Salle!" Mr. Thorn called brightly.

Salle half smiled and turned away again.

Arianwyn's tired mind seemed to fizz and churn with thoughts of the last few days and the excitement of nearly being home again. Somehow, though, she must have dozed off again, as the next thing she knew Mr. Thorn was shaking her gently awake. "We're here, miss. Back in Lull."

Arianwyn's eyes fluttered open and she was looking out across the town square through a slightly fogged-up bus window. The cobblestones, the buildings—all just as they had been when she'd left almost two weeks ago. It was nearly dark now. Bob jumped from her lap and headed out onto the town square, sniffing at the cobbles. Arianwyn and Salle waited for the tourists to disembark and then retrieved their own luggage and followed them off the bus. They strolled across the town square, watching the tourists pause to snap pictures of the shops and buildings at the edge of the square. "Looks like you're going to be kept busy at the Blue Ox," Arianwyn said to Salle.

"I know, very glamorous, isn't it?!" Salle said, poking her tongue out at Arianwyn. She gathered her luggage together. "Right, I'll see you in the morning, Wyn," she said, hurrying to catch up with the tourists who were heading for the Blue Ox, Lull's only inn and Salle's home.

"Good night!" Arianwyn called quietly as Salle made her way home. Then Arianwyn hefted her own suitcase and bag and made her way slowly through Lull's familiar narrow streets toward the Spellorium. Bob the moon hare skipped happily beside her.

A WITCH ALONE: A MANUAL FOR THE NEWLY QUALIFIED WITCH

◆ ◆ ◆

When arriving in your new posting it is essential that you make a good first impression on any local dignitaries who may have influence within the town and local district area.

This may be the parish or town council or the local mayor. They will offer you every support and may well have experience of having worked with several witches during their time in office.

You should make good use of their knowledge, support, and guidance, for a positive relationship will be better for all than one that is strained or suffers from regular conflict. But you must also be wary of becoming too embroiled in local political whims.

CHAPTER TEN

BEHIND WITH WORK

A rianwyn woke suddenly, the shreds of a dream flitting away from her like a red-winged tree sprite. Something of the dream lingered around her . . . a glyph, that was it: the shadow glyph. Her mind had chased the half-remembered fragment and the night ghast had been waiting for her, lurking in the shadows.

She jumped from her bed, shaking the memory off, and walked quickly across the apartment toward the kitchen. She busied herself filling the kettle, lighting the stove, and setting out a mug. Bob lay curled up on the bed, legs twitching as the moon hare chased its own dreams. Arianwyn smiled. "I wonder what moon hares dream about?" she asked the quiet apartment, looking out over the Lull rooftops in the gray light of dawn.

Questions drifted through her mind. Was she the only one to see these quiet glyphs? Could there really be other witches out there like her and Effie, as the High Elder suspected? Or was she actually alone? And what did it all mean?

The kettle gave a shrill whistle, making her jump and stopping her train of thought. Bob gave her a rather thunderous glare at having been disturbed. "Sorry!" Arianwyn smiled.

She rifled through the cupboards in search of something to eat, but all she unearthed was a box of stale crackers, which she tossed straight into the trash. She would have to visit the grocer's as soon as possible. "I wonder if Aunt Grace is cooking anything nice for breakfast?" Arianwyn said to Bob, who sat up straighter when she said "breakfast," head tilted to one side.

Once she'd finished her tea, she washed and dressed quickly, pulling on her uniform jacket as she headed down the stairs into the Spellorium. She cast a guilty look at the stack of unopened letters on the counter as she dashed past. "We deserve a nice breakfast, don't we, Bob?" Arianwyn said as she unlocked the door and stepped out onto Kettle Lane. "It's going to be a busy day and we'll need our energy," she added, locking the door. She could already imagine a plate of Aunt Grace's famous pancakes waiting for her on the cozy table beside the welcoming fire in the Blue Ox. But as she turned to descend the three steep steps to the sidewalk, she almost walked straight into somebody who was standing right behind her.

"Oops, sorry!" Arianwyn turned around and found herself face-to-face with Josiah Belcher, Lull's mayor.

"So, you are back, Miss Gribble!" Mayor Belcher smiled as he peered down at her. "I would have thought you might come to see me as soon as you returned—"

"Oh, it was very late, Mayor Belcher. I didn't want to disturb you." It was only a half lie.

He gave her a look that suggested he wasn't entirely convinced, his mustache twitching a little. "Hmmm."

"I was just heading to—"

"Now, Miss Gribble, I'm pleased you're back early, as it's been rather problematic without you, I must say." The mayor gripped a wedge of small slips of paper. "Miss Prynce was kind enough to keep a log of requests for you in your absence." He shook the pile of paper at her. "I imagine you'll want to get on with them as soon as possible." He thrust the papers at Arianwyn.

She flicked through them quickly. There seemed to be a worrying amount that related to "things" coming out of the Great Wood amid the usual day-to-day issues. The mayor was right: She ought to make sure there wasn't anything urgent. She sighed, her stomach grumbling.

She turned back and unlocked the Spellorium door again. Bob gazed longingly down Kettle Lane in the direction of the town square. "We'll go later," Arianwyn said to the moon hare, trudging back inside and slipping off her jacket. Mayor Belcher followed her, looking annoyingly pleased with himself. She put the pile of papers on to the counter beside her stack of unopened letters and pulled the ledger around, picked up a pencil, and started to log the appointments.

"So, I'll just leave you to it, then, Miss Gribble," said the mayor. "But when you do have a few spare moments, perhaps we could catch up."

"Yes, of course, Mayor Belcher," Arianwyn said, with as much brightness as she could muster to hide her frustration.

"Tomorrow, perhaps?"

"Let's see how I get on with my list first." Arianwyn smiled, prodding the pile of paper.

"Ah yes, indeed—well now, it looks as though you have a customer already. Good morning, Mrs. Emerson."

A harassed-looking woman dashed through the door. "Oh, thank heavens you're back, Miss Gribble. We're in an uproar at home." The woman, who was huffing and puffing, leaned against the counter and took a deep, steadying breath and then placed a jam jar that appeared to be filled with a bright yellow liquid on the counter.

"I'll just get out of your way, then!" Mayor Belcher said, eyeing the jam jar suspiciously. "Cheerio!" he called as he vanished through the door.

"This has been bubbling up out of our kitchen sink for over a week," Mrs. Emerson said, pointing at the jar.

"Oh, well, I'm not really . . . perhaps you need a plumber?" Arianwyn suggested.

Mrs. Emerson fixed her with a glare and then unscrewed the lid. "I've had the plumber in already," she explained. The liquid had begun to wobble and bubble, then there was a bright flash, the Spellorium filled with a shower of sparks, and yellow goop splashed across the counter. "He says it's not really his area of expertise. Any ideas?" Mrs. Emerson folded her arms over her chest and stared hard at Arianwyn.

"Let's just jot down some details, shall we?" Arianwyn asked, wiping the fizzing, sparking yellow goop from her pencil and leaning over the ledger.

She was *never* going to get breakfast now!

There was a constant stream of customers after Mrs. Emerson had left with some powdered gant dung for her mysterious yellow goop. And the next time Arianwyn had a chance to even glance up at the clock, she saw it was nearly lunchtime. Thankfully Salle had come around just after Mrs. Emerson had left, with some warm muffins and a small basket of provisions from Aunt Grace. "That should keep you going," she'd said, smiling, before hurrying off on more errands.

There was still a line of people at the counter. Arianwyn recognized the next man as one of the local farmers. He clutched his cap in his massive muddy hands.

"Did you get my note, Miss Gribble? I'm Farmer Eames from Bridge Farm."

Arianwyn checked quickly through the wedge of paper the mayor had left with her. Bridge Farm certainly rang a bell. "Oh yes," she said. "A bogglin, is it?"

"I reckon so," Farmer Eames said. "About so big, dark brown, and a nasty temper to be sure."

"Well," Arianwyn said, reaching for a large jar on the shelves to her right. "I could give you some jessen seed powder; that might help for—"

"Tried that already, miss," Farmer Eames interrupted. "Think you need to come and take a look."

A few more people came through the door and joined the back of the line.

"I might be able to get to you in a few days . . . it's rather busy, as you can see."

The door banged open again and Millicent Caruthers—
who ran the ladies' boutique next door, which specialized
in the most fabulous hats—came into the Spellorium, a
warm smile on her face. She raised a hand in greeting. She
was followed by two assistants carrying several large boxes
between them.

"Hello, Mrs. Caruthers," Arianwyn called brightly. She
eyed the boxes with a feeling of trepidation.

"Arianwyn, sweet girl, how was your vacation? We all
missed you terribly." She took in the Spellorium, swarming
with people. "Uh—as you can see!"

Arianwyn smiled. "It's nonstop today."

"Yes, well, that's why I thought you might be in need of
your . . . delivery here."

Arianwyn glanced at the boxes again, stamped with
CWA STORES and *FRAGILE*. But she couldn't remember
what it was she was waiting for. She had sent a small order
just before her vacation, to top up her supplies with what
she couldn't find locally, but nothing this large, she was
quite sure. Could it be new equipment from the CWA, perhaps? Had she missed something important in the pile of
letters that she still hadn't had a chance to look at?

"Well, we'll just pop them over here for you." Mrs.
Caruthers pointed to the floor beside the counter and her
two brown-coated assistants moved quickly and placed
them in a neat pile.

"Thank you," Arianwyn said, still racking her brains.

"There are quite a few more in my storeroom," Mrs.
Caruthers said quietly.

"How many more?"

"About twenty-four boxes," one of the brown-coats said.

"Oh, heavens!" Where was she going to put everything? Perhaps she had better take a look quickly. "Excuse me just a moment," she said to Farmer Eames and the line.

She pulled the lid of the first box open and lifted out a wad of scrunched-up newspaper. Nestled in the box were two large glass spheres, each about the size of a soccer ball. "What on earth?" Arianwyn breathed, and then noticed a slip of paper.

Dear Miss Gribble,

We have the pleasure of enclosing your order of Charm Globes Size C.01.

We regret we were unable to fulfill your original order of 500 but have sent our remaining stock. We are not sure when the rest of the order will be available as the larger charm globes have to be specially made now due to decreased use.

Please do get in touch if you need any further assistance.

Gregory Hardy
CWA Stores Manager

"Oh, jinxing-jiggery!" Arianwyn said, getting to her feet, the typed letter crumpling in her hand. "How many more boxes did you say you had, Mrs. Caruthers?"

She looked at the brown-coats. "Twenty-four. There are about thirty boxes altogether, miss," the shorter brown-coat replied.

That was sixty of these gigantic charm globes that she had absolutely no use for whatsoever. How on earth had she made the mistake? It had to be a mistake at the CWA, surely. She'd have to call them to sort out returning the delivery as soon as possible, and certainly before the other four hundred and forty arrived!

Mrs. Caruthers must've noticed her dismay; she reached forward and touched Arianwyn gently on the arm. "Not to worry about moving them all straightaway, though. I'm sure they're not in our way in the storeroom." She smiled. She was being too kind.

"Thank you, Mrs. Caruthers."

"Well, I'd best get back to the shop or the whole place will have fallen apart in the last five minutes, and I wouldn't want to keep you when you are busy. Come along, gentlemen, off we go!"

Arianwyn leaned on the counter as Mrs. Caruthers and her assistants left the Spellorium, the door charm jingling merrily as the door closed behind them.

"Miss Gribble, when can you come and sort out my problem, do you think?"

Arianwyn started; she had almost forgotten Farmer Eames was there.

"Oh, um . . ." She pulled the ledger to herself and scanned the entries she had already made and then glanced up at the pile of messages and notes Mayor Belcher had delivered.

"It's quite urgent, you know," Farmer Eames huffed. "I've had two farmhands bitten in the last week alone."

"Do you have any more of the charms for tamble rats?" a woman asked as she barged up to the counter. Her two children charged around the Spellorium. The girl was clearly pretending to be a witch, flying on her broom, and the boy was pretending to be some sort of dark spirit in hot pursuit, judging from the growling and shrieking.

There was a sudden thud as one of the boxes stacked by the counter toppled off the pile and landed on the floor. The young girl looked up at Arianwyn guiltily. "Sorry," she mumbled.

Arianwyn hurried around the counter and reached for the tumbled box, praying the contents were intact. "It's all right, Mrs. Gubbage, nothing broken." She smiled up at the woman and the small girl.

The woman sniffed and looked straight ahead. "Well, perhaps you ought not to leave things like that lying around—"

"Miss Gribble, what about my bogglin—"

"Tomorrow, Farmer Eames. I'll come first thing tomorrow," Arianwyn snapped quickly.

Farmer Eames smiled, despite her tone.

Arianwyn looked around at the woman, at Farmer Eames, and at the pile of boxes. If she didn't take a break, she felt as if she might explode. "Let me just get these moved out of the way."

Arianwyn heaved a sigh of relief as she left the crowded Spellorium and dragged the boxes into her own small storeroom. As the door clicked shut she paused in the darkness, enjoying the moment of peace and quiet. The noises from the Spellorium, the scuttles of Bob chasing a ball of dust across the floor, and customers arguing over whose job was more urgent, were all muffled by the door. But then a scratching sound came from somewhere at the back of the small room. She stood stone-still and listened—trying to focus.

And she was rewarded with a high-pitched chattering noise as well as the scratching.

She took a few steps forward in the dark. *Perhaps it's just mice?*

But there was a rather nasty smell as well, and as her eyes adjusted to the gloom she saw the cause.

It was certainly not mice!

Under the stone sink, stuck partly to the wall and partly to the small cupboard beside the sink, was a sphere of matted bits of mud and scraps of material.

It was without a doubt a snotling nest!

Snotlings would build a nest out of just about anything. It was small, thankfully. A few snotling droppings littered the floor. "Just perfect," Arianwyn moaned. As if she needed anything else to be dealing with right now!

"Are you going to be long, do you think?" There was an urgent knock on the door that made her jump. It was

Mrs. Gubbage. "Only I do have other errands to run today, you know."

"I'll be right with you," Arianwyn said brightly. She shoved the extra-large charm globes into the storeroom and made a mental note to deal with the snotlings later, then she slammed the door shut and—fixing a smile on her face— returned to the line at the counter.

"So, tamble rats, was it?" Arianwyn asked, reaching for the ledger.

CHAPTER ELEVEN

MUD & MAGIC

"In here, miss!" Farmer Eames called as Arianwyn flew toward the open gate, her broom wobbling as she made the sharp turn into the field.

"Sorry I'm a bit late!" Arianwyn replied, jumping down and crossing over to Farmer Eames.

"Gus said he last saw the bogglin in the corner of the field yesterday afternoon, miss," Farmer Eames said, pointing to a tangle of trees and bushes bordering the field. It looked a bit boggy, an unusual place for a bogglin to build a nest; they usually liked cellars or outhouses, or occasionally coal sheds.

"And you definitely tried the jessen seed powder?" Arianwyn checked.

"Yes . . . ," Farmer Eames said. "Gave my wife a nasty rash, it did!"

"Oh, sorry about that," Arianwyn replied. "Well, I'll see what I can do."

She stood watching the field for a few moments, the dusty yellow corn swaying in the damp breeze, but she couldn't see anything out of the ordinary. The sky was gray and flat.

Arianwyn started to cross the field, Farmer Eames following two steps behind. The corn brushed against her coat and she let her mind wander to all sorts of other thoughts: the book of glyphs, the expedition into the Great Wood, what she would have for dinner, whether or not she had remembered to feed Bob before she left the Spellorium, anything in fact except for the bogglin. So when something dashed through the corn in front of her it was quite a surprise and she gave a little gasp of shock.

She heard the grunting squeal of the bogglin and was just readying a spell orb to stun it when she saw it as clear as day. It had paused and now stood about twenty feet away, staring straight at her.

But it wasn't a standard bogglin at all. The creature squatted among the crops, its lumpy toadlike skin blending almost perfectly with its surroundings, not like the grayish skin of an ordinary bogglin. And its eyes gave it away entirely—bogglins generally had bulging yellow eyes, but these were bright, searing red.

"Oh no," Arianwyn groaned.

"What's wrong?" Farmer Eames asked.

"Well, I know now why the jessen seed powder didn't work. That is a harvest bogglin, and it's quite a different creature."

"Oh," said Farmer Eames. "Why's that, then?"

"Harvest bogglins can camouflage themselves; they're quite horribly vicious and have incredibly thick hides, to the point where standard spells often don't work against them, as their thick skin deflects the magic."

"Oh dear!"

"Indeed!" Arianwyn said.

The harvest bogglin snorted and pounded the ground with a thick, crusty fist that was as lumpy and gnarled as the rest of it.

"Why's it doing that?" Farmer Eames asked.

Arianwyn grabbed the farmer's arm, a sinking feeling in her stomach, and slowly guided him to step backward, away from the creature. "Because it's about to run at us."

They had taken only two or three steps away from the bogglin when it began to bolt straight at them, head lowered and snarling as it charged. Unsure what else to do, Arianwyn shoved Farmer Eames to one side and dived in the opposite direction herself as the bogglin raced past them. It disappeared off somewhere into the field.

"Well, what do we do now?" Farmer Eames asked, peering at Arianwyn through the corn stalks.

She sat in the mud, thinking. "We're going to need some rope!" she said eventually. "Lots and lots of rope!"

Arianwyn stayed beside the field, trying to keep track of where the bogglin was and what it was doing while she thought through her plan. The bogglin seemed to be rushing in a very haphazard fashion around the field, but Arianwyn knew it was marking the field as its territory—she even caught the occasional pungent whiff of its scent and was forced to cover her nose with a handkerchief.

She'd pulled out her copies of *The Apprentice Witch's Handbook* and *A Witch Alone*. Although both had sections on bogglins (standard) and several other types, including bog bogglins, sand bogglins, and even tree bogglins (which it turned out actually weren't dark spirit creatures at all!) neither was particularly useful when it came to harvest bogglins. There was one small sketch of one in *A Witch Alone*, but a single line under the illustration read: "No recorded sightings for seventy-five years." And the book was at least fifty years old. Arianwyn shoved both the books into her bag and looked out across the field, watching the corn wobble this way and that as the bogglin charged around. She would just have to improvise.

She sighed; this was taking far too long. But then from the next field she saw Farmer Eames's tractor trundling toward her. It was pulling a small trailer behind it.

"Been through all my barns and brought as much rope as I had to spare!" Farmer Eames smiled as he pulled up alongside Arianwyn. The trailer held several coils of rope that looked rather like a nest of huge snakes or worms. "Now what do we do, miss?" he asked.

After an hour or so, Arianwyn and Farmer Eames had made a crisscrossing pattern with the various ropes across the field, like a wonky spider's web. Every now and then the bogglin had sniffed at the ropes, occasionally flinging one aside as it continued its charging around.

Once the ropes were placed, Arianwyn knelt and quickly drew alternate Årdra and Erte glyphs into the soil between each rope. She hoped the two glyphs together would form a strong enough spell to hold the bogglin long enough to banish it. She was about a quarter of the way around the field when she heard a commotion from the other side: The bogglin was on the move again, the corn whipping around as though caught in a hurricane.

"Farmer Eames, move!" she called out. But Farmer Eames seemed quite oblivious to what was going on around him as he bit down on a sandwich.

Arianwyn couldn't risk Farmer Eames getting attacked by the bogglin, and she was now worried it might move into the next field once it had finished marking its territory in this one. She would have to set up the spell all over again, and she really didn't have the time.

"Boil it!" she swore. Even though her improvised spell wasn't complete, she would have to go with what she had in place already: slightly less than half the ropes.

But half was better than nothing. She drew one last glyph quickly. She let the seam of magic nearby pour toward her— it was like a warm breeze rushing at you—and her skin fizzed and tickled as the magic connected with the glyphs she had put in place. Ideally the bogglin would have been in the middle of the field, where the ropes overlapped, but this was clearly not going to be one of those afternoons.

The magic surged around her, and Arianwyn directed it at the ropes that spread out nearby. The ropes jolted and rippled as the magic passed into them. And then the ropes closest to her were whizzing away, as though being pulled by strong invisible hands.

There was a squealing noise from the opposite side of the field, and Arianwyn saw Farmer Eames jump, drop his sandwich, and leap backward. The corn nearby was fluctuating and undulating like an angry golden sea under the stormy gray sky. He looked across at Arianwyn at last—she waved her hands, hoping he would take the hint and run, but he was too slow and the bogglin was clearly moving closer. "RUN!" Arianwyn shouted, just as the bogglin lurched from the cover of the cornfield straight toward Farmer Eames, its huge mouth wide open, its knot of stumpy teeth bared.

But then something happened and the bogglin seemed to hang in the air for a second. Arianwyn had been running forward, but she paused, trying to unravel the scene before her. And then she saw the twists of rope that had already wrapped themselves around the bogglin. As the creature hung in midair, the ropes continued to twist and coil, wrapping first around its back legs and then farther around its body and then its front legs. All the while the bogglin turned over and over in midair, snarling and snapping as Farmer Eames backed away.

The ropes were anchored to the earth, holding the bogglin like a rather gruesome balloon. Arianwyn approached cautiously. "Are you okay?" she called to Farmer Eames. He nodded mutely, staring up at the bogglin.

Arianwyn raised her right hand and in the air before the creature she sketched the banishing glyph, feeling the cool slice of the void opening before her, like an icy pull on her heart.

"Return to the void. Your spirit must not linger here. Go in peace. Return to the darkness."

The spelled ropes suddenly fell as the bogglin's physical presence evaporated into the afternoon's gray sky with a spattering of light. At its core hung a little wisp of darkness that hovered for a second before being sucked toward the rift. As the bogglin's dark spirit disappeared through the rift, Arianwyn felt a moment of worry: What if her rift didn't close itself now? What if something else got through? She could feel her heart racing; she felt hot and sweaty, and not just from all the chasing around the field.

But after a few seconds the rift twisted in on itself and collapsed, and the cold pull of the void was gone.

Arianwyn clapped the mud from her hands and turned to smile at Farmer Eames. "There you go, I hope you're happy with that?"

Farmer Eames smiled. "That's wonderful, Miss Gribble, but you did know we've got two of them, didn't you?" He scratched at his head and squinted at her.

It was going to be a very long afternoon indeed!

It was just growing dark as Arianwyn eventually arrived back at the Spellorium, her boots and uniform covered in mud. She was exhausted from her work with Farmer Eames, filthy and roaring hungry. It took all her effort to clamber off her broom and unlock the Spellorium door.

Bob jumped around her excitedly and she paused to scratch the moon hare's long white ears, which were sparkling in the last of the day's light. As she stood, she felt all her muscles stiffen and she gave a little groan. A nice warm bath was exactly what she needed; the mere thought of it was making her feel better. She yawned and kicked off her muddy boots, heading upstairs. She started to run the bath, adding a generous amount of blueberry and star flower bubble bath. Then, as the water filled the tub, she quickly lit a fire, grabbed her book, and made herself a huge, steaming mug of hot chocolate.

Five minutes later she was submerged in the deep bath and sipping on her hot chocolate, letting the aches and pains and mud of the day slip away. She gave a deep sigh of contentment.

And then she heard a furious tapping on the Spellorium door.

CHAPTER TWELVE

HARDLY A DISASTER

"Who can that be now?" Arianwyn grumbled, reaching for a towel. Water splashed onto the floor of the bathroom. There was another knock, louder than the first. "All right, I'm coming." She wrapped herself in her dressing gown, pulled on a thick pair of socks, and went back downstairs into the dark Spellorium.

Bob danced around her feet as she hurried toward the door. A dark shape was silhouetted behind the blind drawn over the window. "Better not be any more harvest bogglins." She smiled down at Bob.

The moon hare sneezed in agreement. She pulled open the door and nearly fell out into Kettle Lane with excitement. "Oh my goodness! Colin!" She couldn't believe her eyes. Colin stood on the doorstep, hair hanging into his eyes as usual. He looked tired and rumpled from traveling. "I didn't know you'd be here so soon!" She moved forward, reaching out to offer him a friendly hug.

But his cheeks bloomed two red spots and he half backed away. "Hello, Miss Gribble," he offered, rather formally.

"I didn't think you were arriving until next week!" In her excitement, Arianwyn pulled him into a tight hug just as he said: "Wait! Arianwyn—"

"MISS GRIBBLE!" A sharp voice rang along Kettle Lane.

In a nearby house a baby burst into tears and a dog started to howl. The voice was jarring and unmistakable. Arianwyn felt her stomach drop as if she were on a roller coaster. But this was much less fun. It couldn't be . . . could it?

"Good heavens," the sharp voice continued, "I trust this isn't how *all* guests from the Civil Witchcraft Authority are greeted?"

"Miss Newam?" Arianwyn said, pulling away from Colin and turning slowly toward the voice, though she was hoping it was some sort of hallucination caused by tiredness and too much bubble bath. But no! Miss Newam stood hunched, arms folded tight over her chest, her thick spectacles sliding down her nose as her hard little eyes fixed on Arianwyn as though she were something she'd found on the bottom of her shoe. Arianwyn felt as if she were at her evaluation ceremony all over again. She could almost smell the smoke rising from the evaluation gauge as Miss Newam's expression grew more disappointed with each passing second. Her mouth pulled into a sour little pout. And then realization hit, like a bucket of ice-cold water straight in the face. Could Miss Newam be the other person, the person the High Elder trusted with their secret mission? No, there had to have been some sort of mistake . . . Arianwyn crossed her fingers. *Please let it be a mistake.*

"Miss Newam works for the Magical Research and Science Department now and was selected to join the team!" Colin said, trying very hard to make it sound like good news.

"Oh . . . *really*?" Arianwyn couldn't mask her shock. Then, remembering her manners, she said quickly, "Welcome to Lull, Miss Newam. It's . . . nice to see you again." She extended her hand.

Miss Newam sniffed and totally ignored the gesture. "Miss Gribble, we've had a very long day traveling, ending with a perfectly awful journey here on a *bus* of all things!" She gestured to Beryl, parked a little farther along Kettle Lane. "Ghastly business, and I'm in no mood for pleasantries. I'd just like to go to wherever it is we are staying, have a warm bath, and lie down." She wiped at imaginary dirt on her sleeves and skirt, her dark gray clothes as drab and ill-fitting as ever.

"Are you booked into the Blue Ox, then?" Arianwyn asked brightly.

"Well, I certainly hope so," Miss Newam snapped. "Naturally you were arranging accommodation!"

She was? Arianwyn had a cold, sinking feeling.

"We sent a telegram ahead to let you know we were coming today," Colin explained quietly.

Arianwyn glanced back inside at the unopened stack of letters and messages still on the counter of the Spellorium.

"With clear instructions to arrange lodging for us," Miss Newam added through gritted teeth.

"I'm sorry!" Arianwyn said in a small voice. "I've barely had time to check all the messages and letters. It's been so busy since I got back—"

"Oh, for pity's sake!" Miss Newam groaned and rolled her eyes to the darkening sky. "So what you are telling me is that we don't actually have anywhere to stay. Is that a fair assessment of the situation?" Tiny black eyes bored into Arianwyn. She felt herself flush.

"Miss Newam, I really am—"

"This is just what I was expecting!" Miss Newam crowed, flinging her hands into the air. "I told the High Elder this would end in disaster—"

"It's hardly a disaster," Colin offered calmly.

"Look, I'm sure I can get some rooms sorted out," Arianwyn said. "Why don't you, uh, wait here. Make your-selves a cup of tea, pop your feet up." She smiled at Colin and pretended not to notice Miss Newam's cold gaze.

"And just what do you suggest we do with all our lug-gage?" Miss Newam snapped.

"I'm sure Mr. Thorn can keep hold of it for now?" Arianwyn gave Mr. Thorn, who waited beside Beryl, a pleading look. He smiled kindly in response.

Miss Newam made a disgruntled sound in the back of her throat that was part cough, part growl. Then she turned her apocalyptic gaze onto Colin.

"I'll be back in a flash!" Arianwyn called as she started to head down Kettle Lane. She'd not gone far, though, when she did an immediate about-face, rushing back past Mr. Thorn, Colin, and Miss Newam, clutching at her dressing gown. "Perhaps I ought to get dressed first, though!"

Aunt Grace slid her hand across the ledger for the Blue Ox and made a face. "I'm sorry, Arianwyn love, we're full tonight. I don't think we can help until tomorrow."

Arianwyn chewed her lip and stared for a few seconds into the cheerful flames of the fire.

"We've got plenty of spare blankets you can take back with you, and I think Mat might have an old cot around somewhere, if that helps? I am sorry. We've been so busy with all the tourists coming to see the Great Wood. The other week, there was even one woman who clambered over the cordon and went in. Constable Perkins nearly had to have her arrested." She gave Arianwyn's shoulder a gentle squeeze. "Just for one night. This Miss Newam can't be that bad, can she?" Aunt Grace smiled reassuringly. She always saw the best in everyone—it was like her very own magic.

"No . . . I suppose I can manage for one night!" Arianwyn sighed. "I'd best go and break the good news!"

As Arianwyn wandered back along Kettle Lane, she could already picture the grimace on Miss Newam's face as she explained the temporary accommodation plan.

The lights of the Spellorium were on, but it suddenly didn't feel as welcoming as it usually did. It was odd to think of Miss Newam being in there. Would she be snooping through drawers and complaining about this and that to Colin? "Oh, heavens, the snotling nest!" Arianwyn moaned to herself loudly, certain Miss Newam would have something to say about *that*.

Through the Spellorium window she saw Colin making tea by the small black stove that was burning cheerfully. Miss Newam sat beside it, still in her coat, clutching her bag as though she were waiting for a train. Bob inched carefully toward her, body flattened against the floor, clearly fascinated. Arianwyn watched as the moon hare sniffed at her boot and Miss Newam yelped, nearly jumping out of her seat, sending the spirit creature skittering around in circles.

Arianwyn steeled herself and opened the front door.

"Well?" Miss Newam's head shot up as soon as the door opened and the bell charm sang out. Her hair, coiled in tight braids on her head, was all wispy and frizzy, and her thick spectacles were firmly positioned on her sharp nose.

Arianwyn took a deep breath, wondering how to explain.

"Oh, I should have known!" Miss Newam groaned. "There aren't any rooms, are there?"

"Not for this evening, no. I'm sorry. You're all booked from tomorrow, though." Arianwyn turned to shut the door as Miss Newam continued.

"And so, where are we going to stay . . . ?"

Arianwyn tried to explain. "Well, I thought—"

"I suppose we'll be sleeping out in the street? Or perhaps the Great Wood!" Miss Newam shrieked. "What is Miss Gribble's marvelous plan?"

"You're . . ." *Just spit it out*, Arianwyn told herself. "Staying here tonight." She made her voice as bright as she could. "Mrs. Archer is sending some blankets and things across from the inn."

Miss Newam's only response was a very loud snort, and then she stared around the Spellorium in horror as though it was the bottom of a sewer, and a very full one at that! "Here?" Her voice was a hoarse whisper now. "Sleep . . . here?"

"Well, there is the apartment upstairs," Colin offered. "You wouldn't have to sleep in the Spellorium itself—"

Miss Newam turned sharply and caught Colin with her hard eyes. "And precisely how do you know about the 'apartment upstairs'?"

Colin blushed.

Thankfully, at that moment the door burst wide open, banging against the wall. A walking pile of assorted and slightly dusty blankets, sheets, and pillows wobbled into the Spellorium. A muffled voice that sounded like Salle's said: "Aunt Grace said you needed these as soon as possible?" Bob scampered forward from his hiding place and ran in tight circles around her feet.

Uncle Mat followed behind with a folded contraption of metal springs and strips of canvas. "Where d'you want this, Wyn?" he asked brightly. He nodded a greeting to Colin and Miss Newam.

Miss Newam stood abruptly. "Absolutely ridiculous to think that it is acceptable for me, in *my* position, to be sleeping above a Spellorium!" She marched to the stairs, still muttering angrily as she went up into the apartment.

"Crikey, who's that?" Uncle Mat asked, making a face and placing the cot on the floor.

"Don't ask!" Arianwyn sighed. Tiredness overcame her and she suddenly felt like a small, hopeless apprentice all over again. Everything she had faced seemed to pale into insignificance beside Miss Newam's utter disapproval.

She rested her head against the polished countertop and closed her eyes.

CHAPTER THIRTEEN

A TALENT FOR CHARMS

"Oh, there you are," Miss Newam snapped as Arianwyn hurried into the Spellorium. It had been a week since Miss Newam and Colin had arrived in Lull. The mayor had promised them some space in the town hall, but until that was ready they were both working in the Spellorium.

Colin was hunched over some charts of the Great Wood. He smiled and waved.

Miss Newam continued. "My goodness, you're entirely covered in—actually, what *is* it you're covered in, Miss Gribble? What have you been doing?"

Arianwyn glanced down at herself; she was covered in messy blue smears. "Harvesting covia berries—they needed bringing in before the first frosts." She raised the bucket she was carrying. "I'll need to dry them first, but they'll be ready to use in a week."

"I see," Miss Newam said, but she sounded entirely bored.

Colin smiled and indicated a large mug and the teapot. Arianwyn felt a surge of gratitude. She wiped her blue-stained fingers on her skirt and took the mug, smiling. "Any news on when we can set off on our expedition?" she asked.

"As it happens, I was just going to call the CWA to see when . . ." Miss Newam glanced around the Spellorium.

"Are you looking for something, Miss Newam?"

"Yes—where's the telephone?"

"There isn't one," Arianwyn said, sipping gratefully on the mug of tea.

"What?"

"The nearest phone is the public one on Old Town Road."

"A *public* telephone?" Miss Newam asked. She turned slowly to face Arianwyn. "I cannot be expected to use a public telephone to carry out official, and I might add, *secret*, CWA business. That's quite out of the question!"

Arianwyn sighed. "You could ask Aunt Grace—I sometimes use the telephone at the Blue Ox."

"I can't quite believe that I have to use a phone in a public bar!" Miss Newam fumed.

"Or you could ask the mayor or Miss Prynce if you could use one in the town hall? I'm sure they would be only too happy to help! You could check on when your office there might be ready, as well." She couldn't wait for Miss Newam to move out of the Spellorium. Secretly she thought Miss Newam and the mayor would quickly annoy each other.

"Well, I suppose I've no alternative," Miss Newam responded, a sour look on her face. She pulled her coat on and headed toward the door.

Arianwyn sighed and rested against the counter, idly playing with an open drawer of fine tiny temerin seeds. They made a reassuring sound as they tumbled through her fingers. She started to feel a little calmer.

She looked up as the door opened and the bell charm sounded. Miss Newam had come face-to-face with Miss Delafield on the doorstep. The two women eyed each other carefully. Miss Delafield towered over Miss Newam but apparently didn't intimidate the smaller woman, who stood her ground.

"Ah, you must be the *legendary* Miss Delafield," said Miss Newam, her mouth twisting a little. "I'd heard you were still incapacitated?" She sniffed. "I'm Hortensia Newam from the CWA."

Miss Delafield glanced over at Arianwyn and then back at Miss Newam, leaning heavily on her walking stick. "I've heard *so* much about you, Miss Newam, and don't you worry: I'll be right as rain in no time. Just you watch!"

"I was just on my way to see the mayor," Miss Newam said, and without any further comment she barged past Miss Delafield and walked off, nearly unbalancing the district supervisor.

"She's so rude!" Colin gasped, burying his head in his hands.

Miss Delafield hobbled inside, her leg still wrapped in a bright white cast, her walking stick clicking against the floorboards. A small wicker basket swung at her side. "Arianwyn, dear!" she called out in her booming voice.

"Miss Delafield!" Arianwyn moved quickly across the Spellorium and was surprised when she was caught up in a hug from her supervisor. She smelled of engine fumes and peppermints.

"Now then, dear, let me get a good look at you." She held Arianwyn at arm's length and studied her carefully for a few moments. "You look well. Your hair's a little longer. How've you been?" She paused for a moment and sniffed the air. "I say, is that . . . snotling? I think you might have a nest, dear!"

Arianwyn flushed as she remembered the nest in the storeroom. She'd still not done anything about it. "Just a little one," she explained, but Miss Delafield wasn't really listening.

"Oh my goodness—young Mr. Twine as well! Tell me, has the whole of the CWA been relocated to Lull for some reason?" She broke into a loud laugh and clapped Colin on the back. He staggered forward a little under the force.

"Hello again, Miss Delafield. How are you?"

"I'll be all the better when I get this wretched thing off my leg!" Miss Delafield smacked her walking stick against the white cast and grinned. "Next week, the doctor said, but in the meantime the whole district is falling into a total shambles, you can't imagine." She eased herself into the chair beside the stove and Bob scampered across the floor to sniff at her cast and then jumped into her lap, purring with delight. "I've had five witches retire in the last few weeks and no sign of a replacement yet from the CWA. I was going to ask if you might be able to pick up some extra duties—"

"Oh, Miss Delafield—" Arianwyn started to speak but broke off, wondering exactly what she would or could say to her supervisor without revealing the High Elder's mission.

"But I was told you have some study to assist Miss Newam with, samples from inside the wood, is it?" She gave a loud, barking laugh. "Whatever will they come up with next!"

"Yes, that's correct," Arianwyn said; she didn't hear any conviction in her own voice at all and felt her cheeks grow warm.

"Hmmm, well, blasted waste of time if you ask me—not that anyone ever does!" She stroked the moon hare's long ears and smiled up at Arianwyn. "But I am pleased you're back, dear. Oh, and I have a little something for you." She lifted the basket from the floor beside her chair.

It looked a little like a basket a fisherman might carry: rounded, with long leather straps and a brass buckle that gleamed. Arianwyn felt a small flutter around her heart when she saw her name engraved on a piece of leather stitched to the top.

"Had a chum of mine in Kingsport make this just for you," Miss Delafield beamed. "As a sort of 'well done' gift."

Arianwyn undid the buckle and the front of the basket dropped forward with a gentle jingle. Inside were several rows of small labeled containers, and strapped into place was a selection of charm bottles and globes of various shapes and sizes.

"I thought it would come in handy when you're out and about and don't have all your charm bits and pieces available."

"Miss Delafield, it's wonderful! Look, Colin!" Arianwyn beamed, showing the case to Colin.

"Well now, just make good use of it, dear. Never known a witch with such a talent for charms as you. And perhaps it will come in handy when you are off collecting your samples . . ." Something in Miss Delafield's voice told Arianwyn she wasn't convinced by the High Elder's cover story, and she felt her knot of unease loosen just a little.

"And I'm sorry about Gimma coming back," Miss Delafield added. "I wasn't given much of an option, if I'm honest. There's such a shortage of capable witches that it's every man, or rather *witch*, to the pump at the moment, dear. And who knows, once we've trained her up, she might be half useful for something. She'll be carefully supervised by both of us. How much trouble can she get into?"

"That's precisely what I'm worried about!"

"But you don't mind too much, do you, dear?" Miss Delafield stared hard at Arianwyn. Her green eyes seemed to bore through her very soul.

"No, of course not. Not at all!" Arianwyn said brightly.

"Well, that's good, then, because I think she's due back in the next day or two."

"How . . . lovely."

What was one more little lie?

CHAPTER FOURTEEN

THE TEA PARTY

Salle and Arianwyn were eating bowls of Aunt Grace's best beef stew by the fire in the Blue Ox, rain pattering gently against the dark windows. Arianwyn was finishing her story about the harvest bogglins as Salle giggled and gasped.

"Well, Farmer Eames was singing your praises to anyone who would listen yesterday evening, so I don't think you have too much to worry about, Wyn!" Salle laughed as she dipped her bread into the rich beef stew.

The door opened and a hooded and broad figure swathed in a long raincoat walked slowly across the inn toward the table opposite Salle and Arianwyn. The figure shrugged off its all-encompassing dripping-wet coat—revealing the mayor underneath.

"Oh, hello, Mayor Belcher," Salle called.

The mayor raised a hand in greeting but didn't even glance at the two girls. He flopped into the seat and sighed. Arianwyn frowned at Salle in concern. The mayor usually had something to say about everything: It was unusual to see him so quiet.

"Ask him if he's all right," Salle hissed at Arianwyn.

"*You* ask him!" Arianwyn replied quickly. She'd not entirely forgiven the mayor for accosting her on her first day back in Lull and interrupting her breakfast plans.

"Oh, for heaven's sake. Fine!" Salle muttered as she turned toward the mayor and tapped him gently on the shoulder. "Everything all right, Mayor Belcher?"

"I'm sorry, what?" the mayor asked, clearly lost in his own thoughts.

"We just wondered if everything was all right?" Salle repeated.

"Oh no, Salle. Not really. You see, Gimma is due back tomorrow and I have a meeting to go to over in Conniston and I won't have time to prepare anything for her arrival."

"Like a parade?" Salle asked. Arianwyn nearly spat her mouthful of stew across the room.

"No, not a parade, Miss Bowen. You do come out with the oddest things sometimes," the mayor sighed. "I just wanted to give my niece a nice welcome back to Lull. I'm"— he paused for a few seconds and then added in a hushed voice—"you see, I'm just so worried about her coming back. She must be anxious and I'm keen that she sees she has, well, friends here."

Salle and Arianwyn exchanged a brief glance. If there was one thing Gimma Alverston didn't have in Lull, it was friends. She'd put the whole town at risk and then tried to blame Arianwyn in the bargain.

"I'm worried people will react badly to her return," the mayor continued. He looked pale and worried. "Do you think people will understand?"

"I . . . I think we have to appreciate that a few people will feel differently about Gimma, but some time has passed now since the summer. Some people hopefully will have put it all behind them . . . perhaps," Arianwyn offered. She hoped Lull would be forgiving.

He looked cheered by the thought of this. "Do you think so? Oh, I do hope you're right, Miss Gribble." The mayor smiled and relaxed back into his seat for a moment but then lurched forward, looking crestfallen again. "But I was going to have a little tea party for her when she arrived."

"Well, that sounds like a nice idea," Arianwyn said quickly, thinking that she couldn't imagine anything worse than tea with Gimma.

"But I won't have time to get anything ready as I'll be in Conniston all day, only just back in time for her arrival."

"Well, we could host it, couldn't we, Wyn?" Salle said, after an awkward pause.

The mayor looked up and smiled, hope shining in his eyes.

"What?" Arianwyn was sure she hadn't heard right. "Us . . . host a tea party . . . for Gimma?"

Salle nodded as though it was the best idea anyone had ever had. "Yes!"

"What are you doing?" Arianwyn hissed, pulling her aside. "Don't cause trouble, Salle!"

"I'm not. I thought this might be a nice way to . . . you know, make things all right with Gimma."

Arianwyn knew that Salle wasn't really capable of being devious; she was sure this was a genuine effort on Salle's part. "Yes, of course we'd like to help," she said, turning back to the mayor, though she couldn't believe her own words.

"Oh, would you? That would be so very kind of you both." The mayor beamed. "It needn't be anything grand, just some sandwiches, cakes, scones of course, cordial, perhaps a trifle? Just a few people—the three of us, perhaps Miss Delafield or Miss Newam, and Mr. Twine maybe?" He got to his feet, his cheeks pink once more. "You are both so very kind to do this. I really do appreciate it." He stooped down and pulled Arianwyn and Salle into a rather awkward and slightly too tight hug. "Thank you! I knew I could count on you!"

The next afternoon found Arianwyn and Salle busily baking cakes, cookies, and scones in Arianwyn's too-small kitchen. "Did you check the scones?" Arianwyn called to Salle, who was flicking through a magazine as a worrying amount of black smoke plumed from the tiny oven behind her. She herself was hastily tidying the apartment, which mostly consisted of hiding things under cushions or under the bed or in cupboards. She glanced at the clock: It was nearly five, and Gimma and the mayor would be arriving any second.

"Salle, the scones!" Arianwyn called again.

"Oh, drat!" Salle spun around and pulled open the oven door. More smoke billowed out into the apartment.

"Open a window, quickly!" Arianwyn called as she tried to hold everything in a cupboard and shut the doors at the same time.

"I hope we're not too early?" Miss Newam's razor-sharp voice cut through the smoky haze of the apartment just as Arianwyn slammed the door shut.

"No, not at all," she lied. "We were just taking the scones out of the oven, weren't we, Salle?"

Salle nodded, holding a tray of scones in her oven gloved hands. One row seemed to be entirely scorched. Miss Newam waited by the top of the stairs in her usual ill-fitting gray suit. Colin stood beside her, his hair brushed out of his eyes, a blue bow tie wonkily secured at his neck. He blushed and said, "Hi, Arianwyn. Thanks for inviting us."

"Shall I put the kettle on?" Arianwyn asked, rushing to the stove.

With her back to the room she whispered Briå—the air glyph—and quickly spelled the smoke away into a swirling vortex that blew straight out the window. She hoped nobody had noticed. "Won't you have a seat?" she asked, pointing to the table that was laid with one of Aunt Grace's best table-cloths and the mismatched teacups and saucers she had inherited with the Spellorium.

Miss Newam eyed the table with suspicion but took a seat, as did Colin.

"Have you baked all of this yourself?" Colin asked, pointing to the cake and cookies on the table.

"With Salle's help."

Arianwyn filled the kettle and placed it on the stove just as more steps sounded on the spiral staircase. She heard Gimma snap, "Stop fussing, Uncle. I told you I'm fine! Why we have to come and see Arianwyn *Dribble*, I have no idea—"

Gimma and Mayor Belcher halted at the top of the stairs staring at the assembled "party." The apartment fell silent except for the rattle of the kettle as the water boiled.

"Hi, Gimma!" Arianwyn said, stepping forward, doing her best to ignore the "Dribble." "We're so pleased to see you back in Lull."

Gimma didn't say anything at first; she looked at the floor and then at her uncle, who made an encouraging "go on" type gesture. "Hi," she mumbled at last.

"Come and sit down, Gimma. Do you remember Miss Newam?" Arianwyn gestured to the table.

Miss Newam sniffed. "Miss Alverston," she offered coldly. "We met at your evaluation."

Gimma stared ahead and sat next to her uncle as Arianwyn poured the hot water into the teapot and placed it at the center of the table. "Well, here we go."

Miss Newam ignored her. "So, I gather you've returned to Lull to retrain with Arianwyn and Miss Delafield?" she asked with all the subtlety of a volcanic eruption.

Arianwyn nearly knocked over the teapot as she stirred in the tea leaves, trying to brew the tea as quickly as possible. "Tea, Miss Newam? Gimma?" she asked, desperate to change the conversation.

Gimma ignored her and glared back at Miss Newam. After a moment she replied, a cool smile on her pale lips:

"And why have you been banished to the backside of beyond, Miss Newam?"

"Gimma!" Mayor Belcher warned.

"Milk, Miss Newam?" Arianwyn said quickly, as she poured weak tea into Miss Newam's cup. She didn't wait for a reply, clumsily sloshing half the milk jug into the cup as well. The tea looked gray and had puddled into the saucer. "Oh, let me get you another." Arianwyn said, whisking the cup quickly away.

"Actually, I'm here to conduct a very important study regarding hex samples on behalf of the CWA, reporting to the High Elder herself, thank you very much indeed." Miss Newam sniffed.

"How *fascinating*," Gimma replied with a sneer.

"Well, really!" Miss Newam gasped.

"When is it that you're off on your expedition?" Salle asked Arianwyn quickly.

"The end of the week, if the weather isn't too bad," Arianwyn replied, as she finished pouring the first proper cup of tea and started on the next. She eyed Gimma cautiously.

"Off to look at mold in the wood. Can't imagine anything more boring," Gimma said derisively. "Apart from being stuck here, of course."

Salle stepped in quickly with her plate of scones. "Mayor Belcher, how was your meeting in Cranniston today?"

"Oh, it was Conniston actually, but yes, it was all right as meetings go." The mayor reached for a blackened scone, but Salle suddenly smacked his hand away.

"No!"

"Salle!" Arianwyn cried as she refilled the teapot.

"I'm sorry—but it was burnt! Sorry! Sorry, Mayor Belcher." Salle blushed.

This really wasn't going very well at all.

"Really—" started Miss Newam, glaring at Salle.

There was an icy silence until Colin said brightly and a little louder than was necessary: "Well, this all looks really delicious, Arianwyn. You must have been baking all afternoon."

"The scones look like they've been baking for about two weeks," Gimma said quietly, though not so quietly that nobody heard her. She glanced at Salle and sipped her tea.

Salle's cheeks flushed red—not only had Gimma been rude about her scones, but she was also too ill-mannered to have even taken her gloves off. Did she think the hot scones might actually burn her stupid delicate Highbridge skin? She was clearly on the verge of replying when Miss Newam sneezed loudly, spilling her tea all across Aunt Grace's pristine white tablecloth. "It's the flowers!" she mumbled through her handkerchief, and pointed at the jug of wild flowers on the table. "I have an allergy!"

Arianwyn reached forward with the tea towel and dabbed at the spreading stain. "Shall I make you a fresh cup?"

"No!" Miss Newam squawked. She looked as though the very idea of more tea terrified her. "I, uh, just remembered I have to go and make a phone call back to my office in Kingsport."

"But it's after five," Colin said, oblivious to what everyone else was aware of: that this was Miss Newam's excuse to escape.

"Yes, perhaps we should be getting back as well, Gimma. You must be tired?" Mayor Belcher asked, raising his bushy eyebrows theatrically.

"Oh? I feel fine. I'd love some more tea, actually." Gimma grinned and held her cup aloft toward Salle. "Less milk this time."

Salle, who was in the middle of slicing a lemon sponge cake, suddenly froze. When Salle and Gimma had first met, Gimma had treated Salle like a servant, ordering her around for this and that. Arianwyn winced, guessing the comment had hit just the right nerve . . .

"How about . . . I shove this cake up your nose!" Salle said, standing suddenly, holding the slice of cake threateningly and looming over Gimma.

"Salle!" Arianwyn gasped.

The apartment fell silent. Salle had turned bright red and seemed unable to believe her own outburst. Her eyes looked watery as she sat back down, dropping the slice of cake on her own plate, while Gimma just sat quietly, looking away, a dark scowl on her face. Arianwyn was worried there was about to be a repeat of Gimma's outburst at the parade. But instead, she suddenly erupted into tears. She jumped up from her seat, tugging the tablecloth a little and upsetting the tea things in the process. A plate slid off the table and smashed on the floor as Gimma fled down the stairs in floods of tears.

"Oh my goodness, I ought to go after her," the mayor said quietly, getting to his feet. "Thank you . . . for the tea, Miss Gribble."

Arianwyn watched the mayor hurry away as Miss Newam also stood up, her cold gaze falling on Arianwyn. "What an interesting afternoon," she said. Then she turned and followed the mayor downstairs. Salle, Arianwyn, and Colin sat in awkward silence for a few moments.

"Sorry," Salle said eventually, blushing.

"I'm not sure a tea party was your best idea, Salle," Arianwyn sighed, reaching for the back of a nearby chair for support.

Salle pouted. "I'm sorry, I really am. But . . . well . . . I was only trying to help. But she is so flaming rude!" Salle threw herself into the armchair near the stove and pouted.

They heard the Spellorium door close after Miss Newam, the bell charm ringing a few times, and then all was silent. "I think that was possibly the worst tea party in the history of the world," Arianwyn groaned.

"Yikes," Colin sighed, picking up a plate. "Anyone want a scone?"

CHAPTER FIFTEEN

THE MISSION BEGINS

Arianwyn, Miss Newam, and Colin stood at the edge of the Great Wood, their tents and provisions loaded and strapped onto their backs. Miss Delafield, Salle, Mayor Belcher, Aunt Grace, and even Gimma (though she hung back and looked far from happy to be there) had come to wish them well on their trip. It was a cool gray morning, but autumn colors of pale greens, lemony golds, and silvers lit up the trees on the edge of the Great Wood.

Miss Delafield stepped out of the small gathering, leaning heavily on her stick. The white cast was gone at last. "Well, dear," she said to Arianwyn. "Good luck with your expedition. Still seems utterly bonkers to me to go off into the Great Wood when there is so much work to do here." She glowered at Miss Newam. "But orders are orders!" She straightened the strap of Arianwyn's new charm kit and looked at her closely.

"It'll be fine!" Arianwyn said, smiling brightly. She felt suddenly less sure under her supervisor's gaze.

"I do hope so. But still, I'd like you *all* to have these." Miss Delafield reached into her satchel, produced three pairs of dark leather gloves, and handed them to the travelers. Arianwyn could feel small tingling vibrations of magic running through the leather. "I've placed a fire spell on these," explained Miss Delafield. "Wear them when you come into contact with any hex in the wood—they will help to keep you safe."

"Thank you." Arianwyn smiled and pulled her gloves on. Colin and Miss Newam did the same. Miss Newam nodded curtly at Miss Delafield.

Mayor Belcher stood in front of the yellow-and-black cord that was still strung partly along the edge of the wood, the warning notices flapping in the breeze. He looked as though he were standing guard against the wood itself. Gimma now hovered at his side, her eyes fixed and staring straight into the trees.

The mayor clapped his hands and then puffed himself up. "Well, before you set off I feel I should say a few words . . ."

"Oh dear," Miss Delafield muttered.

"So therefore, without further ado, I—and indeed the whole of Lull—wish you all good luck with your mission. And we hope to have you all home again soon." He smiled straight at Miss Newam, who blushed and began to fiddle with the buttons on her new gloves.

There was the smallest spattering of applause.

A splash of rain landed against Arianwyn's cheek; she glanced up at a dark, rolling sky, swollen with clouds. "We should get going!"

The mayor lifted the cord, sweeping his other arm toward the trees as if he were ushering them into a restaurant or theater.

"Wyn, wait!" Salle darted forward. She looked at the grass, and then off across the meadow. "I just wanted to say I'm sorry—about the tea party. I didn't mean to ruin it. I shouldn't have said that to Gimma," she said quietly. The girls glanced over at Gimma, who was still watching the Great Wood, just out of earshot.

Arianwyn sighed. "It's okay, Salle. Honestly, I think the tea party was doomed from the start. But you shouldn't let Gimma wind you up like that."

"I know," Salle mumbled as Miss Newam barged past.

"Come along, Miss Gribble. We're already behind schedule!" she barked sourly. She ducked under the black-and-yellow cord and stepped into the wood. She glanced back at Colin and Arianwyn. "Well, are you coming?"

"Try and be nice to Gimma while we're away," said Arianwyn. "I'm worried about her."

Salle smiled. "I will. Good luck, see you soon!"

Arianwyn gave Salle a quick hug and then followed Colin under the cordon.

They had only walked a few miles, according to Colin's calculations, but with Miss Newam stepping carefully over every rock and around every jutting branch as though it might be deadly, they were not moving quickly.

"How long have we been walking?" Arianwyn whispered to Colin.

"Only about an hour and a half." He raised an eyebrow.

"She's going to have to move quicker than that or we'll be in the wood forever!" Arianwyn glanced back over her shoulder at Miss Newam, who was negotiating a small holly bush, very slowly. "Do you need any help?" Arianwyn called.

"No thank you," Miss Newam replied quickly, just as a branch snapped back, narrowly missing her face. Arianwyn stifled a giggle as Miss Newam tried to dodge the branch only to stumble over her own feet. She fell with a cry into the damp undergrowth.

Arianwyn dropped her heavy backpack and moved quickly to where Miss Newam had fallen. She heard Colin following behind. "Are you all right?" She crouched down to help.

"Wretched place!" Miss Newam spat, shoving Arianwyn's hand away. "I'm perfectly able to get to my own feet, thank you, Miss Gribble!"

Leaves cascaded to the floor as Miss Newam stood, though quite a lot clung to her suit and hair. "Perhaps we should stop for a bit?" Colin suggested. "Let you catch your breath—"

"Will you stop fussing!" Miss Newam snarled. She pushed past Arianwyn and Colin, and hefted her backpack onto her shoulder again, muttering. She turned and looked at Arianwyn and Colin. "Well, shall we get a move on? I really can't be doing with this glacial pace of yours, Miss Gribble!"

Arianwyn looked at Colin, the disbelief on his face matching her own. "This is going to be a very long trip!"

she said as she hoisted on her pack again. "Well, come along, Mr. Twine!" she added in her best impression of Miss Newam. "I can't be waiting *all* day!"

They set off again, laughing, but had only gone a few yards when they heard another shout of dismay from beyond the trees ahead: "HELP! Miss Gribble!"

They broke into a run, jumping over tree roots and dodging tumbles of bramble and ivy. They had just cleared a bunch of tangled blackberry creepers when they found Miss Newam, frozen to the spot.

She stood at the edge of a small clearing. It was terribly dark, and for a moment Arianwyn couldn't figure out why. But as her eyes slowly adjusted, she realized the wood was somehow changed. Miss Newam was surrounded by an alien landscape, like something from a nightmare. Half the trees were black, as though they had been burned.

But fire had not caused this devastation.

Arianwyn clamped her hand over her mouth and nose as the rancid stench of dark magic filled her nostrils. Colin gave a low whistle. "What on earth . . ."

"Be careful!" Arianwyn said slowly. "It's hex!"

CHAPTER SIXTEEN

THE HEX

"I've never seen this much!" Colin walked carefully into the clearing. He paused to look at an affected tree more closely. "This is a lot, isn't it, Arianwyn?"

It was. Every inch of the tree's trunk was covered in thick layers of the magical fungus, while its leaves—all blackened—clung limply to the branches.

"Don't get too close!" Arianwyn grabbed Colin's arm and pulled him back. Worry, hot and quick, crawled beneath her skin. She had brought them all into danger already—so early in the mission. "Colin, can I see the map, please?" she asked, her voice fluttering with nerves.

Miss Newam had carefully approached the tree and was already scraping samples of hex into a small glass container. Colin passed Arianwyn the map and she unfolded it carefully, tracing a finger across the path he had plotted.

"We could go around, perhaps?" Arianwyn asked Colin.

He moved closer, studying the map over her shoulder. Then he checked his compass and walked around the clearing, this way and that.

"Well?" Miss Newam asked, slipping the small glass dish into her bag and stowing her scalpel away into a metal tin.

"Okay. So, I think there's a way around, as long as the hex hasn't spread farther." Colin glanced at Arianwyn.

"And if it has?" Miss Newam asked, folding her arms tightly over her chest.

There was a long silence. It seemed as if even the breeze had abandoned this part of the wood. "Well," Arianwyn started brightly, though she felt anything but bright. "Let's hope for the best, shall we?" She caught Miss Newam's glare. "Which way, Colin?"

On the way out of the clearing, Arianwyn's boot crunched against something. She peered down into the dark mulch of the woodland floor, where small shards of glass glistened in the hazy light. Had Miss Newam dropped one of her sample containers? She shook her head and walked on, into the darkness of the wood.

They walked for another hour, reaching a fast-flowing river at the bottom of a deep gorge spanned by a natural, narrow bridge of arching rock. But beyond they found another patch of the Great Wood that was blackened and blighted with tangled strands of hex.

"Any ideas?" Arianwyn asked Colin as he studied the map again.

He sighed. "I think so, but it looks like this area of the wood is a swamp. If we can't get through we'll have days extra to add on, I think." He studied the map again and checked the compass, while Miss Newam busied herself with gathering more samples, lifting various glass tubes and small dishes from the equipment bag along with the silver scalpel.

"Careful, Miss Newam, don't drop any more of your containers," Arianwyn warned.

"I haven't dropped any so far, thank you!" she snapped, laying her tools out on a small canvas square.

Arianwyn frowned, remembering the glass crunching under her shoes. "But—"

"Believe it or not, I do know what I'm doing, Miss Gribble!"

"Sorry," Arianwyn said. "Um, can I help at all?"

But Miss Newam scowled. "I suggest you two occupy your time finding a route to Erraldur and let me do *my* job."

They trudged on, through parts of the wood so overgrown that it seemed to take hours just to move a few feet. They passed trees that were bigger than any Arianwyn had ever seen, their huge trunks and branches arching high above like the vaulted ceiling of a cathedral or castle.

Arianwyn had lost track of how long they had been walking for, but she could feel her feet begin to drag, while her arms and legs felt heavy. Her stomach gave a sudden loud, rumbling growl. "Shall we stop? We should rest and eat, don't you think?" she called back to Colin and Miss Newam, who were lagging farther behind.

Colin's face brightened until Miss Newam said, "Should we not carry on until we pass the swamp? It's likely to get dark soon, surely?"

Miss Newam was probably right—Arianwyn thought it must be dinnertime—but peering up through the high branches overhead, she could see that the sky was bright, flat, and blue: no hint of evening, no tinge of pink or darkness. She checked her watch but it had stopped at ten o'clock, about an hour after they had entered the wood. "Well, I'm hungry. I think we should eat."

She saw an obliging mossy rock, sat down, and started to rifle through her backpack, searching for the sandwiches Aunt Grace had packed for them. Colin and Miss Newam seated themselves on two other nearby rocks. They both looked exhausted. They would perhaps have to think about pitching their tents and resting properly, soon.

"Tea?" Colin asked, stifling a yawn as he pulled out the thermos and three small tin camping cups. He placed them carefully on a smaller rock nearby.

"Here they are!" Arianwyn called triumphantly as she pulled out the parcel of sandwiches, wrapped tightly in thick brown paper. Her stomach rumbled again as she started to unwrap them. But as she undid the last fold of paper she nearly dropped the package; everything inside the wrappings was covered in a thick, fuzzy green mold. The earthy smell of it filled her nostrils. "Oh no!" She held them aloft to show Miss Newam and Colin. "The sandwiches have gone off."

"What? How?" Miss Newam got to her feet and peered at the moldy mess. "You must have let them get wet or something—were they wrapped up correctly?" she snapped. She took the package from Arianwyn and her nose wrinkled. She threw them to the ground. "Disgusting!"

"Well, at least we still have the tea," Colin said as he tipped the thermos up. But instead of a flow of warm, milky brown tea, there was a slow dribble of lumpy sludge.

They looked at one another, trying to figure out what had happened to their food.

"It must be something in the wood affecting it," Arianwyn guessed.

"That's all well and good, Miss Gribble, but what on earth are we going to do for food now?" Miss Newam grumbled as she walked away from their mossy rock seats.

"It's all right; we have some army rations as well, somewhere in one of the bags." She busied herself searching as Miss Newam prowled around the edge of the small clearing, muttering and moaning to herself, occasionally throwing a filthy look at Colin or Arianwyn, at one time even both of them.

"Oh, I think I've got them, Miss Newam. Look, a lovely can of tomato—" Arianwyn glanced up and fell silent. Miss Newam was standing as still as a statue at the far edge of the clearing, surrounded by a small group of assorted odd-looking creatures.

Feylings!

"Who are you?" A voice, rich and delicate, sounded in her ear. Arianwyn was about to turn when she noticed that the sharp edge of a long flat stone—the tip of a short, carved stone dagger—was aimed straight at her.

CHAPTER SEVENTEEN

THE FEYLINGS

A few moments later, Arianwyn, Colin, and Miss Newam were being marched through the wood by the small group of feylings. Every time Arianwyn had tried to ask a question, the sharp stone had been pointed at her again and she had fallen silent.

There was something both exciting and terrifying about seeing these feylings. Each one was a different shape and size from the next. One towered nearly as tall as the trees of the wood and was pale like parchment; another was small, spindle-thin, and dark as slate. A third was about as tall as a child, shimmering as though it were slowly disappearing right before their eyes only to shimmer back into view seconds later. Another was squat, and covered in fine purple scales like a fish—the light flashing against them was mesmerizing. In one chubby hand it clutched a spear, also tipped with a finely carved stone blade, which it kept carefully pointed at Miss Newam. "Perhaps we're somehow closer to Erraldur than we thought?" Arianwyn whispered to Colin.

The lead feyling, who walked on bright yellow claws and was covered in sleek black feathers, turned and glared at her. "Erraldur lost."

"What does that mean?" Miss Newam asked, not even attempting to lower her voice. She was shoved by the squat purple feyling. It babbled something undecipherable. "Well, *really*," she mumbled.

Arianwyn's heart was beating in fear. *Erraldur lost?* Did that mean what she thought it meant?

Ahead, a wild hedge full of bramble and twists of creeping vine loomed like a solid thorny wall from a fairy tale. The black-feathered feyling halted before it and gestured quickly and elegantly into the air. After a moment, a small opening appeared in the hedge, swirling like a whirlpool. The feathered feyling passed through, followed by some of the others.

"What do we do?" Miss Newam asked, her face white, her voice wobbling.

"I don't think we have a lot of choice," Arianwyn said gently, as the spear waved dangerously close to them both. She ducked through the gap.

"We did set out to find feylings, after all," she heard Colin murmur as he followed.

Clambering through the hedge, Arianwyn felt the distinctive tickle of magic, reminding her of the first time she'd met Estar. She stumbled to a halt as she stepped through, Colin trampling on her heel as she gaped at the broad clearing in front of her.

There was a whole camp full of feylings: fifty at least, perhaps more.

The tall-as-the-trees feyling hurried toward another of similar height and shape, though its skin was darker and mottled with patches of gray and green. There was a high, excited sound and the two feylings were suddenly embracing. Arianwyn saw others who were similar in shape or coloring. Several of the squat purple feylings sat around a small fire, tending to a cooking pot and apparently arguing over some of the ingredients. Another group hurried past; they barely reached Arianwyn's knee and were striped and speckled, like insects.

"Oh my word, what is this place?" Miss Newam sniffed.

"It's wonderful." Colin smiled. "Look!" He pointed as yet more feylings emerged from the woods from the opposite side of the clearing, carrying woven baskets filled with nuts and fruits like nothing Arianwyn had ever seen before, all bright colors and strange spiky shapes. A yellow-scaled feyling no larger than Arianwyn's boot floated past them in the air, propelling itself with fanlike crests along its back, arms, and legs. Miss Newam tried to bat it away until Colin grabbed her hand. The yellow feyling turned sharply, poking its black tongue out at Miss Newam. "Excuse *me!*" she muttered.

Arianwyn had been scanning the crowd as they walked through the camp, hoping to see Estar among them, and had noticed that many of the feylings wore a small carved stone around their necks, the carvings similar to those on the spear and dagger stones. There was something glyphlike about the shapes, she thought.

Whispers rose; exotic words and songlike conversations called back and forth. Arianwyn didn't understand them but the voices sounded faintly familiar, like a language she had heard once in a dream. A small gaggle of what she guessed must be feyling children rushed between groups, laughter rising up into the overhanging trees with the smoke and sparks from the fires. The air crackled and hummed with more magic than Arianwyn thought she had ever felt. Her fingertips tingled, her scalp prickled.

"It's amazing . . . ," she breathed.

But as more and more feylings noticed the new arrivals, it was as if a stone had been dropped into a pool. The talking and laughing stopped at once, and fifty or so pairs of strange eyes turned to look at Arianwyn and her companions. From far away a strange song began, a single voice at first, a gentle murmuring chant. Then another voice and another.

"Stay here!" the feathered feyling commanded, raising the sharp stone at them again. All the while, the singing grew and grew. They were now at the very center of the feyling camp around a small fire. A large cooking pot hung above the crackling flames, and the most delicious smell wafted toward them.

Arianwyn felt nervous about what was happening. Were they prisoners of some sort? She searched the crowd again, hoping against hope that she might spot Estar, his shock of black hair and his curving horns and gentle smile, but there were no blue feylings here: none bore even a passing resemblance to her dear friend. Where was he? Were Erraldur and the book close by? Or was Erraldur really . . . *lost*? Surely not. She must've misunderstood. Her mind raced. As the feylings pressed closer, their murmuring song grew louder, stronger. It was the most beautiful sound Arianwyn thought she had ever heard, voices and words overlapping and twining together, and as the voices grew louder the magic fizzed and crackled in the air around her, stronger and stronger.

And then it was over.

The magic fizzed about them for a few more moments, and when Arianwyn looked up she felt as though she had just woken from the most beautiful and refreshing sleep, the aches and pains of the day dissolved, her tiredness evaporated. She felt wonderful. And entirely relieved that, clearly, they were in no danger from the feylings at all. She felt momentarily bad to have thought they might be.

She glanced at Colin and Miss Newam, who had clearly felt the same effects as she had. Miss Newam was even . . . smiling!

"What was that?" Colin whispered.

"Magic!" Arianwyn smiled.

The throng of feylings suddenly split, creating a narrow pathway. A pale white shape moved toward them. For one mad moment, Arianwyn thought it was Bob. But it was another feyling, full of catlike grace, with a long body as white as bleached bone; somehow Arianwyn knew immediately that this feyling was female, and clearly the one who was in charge. A tail flicked this way and that as the feyling drew closer. Arianwyn couldn't help but be reminded of a wild animal hunting prey.

Her hand reached for Colin's and gripped it tightly.

The white feyling came to a halt and then stood, in one elegant, fluid movement, on her back legs. She was smaller than Arianwyn but stared at her confidently. Her face was wide, with delicate, catlike features but huge, wide blue eyes, the color of a frozen lake on a bright winter's day. Eyes that lingered on Arianwyn's silver star badge.

"You are welcome here, friends," the white feyling said. Her voice was not loud, but it carried power. Like Estar, she spoke clearly and well—almost like a fancy Highbridge lady but slowly, as if each word had been carefully thought out. She turned to face the other feylings surrounding them, full of curiosity. "Leave us," she said sternly. "I need to talk to our guests." One by one the feylings dispersed to the other campfires dotted around the site, until only the black-feathered feyling remained, watchful eyes fixed on Arianwyn and the others.

"I'm Arianwyn Gribble," Arianwyn said, bowing low to the white feyling before she sat. The white feyling shot her the most curious of glances and a small smile fluttered across her wide mouth. "These are my friends," Arianwyn continued, "Colin Twine and Miss Newam."

They both replicated Arianwyn's bow.

"I am Virean le-Marrak," the white feyling said, bowing in response, though far more elegantly. Arianwyn noticed that she also wore a stone around her neck, traced with strange carvings and patterns.

"This is Chupak, our head scout."

The black-feathered feyling bowed also, though not as low as Virean had.

"Please, sit down. Would you like some food?" Virean asked, gesturing to the steaming cooking pot.

"Yes!" Miss Newam said suddenly. She blushed at once, mumbling, "Our supplies have gone off!"

The smell of food was almost too much to bear as Arianwyn, Colin, and Miss Newam dropped onto the mossy ground. Arianwyn ached with hunger, and as Virean served out the steaming broth into small wooden bowls, her stomach grumbled loudly. Miss Newam took her serving and was about to lift her meal hungrily to her mouth when Arianwyn gestured for her to wait.

"Thank you," Arianwyn said to Virean. "This is very kind."

"We are feylings; our community is based upon kindness and helping others." She raised her bowl high and said loudly, "We thank the forest for providing food and friends and shelter this day. Please eat."

The broth was delicious, spicy and earthy; it warmed Arianwyn from her toes to the very ends of her curls, after just one mouthful. By the time she finished her second bowl, the aching emptiness in her stomach was long gone.

Now Virean looked at her closely, her eyes falling on the star again. "You are a human magic worker? A . . . witch?" Virean asked.

"Yes," Arianwyn replied.

"Are we near to a human settlement?" Virean asked as they finished their food.

"Our town is about a day's walk away from here," Colin explained, "to the northeast."

"Are you in need of help?" asked Arianwyn.

The white feyling turned and had a brief hushed conversation with Chupak behind her. Then she turned back. "No, we wish to avoid the human settlements if we can. In times past, feylings and humans were friends and neighbors . . . but no more. We teach our young ones to stay away from the human lands and towns. Now we search for others of our kind—have you seen other feylings on your journey?"

Arianwyn shook her head. "No. I'm sorry. Where are you going?"

"There is a feyling meeting place close by. It is the place we go to when there is great danger, when nowhere else is safe for us."

"What's happened?" Colin asked.

Virean had a faraway look in her blue eyes. "Our settlements have been plagued by strange dark creatures, twisted monstrosities the likes of which have not been seen for thousands of years. And in the meantime, the black fungus has been spreading, destroying our homes and our food. Families and communities of feylings have been lost or torn apart by darkness and horror. We fled Erraldur when the dark creatures attacked in force. We were unable to save our city."

So it's true. Erraldur is . . . gone? Arianwyn suddenly felt cold. She could feel her nerves jangle with fear at what this might mean.

Virean continued. "To keep as many safe as we could, we split into small groups and told every feyling to head north to an ancient place feylings used in times of trouble, an old village called Edda. Away from the dark creatures, away from the black fungus—"

"The hex?" Colin asked quickly. "You mean the hex, don't you?"

Virean cocked her head to one side. "Hex?"

"This is hex," Miss Newam said, reaching for one of the glass containers that held a sample.

Virean peered closer. "Hex," she said carefully, nodding. "It is everywhere throughout the wood."

"What?" Arianwyn asked.

"The . . . hex. It is everywhere, south of here. About four days' walk. We tried to double back around, but . . ." Virean shook her head.

Arianwyn stared at the mossy ground. That was it. They would never reach Erraldur—or what was left of it—if the hex had spread so much throughout the wood. They would not find the book. And she would never see Estar again . . . if he had even survived. A crushing emptiness descended, spoiling the magic of the feylings and the warmth the broth had bought. She felt sick, her insides twisting.

"Are you all right?" Virean asked. She placed a cool white hand on Arianwyn's.

"We were trying to get to Erraldur . . . we are looking for someone."

"Erraldur is gone, overrun with the hex and strange creatures. Everything was destroyed, everyone has fled." Virean played with the carved stone around her neck.

Arianwyn looked at Miss Newam and Colin, their faces almost as white as Virean. She saw her own confusion mirrored in their eyes. This had not been how she had imagined their mission would go. How was she going to explain all this to the High Elder? How would they help everyone if they couldn't get the *Book of Quiet Glyphs*? And what about Estar? It felt as though the world had fallen away from underneath her.

"Are you okay, Wyn?" Colin asked.

She shook her head, tears brimming around her eyes. "Estar . . . ," she said quietly.

"I know." Colin swallowed. "But perhaps he'll be all right."

"Estar?" Virean said. She sat suddenly straighter. "You know Estar?"

Arianwyn nodded, wiping away a tear. "He's my friend."

Virean looked carefully at her again. "Estar." She smiled. "I might have known—he has always been curious about you humans."

"What happened to him?" Arianwyn said, hardly daring to hope.

"I tried to persuade him to come with us, but he would not leave without helping as many feylings as he could— other clans, other feyling villages under attack and in need. Estar cannot help but help. I am sorry, but I do not know what became of him."

CHAPTER EIGHTEEN

THE RIVER

rianwyn looked at Colin and Miss Newam. "We'll have to go back to Lull, then," she said, the realization hitting her like a blow to her stomach. Back to Lull—without the book, without Estar.

There was silence for a few moments, and then Virean said, "Then we wish you a good journey." Chupak came forward, carrying three of the carved stones. "We would like to offer you these as gifts," Virean said, reaching out to place the first over Arianwyn's head. There was the faintest tingle of magic from the stone as it fell gently against her chest. "For protection on your travels." Virean smiled. "Stories say river stones gathered at full moon and marked with this symbol can protect from darkness."

She placed a ghost-white hand across her thin chest and bowed low. Arianwyn, and then Colin, copied the gesture. They looked sharply at Miss Newam, who had not.

"I shall get a stiff back with all this bowing," she grumbled, bowing just a little and very quickly.

Arianwyn noticed Virean take it all in, her ice-blue eyes unblinking before she slowly looked away.

"Thank you for sharing your meal with us," Arianwyn said quickly, trying to make up for Miss Newam's rudeness, "and for welcoming us."

Virean smiled.

"Quicker to go south from here," Chupak said. "Follow the river path, hex not yet reached that part of wood. No bad creatures there."

"Thank you," Arianwyn said again, though it felt insufficient for the kindness Virean and the feylings had shown them. Then she looked at her charm basket. "Oh, wait a second," she said, opening the lid, the contents jingling brightly inside the basket. She pulled out a small glass globe, quickly added dried daisy petals, a small sliver of pink quartz, and two silver hoops. She handed the completed charm to Virean and then sketched Aluna, the water glyph, above it.

"It's a friendship charm." Arianwyn smiled.

"How *very* useful, I am sure," Miss Newam said quietly.

"Actually, it's one of the very oldest charms there is. I saw the original recipe, carved in stone in the Hylund museum," Colin said quickly.

Arianwyn was amazed he knew so much about charms. He noticed her looking and blushed.

Virean took the charm in her hand and held it carefully. "Friendship is more important to feylings than magic and power, Miss Newam. Without our friends we are nothing but lost creatures wandering the world alone." She smiled at Arianwyn and bowed low once more before placing the charm around her neck. "Thank you."

Chupak bowed as they passed, his black-feathered arms spread wide as he almost touched the ground.

Arianwyn, Colin, and Miss Newam walked back through the feyling camp. The feylings watched them again, but this time a few hands were raised in farewell. Cooking fires were being extinguished—it seemed the feylings were also getting ready to move on. Before them the tangle of hedge was opening and they passed through, back into the wood once more. And as the hedge opening closed behind them, it was as if the feylings had never been. Only the stone charm hanging around Arianwyn's neck convinced her she hadn't dreamt the whole thing.

Following Chupak's instructions, within an hour they had found the banks of the river, which was wide, calm, and flat. Some way off it tumbled over huge rocks, and farther downstream came the crashing sounds of a huge waterfall. The canopy of trees broke in the very center of the flow and a wide band of blue split the green of the Great Wood. Even though it felt like days had passed since they'd set off, the sun was high in the sky and golden light shifted across the water. Fish darted beneath in silver flashes, while here and there dragonflies zipped across the surface.

"It's beautiful!" Colin sighed. He dropped his pack on the bank and crouched to take in the view. "And if Chupak is right, we should be back home in just a few hours if we follow the river path north." He pointed to a narrow, trailing line on his map.

"It's the Torr River?" Arianwyn asked, peering at the map. How had they come so far east? she wondered.

"A shame we didn't bring a boat!" Miss Newam said, resting against a rock and taking a long drink from her water bottle.

"Just ignore her," Colin mumbled.

The river was so clear you could see every pebble and stone lining the riverbed. But something made Arianwyn feel uneasy. The far bank was hidden in shadow, the trees a thick screen. She lifted a small stone and tossed it across the river. It fell with a gentle plop, the ripples disturbing the water and setting the sunlight dancing in a thousand directions at once.

"I might have a paddle!" Colin said brightly. Pulling off his boots and socks, he rolled up his trousers and headed out into the water, smiling. "Lovely and refreshing!" he called.

He'd only gone about halfway when a breeze moved across the surface of the river. It was warm and carried the scents of the wood on it, warm, earthy smells . . . and something else. "Colin—" Arianwyn called, her nostrils filling with the stench of dark magic.

But she choked on her warning and he didn't hear her. The smell was overpowering and for a second she had to steady herself on the bank, feeling dizzy.

"What's the matter?" Miss Newam asked.

"Hex," Arianwyn whispered, her mouth dry and rough. "More hex!"

"Mr. Twine!" Miss Newam called urgently, her voice high and frightened.

But Colin couldn't hear her over the sloshing sound as he waded through the deeper part of the river, the water around his knees.

Arianwyn didn't wait another second; she skidded down the bank and started to run after him, stumbling and tripping over stones and rocks as she went. Once or twice she thought she might fall headfirst into the water, but each time she managed to right herself. Her trousers and boots were soon soaked through.

As she drew nearer to Colin he turned, alerted by the disturbed water and the sound of Arianwyn rushing and sloshing toward him.

"Colin! Stop!" she shouted, just as he reached the far bank and the shadows of the trees. Though Arianwyn could see now that it wasn't shadow at all; the trees along the edge of the river were swathed in thick layers of black hex.

Colin had obviously spotted it now and stopped, his hand frozen as he had reached out for a black, hex-covered branch where he was about to pull himself up. He turned and looked at Arianwyn, pale. "Thanks."

Arianwyn stood at his side, the water swirling around them both, taking in the sight of the ruined wood before her. The air was full of the cloying stench of dark magic, and she could feel its tug on her. She felt tired and sad. "Come on, we'd best move away from here. It's not safe," she said, moving back across the river to Miss Newam.

Then suddenly from deep in the wood came a thunderous sound followed by an urgent animal call. A loud, trumpeting cry filled the air. And then a herd of staggets surged through the trees and charged out across the river, sprays of water glinting in the sunshine, light glancing off their silver antlers.

"WOW!" Colin said, grabbing Arianwyn's arm. "That's amazing."

The staggets approached the far side of the river, sensed the hex, and came to a stop. They seemed agitated and frightened. They sniffed the air and looked back the way they had just come. Their eyes wide, they panted and moved anxiously around at the edge of the river.

"They know it's not safe to go on," Arianwyn said. She quickly pulled the spirit lantern from its case and held it to her eye. The staggets gave off a soft golden glow, unlike the hex-ravaged woods at the other side of the river, which emanated dark pulsating waves.

There was a loud noise from something nearby, but hidden by the trees. The staggets circled around in the river, clearly unsure where to go.

"Something else is coming," Miss Newam said, pointing back across to the trees.

The call came again: a strangled, terrifying cry followed by a higher-pitched sound that was like a child's shout mingled with a whistling noise.

"What is that?" Colin asked, looking at Arianwyn.

"I have no idea," she replied, just as something small tumbled through the trees, falling with a splash into the river. A gray head broke the surface, skin as dark as stone, huge bright pink eyes wide in terror. The creature gasped in fear and panic.

"What is it?" Miss Newam called as she clambered up onto a rock.

Arianwyn peered closer. "I think it's another feyling," she said. Then she quickly pulled the spirit lantern up to her eye and focused it until she had the small creature framed. The view, as ever, was slightly fuzzy. But there it was, an aura of rainbow colors. "Don't panic!" Arianwyn shouted. "It's a feyling all right." She started forward carefully, not wanting to frighten the feyling, who was scrabbling up the side of a large boulder, trying desperately to get out of the water.

But Arianwyn had only gone a little way when the trees just behind the feyling burst apart and something charged forward and into the river.

It was a male stagget.

Arianwyn felt her tensed muscles relax for a second.

But only for a second.

As the stagget charged from the shade of the trees to the light in the middle of the river, Arianwyn saw that along one side of the creature's body and muddled throughout its once-magnificent silver antlers was a thick, snarled tangle of hex.

CHAPTER NINETEEN

HELPLESS

The infected stagget gave a low, mournful cry and stalked toward the defenseless feyling. Arianwyn took a few cautious steps closer. The feyling had stopped trying to climb the slippery boulder and was now staring at the stagget, frozen in terror. The rest of the stagget herd circled in the river, terrified and confused.

"No!" Arianwyn cried, moving forward through the water.

"Careful, Arianwyn!" Colin called, reaching for her arm.

She shrugged him off. "Stay there!" she warned.

She moved ahead cautiously. The hex had scorched the stagget's antlers, scarring its face and body. As she drew closer to the creature and the feyling, Arianwyn heard the stagget's breathing, shallow and fast, and noticed how its eyes twisted, as if the stagget was struggling against itself. Arianwyn just needed to reach the feyling and . . . but it was too late: Suddenly the stagget snorted in frustration and lowered its head, stamping its front feet in the shallow water. It was about to charge.

"Look out!" Arianwyn shouted to the feyling.

The stagget gave a cry that was full of anger and pain and its eyes darkened, misting over as it charged, churning up the river water. But the feyling moved suddenly, leaping aside just in time: Perhaps it had been planning this all along?

The stagget crashed headfirst into the rock. Arianwyn had turned away, expecting to hear some sort of sickening crack as animal collided with solid stone—but instead there was a loud explosion. When she looked back, the rock had been blasted into a shower of dust and stone that rained down into the river as the stagget reared its head, completely unharmed. *It's so powerful! Unnaturally powerful* . . . Arianwyn thought with a sickening feeling.

The feyling cried out, and was suddenly racing along the river edge straight toward Miss Newam, who looked totally stunned at the turn of events. Arianwyn glanced back at the stagget, which was shaking its head. It called out—a terrifying, sickening scream—and turned around, its black eyes locked on the feyling and now on Miss Newam as well.

Cold dread hit Arianwyn as the stagget charged again. "Run!" she screamed, her voice echoing across the river.

The gray feyling reached Miss Newam, grabbed for her hand, and together they ran along the shoreline as fast as they could. It was the most bizarre pairing Arianwyn thought she had ever seen. Miss Newam glanced back, her face pale as the stagget charged after them, the little gray feyling hurrying at her side.

What do I do? Arianwyn thought, panic wiping her mind of any practical thoughts.

She could see that Miss Newam and the feyling would soon run out of river, a smaller waterfall creating a dead end just ahead. The riverbank was crowded with large boulders, blocking the path back into the wood. They were cornered, closed in by stone on one side, waterfall behind and the hex-ravaged trees on the opposite bank.

The stagget had slowed to a loping walk, realizing its prey was trapped.

What? What can I do? She panicked as she ran, Colin now following close behind.

"Arianwyn, help!" Miss Newam shouted, her voice trembling and broken as the stagget drew nearer. It had stopped and now lowered its head, readying for a final charge. But it hesitated, appearing to struggle with itself. Its legs trembled and it collapsed slightly in the river, shaking its head as though it might be able to throw off the hex that scorched its antlers and body. Arianwyn only had moments to act.

"I . . . I'll have to stun it," she said, her voice shaking. She glanced at Colin.

He grabbed her arm, his face pale. "Who—wait—that's not allowed, Wyn, surely! Not a stagget!" Colin said. He tried to drag her back. "Try something else—there has to be another way!" His fingers gripped her arm tightly.

"Miss Gribble!" Miss Newam shouted insistently, her voice quivering. She and the feyling had edged back against the rocks. "Do something this instant!" The little gray feyling shrank back behind her legs.

Arianwyn's mind raced. Colin was right: these great and gentle spirits were protected by all the laws of the CWA and the Four Kingdoms. She glanced around frantically. She just needed to move the stagget away, that was all, give the feyling and Miss Newam a chance to escape from the river. Arianwyn crouched, her hands plunged into the water. "A̱luna!" she called, and even before she had finished summoning the glyph, she could feel the urgent racing of magic in the river around her. She just needed enough water to move the stagget away from Miss Newam and the feyling.

But something was blocking her. She could feel the stream of strong, pure magic deep under the water, nestled into the earth, but it was trapped.

"Why isn't anything happening?" Colin cried.

Arianwyn looked at the hex-ravaged trees and the infected stagget. The creature raised itself up again. The strange darkness flashed in its eyes as it pawed the riverbed, readying for the final charge.

The hex was blocking her spell. And she had run out of time.

She needed something stronger. More powerful. And she needed it fast.

"Eṟte!" Arianwyn cried.

Summoning the earth glyph in the middle of the river was not the best idea, but it was stronger, simpler, and less complicated than the water glyph. It was still a struggle, but this time she could feel the magic shift down in the earth. The magic moved agonizingly slowly but she didn't need much to create a stunning spell. The stagget started to charge, but then stopped again, its head thrashing around in some sort of horrid, self-destructive struggle, striking nearby rocks, which disintegrated as the first one had. Miss Newam screamed, and she and the feyling tried uselessly to scrabble up the wall of tumbled boulders.

A green stunning orb formed in the air before Arianwyn—it was small, but she prayed it would be enough.

"No, Wyn," Colin said. "It's forbidden to stun a spirit creature. You can't!"

He was right, of course. "But it's not a spirit creature anymore," Arianwyn said, as certain of this as she had been of anything in her life. "It's . . . something else, something dark. And Miss Newam and the feyling . . ."

Could she really do it? Could she go against everything she had ever been taught and stun a spirit creature? She took one look at the struggling creature, at Miss Newam and the feyling, and knew that she could, that she would have to do it.

"Hey—over here!" Arianwyn shouted, kicking the water, trying to catch the stagget's attention and draw it away.

The stagget turned, its black eyes focusing on her. Lowering its head and hex-tangled antlers, it snorted and charged. Before she thought too much more about what was happening, Arianwyn sent the orb flying out across the river, straight at the charging stagget.

The orb hit the stagget full in the chest with an explosion of light. The creature slowed but didn't stop. Arianwyn summoned another stunning orb and sent it after the first.

"NO, Arianwyn. Enough. Stop!" Colin grabbed her arm.

This time the stagget stumbled forward and crashed into the shallow waters with another mournful cry.

Everyone froze.

She wrenched her arm free from Colin and moved as quickly as she could toward the stagget. "What are you doing, Arianwyn? Let's get Miss Newam and the feyling and go!"

Arianwyn turned quickly and pushed Colin away. An idea had unfurled in her mind, a terrible and frightening idea that made her shake with fear. But she knew she had no choice now. "No. I can't leave it like this, Colin. It's cruel. It's wrong."

"What's going on now?" Miss Newam shouted. She was still backed against the rocks of the small waterfall, clinging for dear life to the little gray feyling.

Arianwyn didn't reply. She moved toward the stagget that lay on its side, the water lapping around it. It snorted once or twice in frustration. "Easy now," Arianwyn soothed as she knelt in the water beside the once-magnificent creature.

The stagget's eyes had cleared again now; the strange blackness vanished. It tried to move but the two stunning spells had weakened it, and it only managed to shake its head a little. Carefully Arianwyn placed a hand onto the stagget's neck, its fur slick with sweat, its pulse surging under her fingers, urgent and full of terror. "There, there." There was a sudden lurch as the stagget shifted its head, bringing its massive, silver, hex-ravaged antlers crashing against a nearby rock. "I know!" Arianwyn said sadly. It was so clear now what it was trying to do.

"We should go," Colin said, his voice full of urgency and something else. He was angry with her.

"But I can't leave the stagget like this," Arianwyn said sorrowfully. "It's cruel."

"There isn't anything to be done now," Colin said. "There's no cure for this. *Let's go.*"

Without turning she said quietly, "I have to banish it."

"No!" Colin said quickly. He tried to pull her up, away from the stagget. "You can't do that. It's forbidden—it's *illegal*, Arianwyn!"

Arianwyn got to her feet and whirled to face Colin. He stumbled back in shock. "But we can't leave it like this. I won't do it. Who knows what might happen. It might attack the rest of the herd; it could spread more hex through the wood, infect more spirit creatures. Don't you *see*?"

Colin shook his head sadly. Perhaps he truly didn't understand at all.

The stagget's movements became more furious. Arianwyn could see the blackness clouding its eyes again. The stunning spell was already weakening. "I'm doing it," Arianwyn said, dropping to the stagget's side again.

She sketched L'ier, the banishing glyph, in the air just above its head.

"I'll have to tell the High Elder," Colin said. His voice was low and shook a little. He took another few sloshing steps away from her.

"Colin, you wouldn't—" Arianwyn paused and twisted where she knelt in the river.

"I think I have to," he said, staring at the water, not looking at her. "I'm sorry. I just don't think this is right." He shrugged.

"And I can't see what other choice we ... *I* have," Arianwyn said quietly. She turned back to the glyph and listened to the water splashing as Colin waded away.

The glyph complete, it hung in the air for a moment, dark and full of sadness. L'ier was the only glyph that held a small sliver of dark magic within it, just enough to open a rift to the void.

The void waited on the other side: It was darkness and cold—the place where all dark spirits came from. The icy chill of it wrapped around Arianwyn, her damp clothes making her colder still. From the riverbank, she heard a sudden shout from Miss Newam. "She's doing WHAT?"

Arianwyn ignored the frantic watery sounds of Colin and Miss Newam rushing back across the river. She placed her hand on the stagget's side once more, its eyes totally black now, like the darkest marble. It growled angrily, fighting the last strands of the stunning spell. Flecks of blood flew from its mouth as it gave a sickening cry that was part scream, part roar.

"I am so sorry," Arianwyn said quietly. She took a deep breath, tears blurring her vision. "Return to the void; your spirit must not linger here." Her throat tightened.

"Stop it at once, you stupid girl!" Miss Newam screamed.

"Go in peace," Arianwyn continued, her voice breaking as the physical form of the stagget began to dissolve away. "Return . . . to the darkness." Her tears fell into the river.

Miss Newam snatched at her hand. "Stop it! How dare you."

But it was already too late. They watched in stunned silence as the stagget dissolved into a swirling mass of dark and light, its golden spirit being sucked through the rift and into the void.

What have I done?

The hex-ravaged part of the creature did not dissolve in the same way. As the creature's physical form vanished, the hex floated down into the river, black spores sliding away in the current.

CHAPTER TWENTY

GIRL-WITH-STAR

"Well, I hope you're happy with yourself now, Miss Gribble. Both of those spells were illegal, you know that, I suppose?" Miss Newam said.

"I was trying to help," Arianwyn said quickly. She still knelt in the river. Her legs were numb with cold. "Who knows what the stagget might have done—"

"No buts! No excuses!" Miss Newam snapped. "I shall report this to the High Elder as soon as we are back in Lull."

Arianwyn stared at the river where the stagget had lain just a few minutes before. There was nothing she could say that would make either of them see. She knew that. She heard movement through the water and looked up to see Colin and Miss Newam's retreating backs. Had she been too hasty? Should she have thought it through more? The certainty from moments ago had abandoned her, and she hid her face and cried with frustration. There was the sound of more movement in the water and Arianwyn turned back to see she was now face-to-face with the feyling.

"Oh, hello," Arianwyn said, wiping at the tears on her face.

The gray feyling starred at her quizzically, his head to one side, huge pink eyes blinking. Then he said carefully, "Hell-oh."

She saw now that though his skin was dark gray, it was covered with swirling black designs. Were they tattoos or his actual skin?

The feyling pointed to himself and said, "Tas."

"Tas, is that your name?" Arianwyn asked slowly.

"Am Tas," he repeated, pointing again to his chest.

"I'm Arianwyn Gribble."

"You are girl-with-star!" Tas beamed proudly, pointing to Arianwyn's star badge.

She smiled and nodded.

"All feyling sent away, leave Erraldur," he said sadly.

"I know. I'm sorry. Have you hurt your arm?" There was an angry red cut along his small gray forearm.

"Running from beast. Tas fall. Must find girl-with-star." His huge ears twisted this way and that. "Found you!"

"What?" Arianwyn leaned forward, a little unsure that she had heard correctly.

"Miss Gribble, are you coming back to Lull or do you intend to stay here with your new *friend*?" Miss Newam's voice sliced across the river.

Tas waved at Miss Newam, who flushed and looked away as fast as she could.

"Don't worry about her," Arianwyn said gently. "She can't help it!" She started to get to her feet. "I'm coming!" she called. The air made her legs feel icier still; her coat was heavy with river water. It was going to be a very long walk back to Lull. "We saw some of your people. They were headed to the feyling meeting place at Edda." She smiled, looking down at Tas. "We're going back to our town, to Lull."

"Tas will come also." He smiled, his wide eyes unblinking, staring up at Arianwyn.

"Miss Gribble!" Miss Newam called again. "We don't have all day!"

The break in the trees high above showed the sky turning a soft pink. The sun was beginning to set, finally, on this day that had seemed to stretch on forever. It seemed they would be walking most of the way home in the dark. "Come on, if we get going we might be back in time for breakfast!" She turned and headed across the river, Tas close at her side. Farther down the river the stagget herd were calmly moving back into the woods, their previous panic almost forgotten.

Colin and Miss Newam waited in silence, their expressions stony.

"We should head straight back to the town hall and inform the mayor!" Miss Newam said curtly. Ahead, Arianwyn could see the trees finally giving way to open ground, and glimpsed the high walls of Lull in the first gray light of dawn. Arianwyn was full of relief at being home, but at the same time the crushing disappointment of their failed mission lingered. "You'll have to explain our . . . guest, as well!" Miss Newam eyed Tas with suspicion, as she had done countless times on the long, tiring walk.

They had traveled in silence mostly, all night long. Only Tas occasionally asked a question about Lull or the "human lands," which Arianwyn answered quickly and quietly, in no mood for conversation. Colin had avoided talking to Arianwyn at all, and each time they had caught each other's gaze he had just looked away, his eyes dark and angry.

By Arianwyn's estimate it must almost be breakfast time, and they'd been away from Lull for just under twenty-four hours. It had become incredibly cold, their breath misting the air in front of them. *Rather chilly for early October*, she thought, shivering. She didn't exactly relish the thought of telling the mayor that the hex had spread farther in the wood either and was now closer to town—he really wouldn't be happy. "Can't we leave our report until later?" she asked. She glanced at Colin but he didn't meet her gaze.

"No!" Miss Newam gasped in horror. "We need to report this as soon as possible and not just to the mayor. The CWA will need to be updated as well, you know . . . about *everything*!" She glared at Arianwyn.

Arianwyn sighed. All she wanted was some dry socks and a mug of tea. Then perhaps she would be able to face the mayor and the CWA.

"Ahem!" Miss Newam coughed, drawing Arianwyn to one side so Tas couldn't hear. "You'll need to speak to the High Elder as well, of course, don't forget. I'm certain she will wish to hear why *you* haven't managed to find the book!"

Arianwyn stared at Miss Newam. "You heard the fey-lings. Erraldur was overrun with dark spirit creatures and hex. It wasn't safe to carry on. And *we* couldn't have gotten through the blockages of hex, anyway!" Her words were full of tiredness and frustration and she regretted them at once.

Miss Newam only sniffed, pursed her lips, and raised a single thick black eyebrow. They all tramped silently and slowly through the trees at the very edge of the wood and emerged at last onto the meadow.

Then stumbled to a halt.

There, grazing in the middle of the meadow that skirted Lull, was a herd of qered—tall, horselike spirit creatures. Arianwyn could see four of them, moving away as they saw the approaching party, their strange, whalelike cries echoing around the meadow. They were massive, their huge bodies covered partly in dark scales, partly in coarse hair. They had long, serpentine tails that flowed behind them along with their seemingly never-ending manes. The group of four seemed to be a family, two adults and two younger qered—but there were many more little groups scattered around the field.

"Heavens. Look at that." Miss Newam pointed up at the high walls of Lull.

Arianwyn saw a large cocoonlike shape clinging to the stone high up the wall. The fizz of magic filled the air.

"What's going on?" Colin breathed.

There was a sudden shout from someone high up on the town walls. "They're back! Miss Gribble and the others are back!" There were hurried movements on top of the high wall.

"It *is* Miss Gribble!" another voice shouted excitedly.

"Fetch the mayor!" a third voice called out, echoing off the wall and across the meadow.

What on earth is going on now? Arianwyn wondered.

A WITCH ALONE: A MANUAL FOR THE NEWLY QUALIFIED WITCH

＋ ＋ ＋

As with your training and time as an apprentice, peer support will be of the utmost importance. You should ensure you have an active network for support and also for friendship, for the position of a witch can oftentimes be a lonely one and you will need the advice and companionship of other witches to help you through.

These fellow witches will share skills and help to further develop your knowledge, but you should also take the opportunity to share your own particular specialisms with others too. These new friendships will nourish you throughout your whole life.

CHAPTER TWENTY-ONE

RETURN TO LULL

"Miss Gribble?" Mayor Belcher's face peeked out through the grille in the gate. "Where on earth have you been?" He looked both relieved and frightened. "Open the gates!" he shouted, and there was a rumbling sound as the gates swung inward. Mayor Belcher rushed forward, followed by Lull's chief of police, Constable Perkins. The mayor seized Arianwyn's hands.

She stumbled back a little, shocked by his reaction and the worrying fact that he was still in his pajamas! "Where have you *been*?" he gasped.

"In the wood, collecting samples, of course. You knew where we were going, Mayor Belcher," she explained slowly. "But we had to come back sooner than planned, because of the hex—"

"*Sooner* than planned? Miss Gribble, is this some kind of joke?" the mayor asked, his voice husky. He looked at Arianwyn, then at Colin, then at Miss Newam, searching their faces for an answer. Finally he looked at Tas and gave a little squeak of dismay.

"Hell-*oh*!" Tas said, waving.

Just then, Salle came running to join the group under the high arch of the gateway. Bob followed at her heels, speeding up and dancing around Arianwyn until she lifted the moon hare into her arms, a pink velvety nose brushing her cold cheek in welcome.

"Are you okay?" Salle asked. She studied Arianwyn very carefully.

"Will someone please explain what's going on?" Miss Newam snapped. "Anyone would think we'd been gone for years, not just a day!"

Everyone fell silent. Constable Perkins coughed, his eyebrows so arched they looked as though they might lift off from his face and fly into the air.

"But you've been gone for over two weeks," Salle offered quietly, her eyes wide.

"What?" Arianwyn asked. She suddenly felt rather sick, tiredness and hunger hitting her along with this bizarre news.

"Oh dear—I think you'd all better come straight to the town hall," Mayor Belcher said softly. But he eyed Tas with suspicion. "Ahem, about your . . . companion—" he began.

"I don't think you should allow it within the town, Mayor Belcher," Miss Newam said quickly. "He is a . . . feyling. And for all we know, those creatures could be spreading the hex through the wood. The place was completely crawling with them!"

"But they helped us," Arianwyn said, outraged, but simply too tired and too baffled at that moment to say anything further.

"I think we should follow Miss Newam's guidance. As a CWA official," the mayor said. He turned and walked back through the gate before anyone could argue.

"I'm sorry, Tas, wait here and I'll sort this out in a jiffy. I'll fetch some food as well. But I just have to—"

He shook his head. "Tas okay." But his face remained serious and set. "Tas have to go, find others." He pointed back to the wood.

"Oh, but I thought—"

"Tas have to give girl-with-star something."

"Are you coming, Miss Gribble?" the mayor called from farther along the street.

"I'll be there in a few minutes," she replied. She turned back to Tas. His right arm was extended toward her, holding a piece of paper tightly in his fist. The paper was rolled into a small tube and tied with a thick blade of purple grass. "Oh. That's kind, but you really don't—"

"*He* said, 'Give to girl-with-star.' "

She frowned. "You could have given it to me in the wood; you didn't have to come all this way—"

But Tas was shaking his head. "No. He said: 'Give to girl-with-star in human town by the edge of wood. Must have. Knows what it is. How to use.' "

Arianwyn chuckled gently at Tas carrying out his orders so diligently. She reached out toward the paper, her hand shaking slightly. She felt the faintest murmur of magic run through her arm, like a small electric current.

Is it . . . ?

She took the tube of paper and slipped the grass tie from it. The paper slowly unfurled in her hand like a strange leaf or flower. The page was just like the other one: not really paper at all, something else altogether. And there in its center, bleeding and blooming across the page as though being drawn before her eyes, was a symbol.

It was a glyph. But not a cardinal glyph.

Her heart raced against her ribs.

This was different. It was a new quiet glyph.

"Oh . . . ," Arianwyn breathed. She turned the page this way and that, studying the new glyph, her eyes searching every curve, every line. She looked at Tas. "Is it . . . from the *Book of Quiet Glyphs*?" she asked in a hushed voice.

Tas smiled. "From Estar."

"Estar?" She felt a thrill of hope.

Tas smiled and nodded enthusiastically. "Estar bringing book to girl-with-star!"

Arianwyn felt her heart soar for a moment. But then she remembered the hex, the wood full of unimaginable horrors. What if Estar couldn't get through?

"Okay?" Tas asked.

She had a new glyph and Estar was on his way. She had to believe that everything could still work out. She had to keep that hope alive.

"I'm okay. But must you go now?" Arianwyn asked Tas, taking his hand in her own. "What about your arm?"

He looked back to the wood again. "Others not far. Will see girl-with-star again."

He smiled his broad, toothy smile and then turned and walked slowly back across the meadow. The qered moved toward him and Tas spoke to them in a swooping, hooting call that made them dance around him. And suddenly he was sitting on the back of one of the qered, and being transported speedily across the meadow, which was once more filled with haunting, whalelike cries that seemed to echo through the rustling grass as the rest of the herd called a farewell to Tas and his qered mount.

She looked down at the glyph again, a million questions rushing through her mind at once.

Arianwyn raced into the mayor's parlor. Miss Newam, Colin, the mayor, and Salle were already assembled around his desk and in heated discussion, though it was unclear what it was about.

"Where is the feyling?" Miss Newam asked.

"Gone to find the others," Arianwyn explained quickly. Her hand held fast to the page and she was just about to mention it when Miss Newam sniffed and said, "Well, that's one less irritant to deal with, isn't it?"

"That's not fair, Miss Newam," Arianwyn said, her hand slipping from the page.

"Mayor Belcher, we've only been gone from Lull for a day at most," Colin explained.

"No, no, no! You left on Thursday the first of October and now it's Saturday the seventeenth." He pointed to the calendar on his desk.

What is going on? Arianwyn wondered. Her head ached, pain throbbing in her temples and behind her eyes.

"But that's not possible!" Miss Newam crowed, snatching up the calendar and peering at it closely. "Is this some sort of joke?"

"No joke, dear lady!" the mayor replied, his cheeks flushing quickly before he looked away again.

The room seemed to spin around Arianwyn. She reached out for the back of a nearby chair to steady herself. Had they really been gone for over two weeks? It really had felt like it had only been a day—albeit a very, very long day. She tried to take a calming, steadying breath. Then, with a slight sense of relief, she recalled something Estar had once told her.

"Time moves differently in the Great Wood," she said. "And perhaps the hex is magnifying the distortion . . . Oh, the hex!" Arianwyn exclaimed, suddenly remembering the most important news of all. "The hex has spread throughout the wood. Much closer to Lull."

"Hex?" the mayor gasped. "Oh dear, oh dear."

"It stopped us getting to . . ." She stumbled, suddenly realizing she was about to forget the cover story about gathering samples. "Farther into the wood."

The mayor sat heavily into his seat and rested his head in his hands. "We thought something wasn't right when you didn't return after a week—and *other* things started emerging from the wood." He pulled out his little black notebook, a sure sign of trouble if ever there was one. "You saw those things outside, in the meadow?" he asked.

"The qered, yes. They're not dangerous, though," Arianwyn offered quickly.

"Perhaps not, but they are causing other sorts of problems—as are the *things* nesting against the town walls. I don't suppose you know what they are?"

Arianwyn shook her head. She hadn't gotten a very good view of the cocoon.

"Well, as a security measure we've been keeping the town gates locked and guarded at all times. And I'd hoped Miss Delafield could help, but she's been rushed off her feet too, so Gimma has been doing what she can to help at the Spellorium—"

"Oh!" Arianwyn said, surprised.

The mayor continued. "In light of all that's been going on, we thought it prudent not to be completely witchless."

"She's not been too bad," Salle whispered, squeezing Arianwyn's hand. "I mean, she's still *Gimma*—but at least not weird like in Kingsport!"

Arianwyn wasn't sure what was worse: that she'd been so speedily replaced by Gimma, or that Salle didn't seem to mind. "Has this been reported to the CWA, do you know?" Miss Newam asked, her voice curt and businesslike as usual.

The mayor shook his head. "I am afraid I don't know."

"Well, I suppose I'll deal with that, shall I?" Miss Newam scowled at Arianwyn.

"Oh, won't you use my telephone here?" Mayor Belcher asked, and pulled his seat out for Miss Newam.

"Oh! Thank you, Josiah—I mean, Mayor Belcher!"

Was she blushing?

Salle gave Arianwyn a wide-eyed look, stifling a giggle at Miss Newam and the mayor's odd behavior. "I'd best get back. I'll see you later, Wyn. You can fill me in on all the gory details!" she called as she hurried out of the mayor's parlor.

"I should speak to the High Elder as well," Arianwyn said quietly to Colin, not meeting his eyes.

He nodded. "You'll tell her about the stagget?" His voice was flat.

"Yes, of course. I'll explain what happened—"

But Colin didn't wait to hear any more. He pushed a small card into Arianwyn's hand. "It's the High Elder's private office number," he said quietly, and walked out of the mayor's parlor.

Arianwyn watched him go, suddenly afraid she might cry.

"Mayor Belcher, may I use the telephone in Miss Prynce's office?" she asked.

But he was too distracted to answer, arranging a notepad and pencils on the desk for Miss Newam.

Despite the fact that Miss Prynce never seemed to do much work, Arianwyn was amazed at how untidy her desk was. The telephone was buried under a small landslide of papers. She lifted the ebony phone receiver and carefully dialed the number on the card Colin had handed to her. The phone seemed to ring forever, and Arianwyn fiddled with some pens on the desk and was just about to hang up when the phone was answered.

"Yes?" It was the High Elder's voice.

"Oh, hello. It's Arianwyn . . . Arianwyn Gribble."

"Miss Gribble. I wasn't expecting to hear from you quite so soon." The High Elder sounded a little confused, as though she had just woken up or was in the middle of some all-consuming task.

"Um, it's about the book—"

"You have it?" Her voice was suddenly louder, clearer, sharper.

Arianwyn paused. "Well, no. There's been a complication." She twisted the telephone cord around her fingers.

"And what would that be?"

"We encountered a band of feylings in the wood." She took a deep shuddering breath, overcome with nerves. "They confirmed large-scale outbreaks of hex throughout the Great Wood. Erraldur, the feyling city, is lost—attacked by night ghasts or something worse and ravaged by hex." She felt breathless. "We can't even be sure if the *Book of Quiet Glyphs* is there anymore, or even intact."

Silence.

"High Elder?"

"Yes. I'm still here."

"The hex blocked our way farther into the wood. We had to turn back. But . . . we rescued another feyling, who indicated that Estar is coming to Lull to find me."

"With the book?" The High Elder's voice was rushed, agitated.

"That's what the feyling said."

"Then we wait, Miss Gribble. See if you can learn anything more from this new feyling acquaintance in the meantime."

Arianwyn decided now wasn't the time to mention that Tas had already gone. "Yes, of course, High Elder. There is something else . . ."

"Go on."

"There was a stagget in the Great Wood. It was infected with hex and I"—her throat tightened—"I used a stunning spell on it. The feyling and Miss Newam and Colin were all in danger. We were all in danger, quite possibly. So I stunned it and then I opened a rift and banished it."

She felt both relief and horror at having told the High Elder.

"I see . . . you are well aware that using a stunning or banishing spell on a spirit creature is illegal, Miss Gribble?"

"Yes, High Elder."

"I'll expect a full report within the next two days, please, and of course this will have to go before the council."

"I understand," Arianwyn replied.

"Very good."

And with that the line went dead.

If Arianwyn had been expecting some sort of reassurance, it clearly wasn't going to come from the High Elder. She slumped into Miss Prynce's chair and cried quietly into her hands in the darkness under the stairs. How had everything gone so wrong so quickly? Was it her fault? Should she have done something differently?

A sudden movement in the shadows of the hallway caught Arianwyn's attention. She was about to call out but something made her stop.

Someone was watching her.

Someone had heard the telephone call.

Was it Colin or Miss Newam checking up on her?

Arianwyn looked out of the corner of her eye, not wanting to turn to give away that she was aware. She busied herself with rearranging some of the papers on the desk and then tying her bootlace, though it was perfectly double-knotted as always.

Another movement, and then she heard the soft thud of a door closing.

She scrambled across the hallway, pulling gently and slowly on the doors so they opened just a crack.

Moving across the town was a lone figure dressed in a dark navy uniform, a wisp of white-blonde hair caught in the breeze.

Gimma!

Exactly how much had she heard?

A chill crawled along Arianwyn's spine. The book *had* to remain a secret!

CHAPTER TWENTY-TWO

VERY LIGHT DUTIES

Arianwyn jumped awake, the eiderdown tangled around her legs. For a moment she wasn't sure where she was, or what time it was.

Bright, cold light streamed in through the apartment windows. She could hear the familiar sounds from outside on Kettle Lane.

She was home, in the Spellorium. In Lull.

Since arriving back in Lull the previous day, she'd spent much of her time sleeping in short bursts. Even now, after a whole night's sleep in her own bed, she still felt groggy and tired. Whatever strange magic was at work in the wood had certainly gotten to her.

She glanced at her alarm clock. It was after ten o'clock. *Ten o'clock!*

"Snotlings!"

There was a loud bang, which she thought was from outside, but then she heard someone cough, someone downstairs in the Spellorium. Bob leapt off the bed and stood at the top of the stairs, staring down.

Arianwyn struggled to free herself from the tangled bedding and rushed down the spiral stairs, which wobbled as always. As she took the last twist of the stairs, she saw someone leaning over the counter, consulting the Spellorium ledger. She wore a smart blue uniform, and her blonde hair was held in a perfect bun.

"Gimma?" Arianwyn asked, her voice croaky from sleep.

The other girl turned and jumped a little. "Oh, Arianwyn. I didn't realize you were here. I thought you must be out. It's past ten, you know." She was wearing those pink suede gloves again, and her hands trembled slightly where they rested on the ledger. "Did Uncle explain . . . ?" Her voice wobbled.

"That you've been covering for me? Yes, he did. Thanks for that, but I'm back now. I'm sure I can pick up whatever needs doing." She suddenly didn't like Gimma being here. It felt like an intrusion.

Gimma glanced at the floor. "Well, you see, I think—"

Before she could say more, the Spellorium door flew open and Miss Delafield strode in—well, as much as anyone could stride with a walking stick. "Thank heavens you're back, dear," she said to Arianwyn. "I was starting to get seriously worried—thought we might have to send a search party." Miss Delafield rocked back on her heels and laughed loudly. "Gimma been catching you up on everything, I hope?"

"I was just trying to," Gimma snapped.

Miss Delafield rolled her eyes. "Well, don't let me stop you then, dear." She pulled off her scarf and driving gauntlets and tossed them onto the counter.

"Well, I do know about the qered already," Arianwyn said, frustration ringing in her words.

Gimma scowled. "That wasn't my fault!"

"Nobody's saying it is, dear." Miss Delafield sighed loudly.

Gimma's pale cheeks flushed with a little pink and she fumbled for the ledger. "Well—I've updated the ledger. Including the entries *you* hadn't gotten around to filling in before you went off." She turned the ledger around so that Miss Delafield and Arianwyn could both see it.

"We've kept to light duties, *very* light duties," Miss Delafield said in a way Arianwyn was sure was supposed to sound reassuring. It didn't, though. "Just day-to-day things."

Arianwyn peered closer to the ledger. The most recent page was filled entirely with Gimma's slanted elegant handwriting. Something about it made her feel strange. As though Gimma had been wearing her clothes or sitting in her favorite chair.

"That's wrong." Arianwyn pointed at the ledger. "Mr. Bloom lives at number eleven, Fold Terrace, not number ten." She regretted it as soon as she said it—she could hear how picky she sounded and she didn't like herself for it one little bit.

Gimma folded her arms across her chest and sniffed. "I'm not going to work with her if she's going to be like this."

They glared at each other.

Miss Delafield sighed heavily. "Well, girls, you are simply going to have to find some way to get along—there's far too much work for one witch here at the moment. Now, I don't really care how you go about it but find a way to work with each other, or at least tolerate each other for now. Pass notes if you can't speak to each other. I really don't care."

There was a long moment of silence.

"Well, some of us have work to be getting on with, you know." Gimma sniffed. "Can't stand around all day in our nightdresses." She smiled a satisfied smile and her eyes flicked up and down Arianwyn quickly.

Arianwyn felt her cheeks warm as she caught sight of her reflection in the glass doors of a nearby cabinet: a rumpled nightie and her hair an explosion of curls. "I'll be right back," she mumbled, hurrying for the stairs.

She was just on the first step when she felt a hand close around her wrist. It was Miss Delafield. "I am sorry, dear," she whispered quickly. "I've been put in such a precarious position. The High Elder insisted we utilize Gimma for now. She's not actually been entirely useless."

"I can hear you!" Gimma yelled from the counter.

Miss Delafield turned and called brightly, "Just updating Arianwyn on one or two things, dear, that's all." But she fired Arianwyn a look that said, *Be on your guard.*

As though Arianwyn needed telling twice!

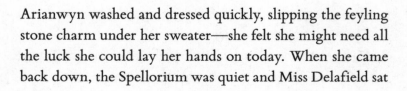

Arianwyn washed and dressed quickly, slipping the feyling stone charm under her sweater—she felt she might need all the luck she could lay her hands on today. When she came back down, the Spellorium was quiet and Miss Delafield sat in the small chair beside the potbellied stove, sipping her famous blue drink from a slender cocktail glass. Arianwyn could smell it from where she stood.

"Has Gimma gone?" she asked.

"Yes, I sent her off to do some work across town, give you a bit of peace and quiet until you're all back to normal, dear. No need to take on too much today."

"I'm fine, Miss Delafield."

"But I heard about the strange time difference; that's bound to have some impact—"

"I'm fine, *really*," Arianwyn said firmly.

Miss Delafield pursed her lips, brow furrowed. "So, I had a message come through from the High Elder's office, something about a stagget?"

The look Miss Delafield gave her said she knew everything already—or at least a version of it. Arianwyn felt her face warm with shame and she did her best to quickly explain.

"I see, dear," Miss Delafield said when Arianwyn had finished her story.

"I am so sorry, Miss Delafield. I didn't see what else I could do." Arianwyn looked away.

"It is a terrible shame, dear, frightful. But I honestly don't see that you had any other choice. I'll write to the council and tell them as much, so don't you fret!"

Arianwyn smiled. It was as if a heavy weight had lifted from her chest. "I wish Colin understood . . ."

Miss Delafield patted her on the shoulder and smiled. "I'm sure he'll come around in time. Sometimes we witches have to make hard choices and others might not always understand at first. But he will, I'm sure. You acted with compassion, as you always do."

But at the back of Arianwyn's mind, a worry still wormed away: What if she'd acted in haste? What if she could have done something else? Something better?

CHAPTER TWENTY-THREE

THE PANGORBAK

Arianwyn stared up at the cocoon fixed just below the top of the town wall. It nestled into the corner next to the tower of the East Gate. She had the spirit lantern by her feet and a pair of binoculars she had borrowed from Uncle Mat slung around her neck. She flicked through the spirit creature glossary in the back of *A Witch Alone*, but so far none of the entries had mentioned this type of cocoon. She'd been watching the walls all afternoon, hoping to identify the creature responsible for it, but if something was inside, it wasn't ready to emerge yet. She'd even flown up twice to try and get a better look, her broom wobbling and bumping against the walls of Lull.

"Any luck?" a bright voice called from the gate.

It was Salle. Arianwyn waved as Salle hurried across the grass carrying a small basket in one hand, a rug folded over her arm. "Aunt Grace thought you might be hungry!" Salle smiled.

"I'm starving!" Arianwyn agreed. "I've not had any lunch yet. I've been busy all day."

"Lunch?" Salle laughed. "It'll be dark soon, it's nearly dinnertime."

Arianwyn glanced around in surprise. She'd been so focused on the cocoon she hadn't noticed the sun lowering in the sky, the shadows growing longer. The qered had moved across the meadow, searching out the last of the day's light, their huge scaly heads moving from side to side, surveying the meadow.

"They're beautiful, aren't they?" Salle said as she laid the rug out.

"They are, but they really should be in the wood. I'm not sure it's safe for them out in the open," Arianwyn said. She turned to look at the cocoon again.

"So still no ideas, then?" Salle asked. She lifted a thermos from the basket, and something wrapped in a red-and-white checkered napkin. She handed these to Arianwyn. "Give me the binoculars and I'll keep a lookout," she offered.

Arianwyn handed the binoculars over and sat down. She unwrapped the napkin—inside was one of Aunt Grace's delicious pastries, the warm, buttery smell filling her nose. She bit down into it and sat in blissful silence for a few moments as she ate. Salle poured them both some tea from the thermos and carried on watching the nest. "How is Gimma getting on?" Salle asked.

"Thankfully we're keeping pretty much out of each other's way most of the time," Arianwyn said, sipping the sweet tea. She'd been back in Lull for nearly a week following the failed expedition into the Great Wood, and both she and Gimma had been busy with the work in the ledger. Their conversations were businesslike—generally they left informative notes for each other tucked into the ledger.

"I heard she seems to be getting on better with her spells but she's still just as much of a pain," Salle said.

"Oh, I don't know . . . ," Arianwyn said, just not in the mood to have a long conversation about Gimma at that moment. She quickly changed the subject. "So how've *you* been?" she asked. "Did you go for that audition in Flaxsham?"

Salle played with a small piece of pastry, looking out across the meadow at the qered as the younglings raced and galloped. "It's next Friday, but I don't think I can make it now. I have another appointment. A sort of interview . . ."

"What for?" Arianwyn asked, her mouth half full of delicious warm pastry and buttery, herby vegetables.

Salle's face went red. "I was going to volunteer . . . to help Dr. Cadbury until he can find a new replacement." She looked across at Arianwyn uncertainly.

"Oh, Salle. That's very good of you."

"Well, I think I could do more to help. But I'm a bit nervous about the interview, so do you think you could come with me and wait while I see him?" She bit her lip.

"Of course I will. I wouldn't—"

But before they could say more, a small commotion broke out by the East Gate and Constable Perkins appeared, followed by several agitated townspeople. He was red-faced as he rushed across to where Salle and Arianwyn were sitting. "Miss Gribble, you're to come at once," he puffed.

"Whatever is it?" Arianwyn asked, jumping to her feet and brushing the pastry crumbs off her skirt.

"Miss Alverston was called to the Guthries'. Mr. Guthrie said he'd been bitten by something over at Caulls's Farm this morning. Seems things have taken a turn for the worse and Miss Alverston sent for you." The constable put his hand on his knees then, and took several deep breaths.

Arianwyn looked at Salle.

Salle smiled. "I'll pack this all away and take it back. You go."

Arianwyn grabbed her broom. "Come on, we'll get there faster on this," she said to the constable.

He clambered onto the broom behind her, and seconds later they were flying across the meadow toward the gate.

Arianwyn charged through the door, Constable Perkins close behind her. The Guthries' kitchen was small, but seemed even smaller now, so packed with people. She heard someone call, "It's Miss Gribble, let her through."

She was ushered through the kitchen and into the dark sitting room. The curtains were drawn and only a single weak lamp offered any light. Arianwyn saw Gimma at once, her face like a pale beacon in the gloom.

"Gimma? What's the matter?" Arianwyn asked.

Mr. and Mrs. Guthrie sat on the sofa. Both of them looked beyond terrified. Arianwyn noticed that Mr. Guthrie was draped in a towel but didn't appear to have a shirt or sweater on.

First things first, thought Arianwyn—she wouldn't be able to do anything properly in such a dark room, and certainly not with all those people watching from the kitchen. She shut the sitting-room door quickly and heard moans from the assembled watchers as she did so. "I think we could do with some more light as well. Can you open the curtains, Gimma?"

Gimma appeared to be glad for something to do. She crossed the room quickly, flooding the room with late afternoon light as she pulled the curtains back. Mr. Guthrie turned away from the light, wincing.

When Gimma crossed back, she grabbed Arianwyn's hands in her own, still covered with her pink suede gloves. "They said it was brownie bite, Arianwyn. I didn't know what to do and everything I tried just seemed to make it worse." She was shaking, and suddenly she burst into tears, burying her head against Arianwyn's chest.

"It's okay," Arianwyn said slowly, patting Gimma's back awkwardly. "Why don't you sit down there for a second, Gimma. Mr. Guthrie, can you tell me what's happened?"

"He can't talk," Mrs. Guthrie said. She fiddled with a thin gold chain around her neck. "It's the thing, you see."

"I'm not sure I do." Arianwyn felt a cold, dead weight in her stomach. She glanced at Gimma, who wiped her tears away.

"Show her," Gimma said, her voice wavering. "She'll know what to do."

Mr. Guthrie stood slowly; it seemed to take all his effort to do so, his face twisting in pain as he tried to stand upright. Mrs. Guthrie stood at his side, then she reached for the towel and Mr. Guthrie gave a small nod.

As she pulled the towel from his back, Mrs. Guthrie looked away and Arianwyn saw something coiled around

Mr. Guthrie's neck and chest, dark and scaled like a snake. Arianwyn couldn't stop herself from gasping.

"He got home from work and said his back was sore where he'd been bitten by a brownie up at the farm," Mrs. Guthrie explained as Arianwyn moved slowly across the room. "And when he took his shirt off so I could put some ointment on, well . . . there it was." Mrs. Guthrie started to sob quietly into the towel.

Mr. Guthrie turned slowly then, and Arianwyn saw exactly what they were dealing with. Clinging to Mr. Guthrie's back was a creature, dark green and scaled just like the tentacle around his neck and chest. It was about the size of a large dinner plate, spined with numerous shorter tentacles spreading out across Mr. Guthrie's back. The skin under the tentacles was gray-green.

This was not good.

"What is it?" Gimma asked.

"I don't know," Arianwyn said slowly. Mrs. Guthrie started to cry again. "Have you tried stunning it?" Arianwyn asked Gimma.

She nodded. "Every time I tried it just got bigger and the tentacles pulled tighter."

As they stood there watching the creature, it shifted slightly and then seemed to grow suddenly from the size of a dinner plate to a dish-washing bowl. Mrs. Guthrie gave a cry of fear, reaching to take her husband's hand, and Gimma gripped Arianwyn's arm. "You have to do something!" she hissed.

Arianwyn went to the door and found Constable Perkins in the kitchen. "I need you to fetch Miss Delafield as soon as possible, please. She'll be on duty in Flaxsham today," she said. The constable nodded and left the kitchen.

An hour and several failed spells later, the whatever-it-was had grown bigger still, and Mr. Guthrie was struggling to breathe as the tentacles tightened. Arianwyn was desperately attempting a charm, though her hands were shaking and she had dropped the errony stones and carrum flowers twice by the time Miss Delafield hurried through the sitting-room door.

"I'm here!" she called.

Arianwyn felt hope flutter against the worry and fear in her chest, like a butterfly against a window.

"Oh, heavens," Miss Delafield breathed as she took in the full horror of the situation. She stood beside Arianwyn and Gimma and placed an arm around each of them.

"What is it?" Arianwyn asked.

"A pangorbak. Nasty little things as well. Haven't seen one in years, thankfully." Miss Delafield stepped away and took off her coat, then turned to Constable Perkins. "We need everyone to leave, all those people in the kitchen—send them home. Right now."

The constable went away and they could hear the sounds of people leaving from the kitchen. Miss Delafield rolled up her sleeves. "We tried everything we could think of,"

Arianwyn explained as her supervisor approached Mr. Guthrie and examined the pangorbak more closely. "But everything just seemed to make it get bigger. Was it feeding off the magic?"

Miss Delafield sucked air in through her teeth. "No, it's not the magic." She straightened and folded her hands together, then looked first at Mr. and Mrs. Guthrie and then at Arianwyn and Gimma. "You have to follow my instructions to the letter, do you all understand? No questions, no disagreeing."

They all nodded.

"All right, then. The secret to defeating a pangorbak is simple, but may seem strange. When I say so, everyone has to turn away from Mr. Guthrie. Don't look at the pangorbak. Try not to even *think* about it."

"What? Miss Delafield, are you sure?" It sounded crazy.

She gave Arianwyn a hard stare. "Quite certain, Miss Gribble."

The room fell silent. Miss Delafield turned to Mr. Guthrie and took his hands. "Now, Mr. Guthrie. At first the pangorbak will double its grip, but that means it's weakening. You need to be prepared. Do you understand, dear?"

He nodded.

"Good. Everyone ready? One, two, three. NOW!"

As Arianwyn turned to face the kitchen door, she cast one quick look at Gimma, pale and shivering. The room fell silent. Arianwyn fixed her eyes on the wall and in her head she counted, trying to think of anything but the pangorbak. After a few minutes the room was filled with the sound of Mr. Guthrie's labored breathing. Arianwyn wanted to hold her hands over her ears.

Surely it's over by now?

And then she heard a soft thud.

"Quickly!" Miss Delafield said, and everyone turned around.

Mr. Guthrie had collapsed onto the sofa, the pangorbak gone from his back. It lay on the rug, its tentacles moving slowly this way and that.

"Don't go near it!" Miss Delafield warned, and then there was a bright flash as she sent a stunning orb toward it. Its flicking tentacles immediately stilled.

"Now does anyone want to do the honors?" Miss Delafield asked. She meant banishing it, of course.

Gimma shook her head quickly. "No."

"Arianwyn? Not every day you get to banish a pangor-bak, dear."

"Yes, all right, then," Arianwyn said carefully.

She took a few slow steps forward and knelt down beside the pangorbak. Mrs. Guthrie was tending to her husband, Miss Delafield was watching Arianwyn, and Gimma stood by the fireplace, shaking.

Arianwyn sketched L'ier, the banishing glyph, and recited the banishing spell as the pangorbak's body slowly started to dissolve into small flecks of light.

"Oh my goodness," Miss Delafield sighed as they walked into the dark Spellorium.

"That was horrible," Arianwyn said, flicking on the lights. Bob skittered toward them.

Gimma had been silent since they left the Guthries'. She stood quietly by the counter.

"This is not good," Miss Delafield said. "Things are getting out of hand. We need something to slow the hex or we'll soon be overrun with all manner of creatures. We certainly don't want any more pangorbaks, do we? Any ideas, girls?"

Arianwyn thought about what Virean had said about Erraldur. Could the same future face Lull if they didn't act fast? She looked at Gimma, who simply shrugged her shoulders and mumbled, "A protection spell?"

Miss Delafield tutted. "As a last resort, perhaps, but no, dear, that wouldn't work. Someone would have to maintain it all the time. We need something we can leave in place while we get on with our duties."

Arianwyn's eyes fell on a batch of charms hanging from a hook by the window, mostly weather charms for the local farmers. Below them were stacked some of the large charm globes that had arrived by mistake. Her mind began to click as ideas filtered through.

"Charms?" Arianwyn said partly to herself.

"You mean issue everyone with a charm, dear? I don't see how that would help much."

"No, we could string charms up at the edge of the wood to hold off the hex," she said, as the idea unfolded in her mind. "The feylings were wearing a stone that they said warded off dark magic . . ." She felt for the feyling charm under her clothes and pulled it out.

"And you believed them?" Gimma laughed. "That's just a stone with some markings carved on it!"

Arianwyn blushed. "Well, if the feylings say it works, I think it's worth a try. The stones have to be from the river and gathered at full moon, they said, and they use this symbol." She traced the line of the carving with her finger. "And if we use Miss Delafield's fire spell that she placed on our gloves and use other ingredients that might fend off hex as well, it *might* work." She looked hopefully at Miss Delafield.

"Well, it's the full moon early next week, and if anyone *can* make it work, I'm sure it's you, dear." Miss Delafield smiled. "It's a good idea."

"Oh, of course it would be!" Gimma sniffed.

CHAPTER TWENTY-FOUR

THE NEW GLYPH

"Thank you, Mr. Brown!" Arianwyn called as the gentleman stepped out of the Spellorium, his package of charms safely tucked under his arm. "Those should keep the krecks away from your aviary! But come back if not, we can always try something else!"

Mr. Brown turned and waved gently.

Arianwyn gave a deep, tired sigh and closed the door. The Spellorium had been packed all morning; she hadn't stopped for a second—especially as Gimma was taking a day off and had gone into Flaxsham with her uncle. The increased sightings of spirit creatures and dark spirits seemed to have everyone worried. The incident with the pangorbak earlier in the week had sent them into a positive tailspin, and she'd been busy making charms since news broke.

Now, as the door clicked shut behind Mr. Brown and the bell charms sang out in the empty Spellorium, she had a moment to gather her thoughts.

She glanced up at the clock: It was after noon. Her stomach rumbled.

"Lunch, I think!" she said to Bob, who immediately scampered up the stairs to the apartment above. Arianwyn knew she would find the moon hare waiting on the kitchen rug, staring at the cupboard where she kept the ginger cookies. They were Bob's favorite.

She turned and flipped the open sign to closed before heading upstairs to make a sandwich and some tea and give Bob a cookie.

While the kettle boiled, she sat at the small table and flicked idly though her copy of *A Witch Alone*.

As she turned a page, absorbed in a chapter on how brownie droppings could be used to treat bogglin bites, she came across the page Tas had given her: the page that held the new glyph. Miss Delafield's words of warning echoed in her mind—charms were all well and good, but what if this new glyph was somehow the key to fighting the hex?

Her fingers hovered over it for a second, the glyph blooming faintly like its own ghost. Then the kettle whistled loudly and Arianwyn stepped away and carried on with preparing her lunch.

A few moments later and she was back downstairs in the Spellorium with her mug of tea and a cheese sandwich. She sat at the counter, staring hard at the now-empty piece of paper.

Arianwyn tapped her fingers against the page, the glyph appearing and vanishing over and over. Would she summon the glyph? She'd had it tucked away this long and not tried to summon it. Why? Part of her wanted to know what she had before she showed it to Colin and Miss Newam. But part of her was scared of what power it might hold. Would it be like the shadow glyph? Dark and menacing?

There was only one way she would find out.

"Right, then!" she said, feeling suddenly confident. "Let's see what you do, my little friend!"

Arianwyn pulled the small square of paper flat, the symbol becoming bolder as each second passed.

A swirling spiral, a soft curving line and three dots.

Energy shimmered from the page.

Something told Arianwyn to start at the center of the swirl and work her way out.

Almost at once she felt the fizz of energy from the glyph as she sketched it in the air. A seam of magic poured forth and connected with the glyph.

There was a flash as glyph and magic connected. Arianwyn felt pressure on her ears, as though they might pop, but the sensation disappeared quickly.

She glanced around the Spellorium, looking for some indication that something had changed, that anything was different. But everything looked exactly as it had before. As it always did. There was the curving counter, polished until it gleamed like a dark mirror. There were the white painted shelves that held supplies, and books.

It was Bob who noticed it first—sniffing at something barely visible between the counter and the Spellorium's bay window. Floating nearly three feet off the floor was a sphere so clear it was almost impossible to see, like a large bubble.

Arianwyn approached the sphere cautiously. She didn't notice straightaway, but drawing closer, her footsteps became almost totally silent. She beckoned to Bob, who skipped across the floorboards toward her, but instead of the usual scratchy sound of small claws on the wood, there was nothing.

"Well, that's odd, isn't it?" Arianwyn said, her voice now the softest of whispers, almost inaudible. What was going on?

She was right beside the sphere now, and reached carefully toward it.

Magic flowed from it in waves, pulsing toward her. It felt nothing like the shadow glyph, thankfully. But she could still feel its great power nonetheless. Her fingers brushed the sphere and created a muted vibrating noise, as if the sound was coming from deep below the earth.

"Hmmm," Arianwyn murmured to herself, "you're a curious one." The sound was still dampened, as though her ears were blocked. From the corner of her eye she caught sight of the radio. "I wonder . . ."

She crossed the Spellorium quickly and turned the large dial on the front of the radio. The display lit up and the soft strains of a tune wafted to her. "Moonlight Magic"—it was one of her grandmother's favorites. She turned the dial a little more, increasing the volume. Then she moved back to the sphere, which hung in place as before.

Standing with the sphere between herself and the radio, Arianwyn moved her hands around its outside, a few inches from the surface. The sphere contracted and expanded as she had hoped it might.

The moon hare flattened itself against the floorboards of the Spellorium. "It's okay, Bob. It's not like the other one!" Arianwyn said, but it was as if her words were stolen away even as she uttered them.

She drew her hands toward herself. She then pushed them at the sphere, sending the orb sailing across the Spellorium toward the radio, expanding as it moved, doubling and then tripling in size.

Arianwyn felt a small pang of fear as the sphere bumped into the radio, worried it might spark or even blow up, but the sphere simply absorbed the radio inside itself with a gentle wobble. And as it did, the Spellorium fell into complete silence.

The radio's display was still lit, the fine needle twitching a little, but there was no sound at all. Arianwyn felt a smile spread across her face as she dashed across the Spellorium, and without a second thought plunged her head inside the sphere.

The wailing trumpets from the song came to her as though she were underwater now, and all sounds from beyond the sphere were completely gone. She gave a small laugh of surprise, but it was only the faintest of whispery sounds. She reached forward and turned the dial on the radio as far as it would turn, but there was no increase in the volume from the song.

Arianwyn pulled away from the sphere and gave a small cry of surprise to see Millicent Caruthers standing next to her, a look of great concern on her face.

"Uh, Miss Gribble, your"—she gestured to the sphere—"*thing*, is poking through the wall into the ladies' underwear department." She flushed a little. "I wonder if you could . . . make it stop, please. It rather alarmed one of my customers."

"Oh, Mrs. Caruthers, I'm so, *so* sorry. Of course." Arianwyn looked at the sphere, unsure now how to undo the spell. After a couple of moments where she moved her hands this way and that—only to make it bigger again—the sphere did at last contract and vanish with the smallest flash and a tiny pop. But as it did, the music from the radio blasted throughout the Spellorium. Millicent Caruthers speedily covered her ears and Bob took cover under the chair.

Arianwyn quickly reached for the dial and the radio clicked off.

"Heavens, whatever sort of a spell was that?" Millicent Caruthers asked, peering at the radio.

"Something . . . new," Arianwyn said, blushing. "I'm sorry I disturbed you!"

"Oh, it's quite all right, you know. I was happy to escape for a moment or two. But if you could refrain from sending any more new spells through the wall, I would be ever so grateful." She smiled warmly.

"Of course, sorry—again!" Arianwyn called as Millicent Caruthers left the Spellorium.

As soon as the door clicked shut Arianwyn moved to the counter and gazed at the page, which was blank once more. Her hand shaking slightly, she lifted a pencil from where it rested on the open ledger and, pulling the page toward her, she carefully wrote across the bottom:

The Glyph of Silence

CHAPTER TWENTY-FIVE

ALWAYS SOMETHING...

A rianwyn glanced at the clock: It was a quarter to three. She had agreed to meet Salle at exactly three o'clock and walk with her to Dr. Cadbury's office for her interview. She was determined not to be late.

She was just finishing up one of the new giant charms they were planning to hang on the edge of the Great Wood—they'd collected the river stones during the full moon just a few nights ago, and she and Gimma had spent a long evening of awkward silence and half-started conversations carving the feyling markings into the stones' surfaces. There was a small pile of the stones on the counter. Now she placed a handful of bright kartz stones inside the huge glass sphere and secured its stopper, placing the completed charm into the box alongside the others she had made that afternoon. She just had another two boxes to complete and then they would be ready to be hung. Gimma had made three so far, and one of those Arianwyn had had to remake.

She hoped her idea would work, at least in slowing down the spread of the hex, though she worried that it was a long shot.

She pulled on her coat and hurried to the door, ready to leave, just as Gimma barged through, nearly knocking Arianwyn off her feet. She was in floods of tears. "It wasn't my fault!" she snapped, slamming the door behind her.

"What's the matter now?" Arianwyn asked.

"That wretched woman screamed at me." Gimma pouted and flopped into the small armchair beside the stove.

"Who? Not Mrs. Myddleton?" Arianwyn asked. She'd had her own run-in with Mrs. Myddleton shortly after she had first arrived in Lull, when she was still just an apprentice witch. She knew how difficult she could be.

Gimma nodded. "Stupid old bag. She kept interfering and I was trying to activate the charm she ordered and . . . well, I just couldn't do it." Gimma looked out the huge window. "I suppose you'll tell Miss Delafield and my uncle how useless I'm being?"

Arianwyn sighed. *Well, you're not helping yourself*, she nearly said, and then thought better of it. Gimma looked utterly miserable. "What happened?" she asked with a sigh, moving closer. "Tell me exactly and I might be able to help." She glanced at the clock: She had ten minutes before she needed to meet Salle—enough time to run through a simple charm. "Why wouldn't the charm activate? Did you follow my instructions?"

Gimma produced the charm recipe from her pocket. It was crumpled and had a gummy sweet stuck to it. "And do you have the charm you made?" Arianwyn asked.

"Oh, I dropped that," Gimma said, as though it really didn't matter in the slightest.

"Okay, well, why don't you show me what you did?" Arianwyn crossed to the counter. Without looking at the recipe, she quickly retrieved the components for the charm and a small glass orb. She placed them all on the counter and looked expectantly at Gimma.

"Do I have to?" Gimma groaned, sinking lower into the chair and fiddling with her hair.

"Yes," Arianwyn said. "You're never going to learn otherwise." She could hear her grandmother in the words and she half smiled to herself. She would have to tell her all about it when she next wrote to her.

Gimma moved slowly toward the counter and peered at the charm components and the recipe. She sighed heavily and looked at Arianwyn. "I can't!" she spat, brushing some of the components off the counter. She tried to move away, but Arianwyn blocked her path.

"Let's take this one step at a time, shall we?" Arianwyn said gently.

Over an hour later there were three smashed charms on the counter, evidence of Gimma's foul mood. But she did hold one completed charm in her hand, evidence of Arianwyn's perseverance.

"I still just don't understand the boggin thing!" Gimma sighed. "But. Well . . . thanks, I guess," she mumbled.

The bell charm on the door jingled and Gimma glanced up, her eyes narrowed. "Oh, Salle," she said, sounding bored. "Wyn was helping me with some charms."

Arianwyn felt her blood turn to ice as she turned and saw Salle standing frozen in the doorway. Her face was white, her eyes red-rimmed. She'd been crying. Arianwyn had totally forgotten about Salle's interview with Dr. Cadbury! She glanced up at the clock on the wall. It was after four now.

Salle fixed Arianwyn with a hard stare. "I can see you're *busy*. Sorry to interrupt." Her words were flat. She turned and walked away, leaving the door open.

"Boil it!" Arianwyn moaned, and rushed to the door.

She stumbled to a halt. The postmistress, Mrs. Attinger, was on the doorstep. "Post, Miss Gribble," she said, reaching into her delivery bag.

"Just pop it inside, please!" Arianwyn called, swerving around Mrs. Attinger as she chased Salle along Kettle Lane. "Salle. Wait!" Her feet pounded against the cobbles. She weaved in and out of shoppers and people going about their days. "Pardon me!" she called as she ran.

Salle was just a few feet ahead now. Arianwyn reached out and grasped the edge of her coat sleeve.

"Salle! I'm sorry—" she began to explain, slightly out of breath. "I didn't forget, but Gimma needed some help with—"

"It's fine. No problem," Salle said with a small smile, and then she turned and carried on, sliding past Arianwyn.

It all seemed a little too easy.

"Salle, wait. Aren't you *mad* at me? Because I totally understand if you are."

Salle turned quickly now. "Mad at you? No. I'm not mad at you, Wyn, but I am hurt that you forgot about me."

"I didn't forget, Salle. I just said I had to—"

"Had to what? It's always something, isn't it? There's always something that crops up that's more important. Something for the mayor or, these days, for Gimma." Salle made a face.

"I'm sorry, Salle, but I do have to do my job."

"And I said it's fine." Salle stared at her, lips clamped tight. She didn't blink or glance away.

"So . . . how was it, then?" Arianwyn asked. "Your meeting with Dr. Cadbury?" It all felt horribly forced and uncomfortable.

"No idea really. I thought it would be like an audition, but it was a bit more complicated than that . . . I don't think I did very well, actually," Salle replied.

"Oh, I'm sure it was okay really." Arianwyn reached out to touch Salle's arm, but she quickly pulled away. "Salle, I'm truly sorry . . . shall we go and get cake or something, my treat? Ice cream at Bandolli's?"

Salle shook her head, staring at the floor. "No. I just want to go home. I'll see you . . . sometime," she said. Her voice was full of sadness, and she didn't seem to believe her own words. The usual bounce in her step was gone as she turned and walked away. Arianwyn waited, expecting her friend to turn around and wave as she often did. But Salle carried on straight along Kettle Lane without turning back once.

"Snotlings!" Arianwyn spat in frustration.

CHAPTER TWENTY-SIX

HAPPY BIRTHDAY

Arianwyn slammed the Spellorium door, the glass rattling in a satisfying way. The bell charms clattered, their usual bright song lost in the crash of metal on glass and wood. Bob came skittering across the floor toward her, ears flapping happily.

Thankfully Gimma had gone.

"Oh, Bob!" Arianwyn muttered, crouching down to rub the moon hare's back. "I've made a right blooming pickle of it all today, I can tell you. I don't know what I'd do if I didn't have you for company." Her throat felt suddenly tight, as though she might cry. She let the moon hare lick her hands for a few moments and then she noticed the pile of letters on the floor.

A couple were in brightly colored envelopes, the handwriting familiar and welcome on this cold afternoon. One was from her grandmother and the other, her father!

She flicked on the lights and quickly tore open the yellow envelope with her grandmother's writing on it. A jolly-looking card tumbled out onto the counter and for a moment Arianwyn's heart stopped.

It was her birthday!

She clutched the card tightly for a moment. And looked at the calendar behind the Spellorium counter.

October thirtieth.

She had been so preoccupied with everything that she'd entirely forgotten her own birthday! She flipped open the card from her grandmother:

> Happy birthday, my Arianwyn.
> Wishing you many happy returns!
> With all my love
> Grandma xxx
> P.S. Will call soon! Traveling in Grunnea.
> Hope this reaches you in time x

So Grandma was in Grunnea, looking for other witches who might be able to read the quiet glyphs. Not that it mattered, as they only had two so far! Arianwyn stood the card on the counter and smiled at it. "Happy birthday to me," she said quietly, and her eyes were suddenly watery, her vision blurred.

She sniffed and turned to the other letter, the one with her father's familiar writing. She tore open the envelope and pulled out the card: A basket of impossibly bright flowers shone out at her. She flipped it open and saw her father's slanting bold writing:

October 10

My darling girl, happy birthday!

Thank you for your letter. I can't
wait to visit Lull and meet all
your new friends there. I don't know
when I will get back to Hylund
next. Some days it's as if there
is no war at all and then the
fighting starts again. We have seen
some strange sights here, creatures
and weirdness that I can't begin to
fathom. But thankfully, now, we
have three witches detailed to our
platoon. They are very brave and
hardworking and I keep telling them
all about you—my clever little
witch!

We even met a Vrisian who called
himself a witch—but we thought
there was no magic in the Uris
anymore. He was a strange fellow,
all covered in odd black markings
like tattoos. I took a photo and I'll
show you when I am home. Well, I
must go, our supper is nearly ready.
Remember, I LOVE you and I am

proud of you, so proud, my girl, and your mother would be too—you are so like her.

Take care of yourself.

DAD x x x

Her tears flowed freely then. She buried her face in her hands and sobbed, loneliness suddenly wrapping itself around her. Not even in the grip of the shadow glyph, or when her mother had died, had she felt this sad and alone.

She read the cards through twice more, her hands shaking so much that at times she could barely see the letters clearly. More tears came and the moon hare whined at her feet, sharing her sadness.

Her only family were now thousands of miles away. Colin was still avoiding her and now she had upset Salle too.

What's more, she'd failed to find the book, and in the process she'd used two illegal spells on a spirit creature. Had the CWA made a mistake in giving her the silver star of a qualified witch? Most days she still felt like an apprentice. Bob took the chance to leap onto her lap, soft ears tickling her cheek. She pulled Bob close, burying her face deep into the warm white fur and shimmering scales. She hugged the moon hare tight and let the tears flow.

She didn't know what else she could do.

CHAPTER TWENTY-SEVEN

SHRIEKING RITTS

Arianwyn and Gimma were returning from a visit to Farmer Eames at Bridge Farm to check he'd had no returning harvest bogglins. Thankfully he hadn't! As they drew nearer to Lull, the air was filled with a piercing, shrieking sound.

"What is that?" Gimma cried, her hands held tightly over her ears.

"I don't know!" Arianwyn shouted back. But as she glanced up, she saw swift dark shapes swooping high over Lull.

As the North Gate came into view, they saw Mayor Belcher, wearing not one but two pairs of earmuffs. He rushed toward them. "Oh, Miss Gribble. This terrible, awful noise." The mayor had to nearly scream to be heard. "I don't think I can take it for a second longer. It's that cocoon thing, by the South Gate. It's been this way for nearly two hours. I've had complaints from just about every residence in Lull. You have to do something. Right now!" He gave her a steely gaze, which she knew meant the subject was not open for discussion.

They headed for the South Gate, where the cocoon was still fixed high to the town walls, but as they emerged onto the meadow, Arianwyn could see now it was not a cocoon at all: It was a nest! And a creature was crawling from an opening near the bottom.

Arianwyn rummaged in her satchel and thrust *The Apprentice Witch's Handbook* and *A Witch Alone* into Gimma's hands. "Look for anything you can on nests that are shaped like that, quickly, Gimma!" Why hadn't she thought to look for nests last time? What a stupid mistake!

"They can't stay there. It's driving the whole town to distraction," Mayor Belcher wailed, his hands now clamped over both sets of earmuffs.

Arianwyn moved farther along the bottom of the wall, watching the nest as another creature emerged. Its body was small, about the size of a crow; but its wingspan, she guessed, was more than ten feet wide. Its flight was strange: It looked more like a twisting scrap of dark cloth than a bird, and there was an oily rainbow glimmer to its dark skin.

Arianwyn pulled out the spirit lantern and, peering through the viewing aperture, she tried to focus on one of the creatures, but they moved so quickly it was nearly impossible. "Anything yet?" she called back to Gimma, who was flicking furiously through both books. Just then she fixed on one as it landed and crawled back into the nest—and there was the unmistakable golden aura of a spirit creature.

"It's all right, they're not dark spirits," Arianwyn shouted, turning back to the mayor. He didn't seem entirely thrilled by that discovery, though.

"Here!" Gimma turned the copy of *A Witch Alone* around and pointed to a small entry at the bottom of the page, entitled: *Velastamuri, commonly referred to as "shrieking ritts."*

"Well, now you know what they are, get rid of them, please!" the mayor hollered at Arianwyn.

"But they're not dark spirits, Uncle," Gimma cried. "We can't simply destroy—"

"Spare me the details. Gimma—I think you'd best come with me before your eardrums burst." He clamped his second pair of earmuffs over her head. "Miss Gribble," he continued, "just . . . MAKE THE NOISE STOP!"

The mayor didn't wait for a response, but turned and retreated back across to the South Gate, leading a protesting Gimma by the arm and leaving Arianwyn staring up at the shrieking ritts swooping around the nest. Well, at least she knew what they were now. Arianwyn glanced again at the book to see if the entry had any suggestions. It didn't. Her head was starting to ache with all the noise.

If only there was a spell we could use to silence them, Arianwyn thought, and then realized there was: the new glyph.

Could she risk using it out here in the open? Nobody knew about it yet.

The shrieking grew ever louder, and it felt as though it might never be quiet again. Arianwyn thought she might go crazy if it went on much longer. She closed her eyes, took a deep breath, and tried to still her mind, though it was almost impossible with all the noise. But somehow the glyph was there, waiting for her in the darkness behind her eyelids. And, for a second, everything was quiet.

With her eyes still closed, she raised her hand and began to sketch the new glyph before her. She felt the weight of magic from the Great Wood nearby, and as she drew the last curl of the glyph of silence, she felt it rush toward her like a tide.

She could feel the glyph and the seam of magic connect. She opened her eyes and, hovering just off the ground of the meadow, was a clear, colorless, and slightly rippling sphere, just like the one she'd summoned in the Spellorium.

But what to do with it now? Could she cover the nest with the orb? Would the creatures still be able to fly around? What if they flew farther from their nest? Would the orb then be able to reach far enough to silence them? She hadn't quite thought this through! She tried to send the orb forward, twisting her hands to manipulate the spell, but the sphere wobbled, buckled, and collapsed into a shower of sparks.

"Boil it!" Arianwyn muttered to herself. *Why didn't that work?*

She tried again, but no matter how hard she tried, she couldn't get the large sphere to move, or to increase further in size. To do anything, in fact. And after a few seconds the spell either collapsed or wobbled and faded away.

"Oh, come on!" Arianwyn groaned.

The shrieking ritts' nest was high on the wall; they were still circling it, screaming out across the meadow. The sound was almost unbearable.

She decided that all she needed to do was to get a small spell orb near to the nest, and that would hopefully absorb enough of the noise. It had worked in the Spellorium with the radio!

She summoned the glyph of silence again. Sketching it in the air before her, she waited until she felt the pull of magic. She could feel the magic of the Great Wood, but now she could also feel it was tainted with dark magic from the hex. She slowed her breathing and waited, hoping there would be a closer seam of magic that she could use.

And there it was: a small pocket somewhere in the meadow. It connected with the glyph and, as before, a small colorless sphere formed in front of Arianwyn.

This time she didn't try to make it so large: Instead, she kept the bubble small and sent it drifting toward the nest, moving her hands slowly, carefully. It had just started gaining height and was about halfway up the wall when a hand grasped Arianwyn's arm.

She jumped in surprise and immediately lost control of the sphere, turning toward the owner of the hand: It was Gimma!

"What is it?" Arianwyn cried.

Gimma looked upset. "I . . . just wondered if I could help . . ."

Arianwyn glanced back at the orb: Instead of floating gently toward the nest, it was now hurtling fast, as if she had fired it from a cannon.

It was heading straight for the nest and the top of the town wall.

"Watch out!" Arianwyn shouted.

The girls jumped back as the orb exploded and the shrieking ritts took flight, screaming louder than ever. Chunks of nest and stone tumbled down the walls into a heap just a few feet in front of them.

Arianwyn glanced over to where the mayor was watching, his earmuffs still in place, his mouth wide in shock. "Snotlings!" she muttered under her breath.

She stared helplessly up at the gaping hole in the town wall. The shrieking ritts circled back over the wall. They swooped down to where the nest had been, then around and back again as though this might make the nest appear. After another few attempts they wheeled away, flying out across the meadow and then off over the tops of the Great Wood, the sound fading as they flew farther on.

"Well done, Miss Gribble," Mayor Belcher said, coming toward them and removing his earmuffs.

"I'm sorry about the wall, Mayor Belcher. I—"

"The wall can be repaired. Though I will bill the Spellorium for that, of course. I thought you'd said the nest couldn't be destroyed?" He glanced at Gimma.

"The nest shouldn't have been destroyed, Mayor Belcher," said Arianwyn. "And I didn't mean to destroy it. The spell went wrong, I don't know why." If Gimma hadn't distracted her, perhaps it would have been all right.

Or perhaps she shouldn't have tried to use the new glyph before she was ready?

For a moment she thought the mayor was reaching for his little black book, but his hand paused and he smiled.

"Well now, they're gone, and although that might not sit well with Miss Delafield, the result is peace and quiet, Miss Gribble. Thank you." The mayor glanced up at the new hole in the top of the town wall. Then he turned and strode off back toward the gate. "Come along, Gimma."

Gimma glanced at Arianwyn. Her face was ashen, her lips dry and sore. She looked tired. "I'd better go," she mumbled, following her uncle.

"Don't forget about the charm-hanging later," Arianwyn called after her.

It wasn't all Gimma's fault, and Arianwyn knew it. She stared at the rubble and smashed nest at the foot of the wall. Why hadn't the spell worked this time when it had been so pliable and obedient in the Spellorium?

Perhaps it wasn't even the spell; perhaps it was her. Perhaps she had lost her knack for some reason. She was certain when the council heard about this and the stagget they would be asking for her star badge back pretty soon.

CHAPTER TWENTY-EIGHT

THE TELEGRAM

As Arianwyn walked slowly along Kettle Lane, replaying the day's events over in her mind, she noticed someone waiting outside the Spellorium, even though it was nearly closing time. As she drew closer she saw that it was Jonas Attinger, the eldest son of Lull's postmistress.

"Oh, hello, Jonas. What can I do for you? Not brownies again, is it?" Arianwyn smiled as she unlocked the Spellorium door and went inside, flicking on the lights. She dumped her satchel on the counter.

Jonas hovered by the door. "Uh, no, miss . . ." He looked down at the small piece of paper in his hand. "This came for you." He didn't move any farther forward. "It's a telegram." His hand shook a little.

"Oh, it's probably something from the High Elder," Arianwyn said, suddenly worried that it was to do with the stagget.

"Sorry, Miss Gribble, but . . ." He took a deep, shuddering breath. "It's from the war office." Jonas let her take the piece of paper, and suddenly Arianwyn's own hands were shaking. She paused for a second. A million nightmarish things raced through her mind before she pulled the folded piece of paper open and stared down at the neatly typed letters:

```
(PRIORITY COMMUNICATION)
  MISS ARIANWYN FLORA GRIBBLE, THE
SPELLORIUM, 38 KETTLE LANE, LULL
     THE SECRETARY OF WAR DESIRES ME TO
EXPRESS HIS DEEPEST REGRET TO INFORM
YOU THAT YOUR FATHER SGT. OLIVER E.
GRIBBLE S/KD6911779 HAS BEEN REPORTED
MISSING IN ACTION ON WAR SERVICE SINCE
OCTOBER 17 IN NORTHERN VEERSLAND IF
FURTHER DETAILS OR OTHER INFORMATION
ARE RECEIVED YOU WILL BE PROMPTLY
NOTIFIED
     J. A. GREENFIELD ADJUTANT GENERAL
```

"I am sorry, miss," Jonas offered quietly, his voice shaking. "Can I get you anything?"

Arianwyn looked up, but Jonas was just blobs of color through her tears. "I . . ." She didn't know what to say. Fear and terror gripped her in a way she hadn't thought possible. It felt as though the walls of the Spellorium were closing in on her now, and her only thought was to run.

The telegram slipped from her hands as she dashed out of the door and ran down Kettle Lane, hoping that the whole world would collapse around her or at least stop while she tried to make sense of the words so efficiently typed on the telegram.

She ran and ran and ran.

Arianwyn sat on the grassy riverbank, her face buried in her hands as though that could keep the news, everything, at bay. The river flowed past, careless of how Arianwyn's world seemed to be ending.

She sobbed, but the river just murmured gently, and she could still hear the calls of the birds above and occasional sounds from Lull, safe behind its high walls. How could the world carry on as though nothing had changed, when everything had?

When she felt she could cry no more, when her throat was dry and her eyes sore, she glanced up to see that the sun had started to set and the walls of the town were bathed in a glorious warm pink light. But huge gray clouds were moving fast across the sky. A storm was coming.

She wiped at her face and slowly got to her feet, though she didn't know where to go. Suddenly everywhere felt strange and alien to her. She wanted her grandmother but there was no easy way to reach her.

She had never felt so alone.

"Arianwyn?"

She turned quickly, startled.

Colin was making his way toward her.

"Miss Newam and I just went to the Spellorium to see you and . . . I'm so sorry, Arianwyn." He stopped where he was, the telegram in his hand.

"I'm not sure I want to talk about it right now, Colin," Arianwyn said, turning back to the river.

Perhaps he would go away?

There was a rustling sound as he moved through the long dry grass, and then he was at her side.

So, he wasn't going away, then.

"Are you here to check up on me?" she snapped.

"No, of course not—"

"Because I've had enough of being told off by my friends recently."

Colin sighed. "I wasn't telling you off, but it's just not like you to give up on something like that, Arianwyn."

She swallowed hard.

"I'm not angry with you, I'm still your friend," Colin said, "if you're still mine?"

She nodded, but she didn't feel she could look at him yet. If she saw a pitying look in his eyes she would burst into tears again.

"I won't talk about it, then," he said quietly. "I'll only say that if you want anything or want to talk then I'm here, okay?"

She nodded.

"But it did only say he was missing, the telegram. So, don't give up hope."

They sat for a few more moments watching the water flow past. Large circles bloomed on the surface of the river as the rain arrived.

"I should get back. I have to meet Gimma and Miss Delafield—we're hanging the charms this evening," Arianwyn said, though the thought of returning to the Spellorium didn't fill her with enthusiasm.

"Don't you think you should . . . I don't know . . . rest? You've had a terrible shock, Arianwyn. I'll tell Miss Delafield—"

"No, Colin, please. I don't want everyone to know. Not yet."

He looked at the ground, his sweater darkening with spots of rain. "Are you sure?"

Arianwyn nodded. "At least with Gimma around I'll have something to take my mind off things."

"Well, let me walk you back, then?"

They headed along the bank, the calls of birds and the patter of rain the only sounds. Arianwyn was grateful that Colin didn't mention the telegram any more. She saw him slip it into his back pocket and they walked to the Spellorium in companionable silence.

A WITCH ALONE: A MANUAL FOR THE NEWLY QUALIFIED WITCH

✦ ✦ ✦

Dark magic is commanding: Where it is prevalent within the world it has the power to bend and shape a witch's spell in the most extraordinary and unexpected of ways. A poorly trained or inexperienced witch may struggle with basic spell craft if there is a large buildup of dark magic nearby. While a small amount of dark magic is sometimes useful and indeed used, as with the banishing spell, too much of it will contaminate the purer magic a witch must seek to uphold. And if there is prolonged exposure it can sometimes affect the witch herself. Guard yourself against dark magic at all times.

CHAPTER TWENTY-NINE

FIREFLY LIGHTS

"Typical that it would rain this evening, isn't it, dear?" Miss Delafield said, wrestling her way into a long waxy raincoat in the Spellorium.

Arianwyn mumbled something in reply, not really listening as she pulled on her own matching CWA raincoat, which was secondhand and far too big. She carefully folded the sleeves over several times, but the hem was only a few inches from the floor, like a cape. Whoever had owned it before must have been a giant.

"Are you all right?" Miss Delafield asked. She stopped and gave Arianwyn one of her appraising looks, as though she might sum up at once what was wrong with her.

For a second, Arianwyn decided to tell her about the telegram. But before she could, the door opened and, in a swirl of rain-laced wind, Gimma stepped into the Spellorium. Her raincoat was definitely *not* standard CWA issue.

"We're not seriously doing this tonight, are we?" she asked, looking at Miss Delafield and then at Arianwyn in disbelief.

Miss Delafield folded her arms across her chest. "We most certainly are! You girls have done wonders getting the charms ready so quickly; now we need to get them in place as soon as possible. No time like the present, you know."

Gimma sighed and then, glancing at the stack of boxes by the counter, said, "We're not carrying them all the way to the wood ourselves, though, are we?"

"No, dear. I'm going to nip down there with them in my car. You and Arianwyn will have to follow, I'm afraid! No room."

"Oh, joy!" Gimma scowled. "Can't we go on Wyn's broom, then?" She looked longingly at Arianwyn's broomstick propped against the wall near the Spellorium door.

"I'm not flying in the rain," Arianwyn said quickly, pulling up her hood and tightening her satchel. She wasn't even going to discuss it.

"So then all ready to go, girls?" Miss Delafield asked, tightening her own bag strap across her chest.

Arianwyn glanced through the window at the wet and wild evening. "I guess so!" she replied.

But her eyes strayed to the bookshelf behind the counter. High on a shelf sat her copy of *A Witch Alone*, and trapped between its pages were the glyph of silence and now the telegram, which Arianwyn had reluctantly taken back from Colin once they'd returned from the river, neither of them saying a word.

Secrets and more secrets.

After Miss Delafield had zoomed along Kettle Lane, Arianwyn and Gimma walked in silence, each cocooned in her raincoat as the rain grew heavier and heavier. The occasional gust of wind blew icy needles into Arianwyn's face, adding to her gloom. She imagined the charms—hours of hard work—chinking and rattling in Miss Delafield's racing car, roads dampened by the rain, and hoped her supervisor was driving unusually carefully. Lull was dark and quiet: Only the bright lights in the windows gave any indication the town was inhabited. As they passed through the town gates, Arianwyn and Gimma switched on their flashlights. They would need all their energy for spells later, so no light orbs this evening.

They met Miss Delafield at the edge of the Great Wood, just a few yards from the mayor's cordon. The car's headlights were turned on, and all along the edge of the wood the floor was strewn with bloodred leaves that glistened damply in the beams. The last chatter of the woodland birds sounded about them, and the tang of wood smoke from town drifted to them with the occasional whiff of cooking smells.

Miss Delafield had set the stack of boxes on the ground underneath a tree, but they still looked rather soggy. Rain dripped from the branches. Somewhere off across the meadow Arianwyn heard the call of the qered, low and mournful.

"Well now, what's the plan again?" Miss Delafield asked, looking at Arianwyn.

Arianwyn took a deep breath and looked at Gimma and Miss Delafield. "If we hang a charm from a branch every ten yards or so along the border of the wood, and activate them with Årdra, they will hopefully stop the hex from spreading closer to town." The fire glyph, they all knew, had strong protective properties.

Gimma rolled her eyes as Miss Delafield said, "Bravo, dear!" clapping her hands together. "Well, you girls go that way and I'll head toward the river." She pointed off along the edge of the wood.

"Are you sure you don't want me to help you, Miss Delafield?" Arianwyn asked. Today of all days, she just wasn't sure she could face spending more time with Gimma than was absolutely necessary.

"No, dear—you girls stick together. I'll be perfectly fine on my own. I'll shout if I need anything."

Arianwyn handed Gimma a box of charms and grabbed her own and they wandered off along the edge of the wood. After a few yards Arianwyn stopped, put her box down, and lifted out the first charm. She glanced back along the tree line to where Miss Delafield was already absorbed with her own work.

"What is it we have to do again?" Gimma asked, stifling a yawn. She stood next to the box and didn't move to help Arianwyn as she lifted the first charm free. The contents rattled inside the glass sphere.

"Once we've hung them, they need activating, with Årdra," Arianwyn explained again.

"And do you honestly think these will help?" Gimma asked as she lifted a charm orb from the box. She held it in both hands and studied it carefully. The kartz stones gave off a faint glow, lighting the little feyling stone nestled at their side.

"I can't think of anything else," Arianwyn replied. *If only we had the Book*, she thought. *But then the glyph of silence was hardly a roaring success . . .*

A bird cry rang out from the forest, startling Gimma. "I don't know why I feel so nervous," she said. She glanced over at Arianwyn, and her eyes seemed to sparkle in the darkness. She smiled. Not her usual sneering smile, but something gentle and almost friendly. Arianwyn smiled back as she started to tie her charm orb to a secure and sturdy branch. She watched Gimma copy her with a tree a little way off. "Like this?" Gimma called as she tied the cord in loops around the branch.

"That's it, and then you need to sketch Årdra onto the globe, to activate the charm."

Arianwyn drew the glyph onto her charm globe and felt a tug of magic from nearby. The magic flowed straight toward her and, as it connected with the glyph, the charm unexpectedly began to glow brighter, like a large but rather dim light bulb. It was such a surprise that she gasped and stepped backward, watching for a second. The light seemed to pulse slowly, like a heartbeat. A gentle wave of heat rolled toward her. *This has to be a good sign, surely?*

"Oh, is this right?" Gimma asked.

Arianwyn turned and saw her charm globe was glowing in the same way. She smiled. Something had gone right for Gimma at last. "Well done, Gimma."

"It's beautiful, Arianwyn." And suddenly Gimma laughed softly.

Arianwyn realized she had never heard Gimma genuinely laugh before. It was a sound of pure joy, and it threw Arianwyn completely off guard: She forgot her own worries for a moment, and instead found a happy smile spreading across her face.

After an hour, a string of charms looped across the edge of the Great Wood all the way around Lull, their faint pulsing light flickering like giant fireflies. Arianwyn, Miss Delafield, and Gimma were soaked through, but the charms had kept them surprisingly warm. Gimma came jogging toward Arianwyn after activating her last charm. Her pale blonde hair was plastered to her head in wet strands, but her cheeks were rosy and her eyes shone.

"Are you okay?" Arianwyn asked, afraid Gimma had caught a chill.

But she smiled again, in that same way that had taken Arianwyn by surprise earlier. "I feel fine actually—I could do this all evening. I've not felt this good in—"

There was a loud cry from within the wood. It sounded like something in pain or frightened. "What was that?" Gimma asked, peering through the dark trunks and branches, the rain still splashing about them.

"Probably just an animal or something," Arianwyn said hopefully, and started to turn back toward Lull. But, just then, a gust of cool, rain-flecked wind blew leaves around her ankles and, breathing in, she detected a rancid stench of dark magic on the air that hadn't been there a moment before.

The cry sounded again, but this time she heard faint words: "HELP ME! Please!"

That was certainly no animal. She looked at Gimma, whose eyes were wide.

There was another undecipherable cry and Arianwyn was suddenly running into the forest, branches snatching at her raincoat. She allowed herself to be swallowed up by the trees. She heard Gimma following.

"Go back, fetch Miss Delafield. It's not safe!" Arianwyn shouted over her shoulder.

But Gimma ignored her, drawing level with Arianwyn as she ran on.

Arianwyn wasn't sure exactly how long they ran for, but there were no more cries for help. Had they imagined it? She stopped and stood still, trying to catch her breath. She glanced at Gimma, who looked as confused as Arianwyn felt. But then Gimma's hand flew up to her mouth.

"Oh no—look!" She pointed past Arianwyn into a thick snarl of vines and creepers.

There in the gloom of the Great Wood lay a small blue figure, yellow lamplike eyes wide in terror.

"Help!" the blue thing croaked, its voice hoarse and cracked from shouting.

"Estar? Oh my goodness!" Arianwyn darted forward, falling to the wet floor of the wood before her friend.

He was battered and bashed, his blue skin dark with bruises and dirt, his arms lined with cuts and scratches. *Could it really be Estar, here at last?*

"Hello, Arianwyn Gribble, my friend," he whispered.

"Oh, Estar. I didn't think I'd ever see you again." Something urgent bubbled up from inside her then: the worry, fear, everything from the last weeks. Suddenly it all erupted in a burst of tears as she wrapped her arms around Estar and pulled him close.

"Of course, it's very lovely to see you again as well, Arianwyn," Estar said, patting her back gently. "But the thing is, there is a rather horrible creature just over there, and I think it may wish to eat one or indeed all of us!"

CHAPTER THIRTY

BLACK LIGHTNING

Arianwyn pulled herself up, wiping her tears away and gulping a lungful of air. "What?"

"It's a skalk," Estar said calmly, trying to get to his mismatched feet: one was hooved like a goat's, the other scaled and clawed like a lizard's. "My suggestion would be that we move quickly and quietly away as soon as possible." He secured a small pouch around his waist and lifted a small knife-shaped stone, rather like the one the feathered feyling had carried.

"Oh dear," Arianwyn breathed.

"Do you need help?" Gimma stepped forward.

"Oh, it's you . . . again. Hello," Estar said uncertainly.

Gimma's face had grown pale again, the bright sparkle in her eyes gone. She looked scared and remote once more.

"Are you okay?" Arianwyn asked.

"I'm fine—stop fussing," Gimma snapped. "Let's just get out of here, shall we?"

Gimma swung her flashlight around, looking for the way they had come. And that was when Arianwyn saw it: the flashlight beam illuminated a huge dead tree about five yards away . . . and something that clung to the dark, wet trunk. Its skin was pale, pink, and raw, like too-cold hands. It looked almost human but for its bones, jutting under the skin at odd angles, its spine a twisted mess. It had a knotty tangle of too many arms and legs, and its head was hidden from view under thick, shaggy, matted hair.

It hadn't moved, so perhaps it hadn't detected them . . .

Arianwyn put a finger to her lips and glared at Gimma and Estar, willing them to stay quiet. She took a few cautious steps backward, grabbing Gimma's raincoat and Estar's arm, pulling them along with her. The flashlight beam wobbled and the creature was swallowed up in the darkness.

And after another few backward steps they turned to run, but Gimma stumbled—Arianwyn tried to hold on to her but she fell to the ground. The flashlight slipped from her hands and there was the sound of breaking glass as it smashed against a tree stump or a rock.

Darkness swallowed them.

"Gimma? Are you okay?" Arianwyn hissed. She breathed Oru, the light glyph, and a faint orb of light formed just ahead of her.

"I'm here. Watch where you're going!" Gimma snarled angrily.

Arianwyn could see Gimma sprawled across a huge tree root, covered in damp leaves and mud, the remains of the broken flashlight shattered near her hand.

There was the sudden sound of many hurried feet—quick and scuttling. *It's seen us*, Arianwyn realized, a sick feeling rushing over her. She glanced at the fallen tree, but the skalk was not there. *Lurking in the shadows?*

She twisted her hand, pulling magic toward the light orb, which glowed brighter at once.

Arianwyn glimpsed movement to her left, behind the closely grouped trees. She ducked forward, pulled Gimma to her feet, and grabbed Estar by the hand. "Come on!" she said, dragging them into the trees in the opposite direction, back the way they'd come. The light orb flickered and dimmed, but Arianwyn pushed it ahead: clouds covered the moon, and the wood was pitch-black—they needed something to light the way.

They turned onto a narrow path, their feet pounding quietly against the soft, damp carpet of leaves as they dodged in and out of trees, barely visible in the spell orb's half-light. They bounded over tangles of bramble and vine. Arianwyn's raincoat caught on sharp spines or snagged on branches that reached out to her like eager, menacing hands. Once or twice she stumbled over lumps in the ground, but thankfully she righted herself or Gimma reached out for her, pulling her to her feet. Estar limped a little behind, slowed as ever by his mismatched legs.

The skalk thundered behind them, occasionally launching itself into the trees and swinging above them, like a bald ape, but always landing back on the ground and—thankfully—each time it was still behind them, but the gap was closing. All of a sudden, the skalk was beside them and Arianwyn saw it clearly for the first time: a snarled mess of white arms and legs, scuttling across the ground like a fleshy spider. It swiped out at their ankles as they moved. Gimma screamed and they ran faster, Arianwyn pulling a weakening Estar by his hand.

They were near to the edge of the forest now, the trees thinning, and Arianwyn glimpsed the walls of Lull across the wide dark meadow. She could hear the gentle haunting call of the qered.

She couldn't let the skalk beyond the boundary of the wood. Without the trees to slow it down it could attack the qered—and worse, if it found its way beyond the town walls . . .

Arianwyn summoned and hurled a spell orb at the skalk, but the orb evaporated in midair before it got anywhere close. "Boil it!" Arianwyn spat, and she shoved Gimma and Estar to one side so they were running along the edge of the wood now, the meadow parallel to them but still a short way off.

"Where are we going?" Estar panted. He was barely running. It felt to Arianwyn as though she were dragging him through the wood.

"Get on my back," Arianwyn said, pulling Estar into place, his arms reaching around her neck to hold on. "We can't lead it into the meadow—we'll put everyone in danger. And the trees are slowing it at the moment!"

"This is slow?" Gimma gasped.

The change of direction seemed to have thrown it off, and for a second Arianwyn wondered if they had lost it. She paused, hoping and listening.

Gimma panted beside her, trying to catch her breath.

"Did we lose it?" Estar asked, his grip tightening on her shoulders.

"I don't think so . . ." It just seemed a little too easy.

The light orb now hovered just behind Arianwyn, illuminating the patch of wood directly ahead of them. The ground looked churned up but there was no sign of the skalk. Then, from above, came a strange clacking sound. Arianwyn tipped her head back and found she couldn't breathe: the creature was hanging upside down from the branches above, gripping on to the tree with a mixture of feet and hands. Its bonelike beak snapped at them again.

And then it dropped!

She and Gimma dived in opposite directions as the skalk landed with a thud and a whoosh of leaves and twigs. It cast its snapping beaky head, covered with matted hair, this way and that, sensing each of them, picking its prey. Estar clung to Arianwyn's back, his hands shaking with fear.

"Run!" Arianwyn shouted to Gimma. "Get to town. I'll try and draw it back into the wood!"

"But—"

"Just do it, Gimma!" Arianwyn ordered.

She tried to ready a spell orb, but all she got was a handful of sparks and a brief blinding headache. She tried again but still no orb would form . . . what was going on? She turned to run again, Estar clinging tightly to her back. She'd only gone a few steps when she felt something crash into them and they were falling, tumbling headfirst to the ground—Estar flew off her back and landed nearby, lying very still. Mud and leaves filled Arianwyn's mouth and blocked her nose. She tried to scramble to her feet but she was too slow and the ground too slippery. The skalk pounced again, wrapping its legs and arms around her.

She was pinned. The skalk had her firmly in its grip!

Estar lay stunned, unconscious a couple of yards away. She tried to reach for him but it was no good. She tried to move, to wriggle, anything, but she couldn't even flex her fingers to finish a spell. She wasn't sure she even had enough air in her lungs to summon a glyph, so tight had the skalk enfolded her. It snapped its yellow-white bony beak close to her face, and she glimpsed fiery red eyes through matted hair. Its beak snapped again, the sound echoing through the wood.

And now it was so close, she could smell its rank hot breath. Was this how it would all end, here alone in the Great Wood?

Arianwyn felt the burst of energy more than saw it, and the skalk was suddenly flying away from her. She turned quickly and saw it crash against a nearby tree trunk—and then it was still, just for a second. Arianwyn tried to scrabble toward Estar, but the skalk had found its feet again, flipped itself around, and was charging back toward them.

This time she saw something dark shoot across the wood, like a bolt of black lightning. It smashed into the skalk head-on. The creature cried out as it was slammed hard into another tree. There was the sickening sound of bones and bark cracking. The skalk fell to the ground and the full-grown tree it had hit snapped in half as though it were a mere sapling. Arianwyn shielded her head as a shower of twigs and wet leaves flew down from the canopy. When she looked up, the skalk had been buried in the flurry of leaves and roots and bark. Arianwyn twisted to see who had sent the strange spell—who had saved them.

Highlighted by a wavering flashlight beam at the edge of the wood was a pale-faced Gimma, her wet hair whipped around her like tendrils.

CHAPTER THIRTY-ONE

POLICY & PROTOCOL

"Can you stand, dear?" Miss Delafield was suddenly at Arianwyn's side, helping her to her feet. A light orb bobbed beside her. Arianwyn felt every part of her ache, every single muscle.

"Whatever it was you did worked like a charm, I would say . . . it is gone, isn't it?" Miss Delafield asked, her eyes shifting to the tumbled, broken tree.

"I didn't do it," Arianwyn said, straightening. "It was Gimma."

They both looked over to Gimma now, who stood still as a statue. She was staring straight past them, and looking deep into the wood. "Well *done*, Miss Alverston. What spell did you use, dear?"

Gimma mumbled a reply too quiet to hear, pulling her gloves straight and rubbing at her wrists.

"Best get it banished, dear," Miss Delafield said. Gimma wandered past them as if she were in some sort of daze. She crossed to the fallen tree and sketched the banishing glyph close to the trunk. Arianwyn could see, could feel, the small rift open, a sliver of darkness far darker than the nighttime shadows of the wood that surrounded it.

A wet gust of wind hit Arianwyn and she caught another hot rancid sniff of dark magic from the Great Wood.

"Estar!" Arianwyn said as she turned and saw her friend lying so still among the churned-up earth and leaves of the woodland floor. She hobbled across to him and gave him a gentle shake, but he simply moaned, his eyelids fluttering.

"Well, that was a surprise, wasn't it?" Miss Delafield whispered, her eyes flicking across to where Gimma waited, facing back to Lull.

"But don't you think it's a bit . . . odd?" Arianwyn asked quietly.

"How do you mean, dear?"

"Where did that come from? Gimma was never the best with any sort of spell. She could barely handle one bogglin in the summer and now she's just seen off a skalk—a creature no one has seen in decades!"

Miss Delafield's expression suddenly hardened. "Don't be jealous, Arianwyn—it really doesn't suit you. Besides, who knows what might have happened if Gimma hadn't been here to help."

Arianwyn lifted Estar easily and held him close, his small blue chest rising and falling with every breath. She glanced back at Gimma, who had turned back, gazing into the Great Wood again—though not with fear or worry but with something different, something that Arianwyn couldn't quite put her finger on.

"I should get you all back to town at once," Miss Delafield said calmly. "It's not safe out here. Whatever were you thinking, running off into the wood alone like that?

You should have called me!" She shepherded them all into the car, Arianwyn holding Estar close, Gimma wandering in a stunned daze.

They were back at the Spellorium in just a few minutes. Arianwyn was surprised to see Salle waiting on the doorstep. Miss Delafield hurriedly clambered out of the car to unlock the door as Arianwyn climbed down into Kettle Lane. Salle stepped forward, a small parcel wrapped in red checkered cloth in her hands. "I didn't want to disturb you, but Aunt Grace asked me to bring you . . ." Her words trailed off and her face darkened when she saw Arianwyn's burden. "What's happened? Is that Estar?"

"He was hurt in the Great Wood—I need to get him inside." She hurried past Salle. No time for sympathy or recriminations now.

Gimma followed them all inside, apparently still stunned and in shock. She waited near the door, fidgeting with her gloves. She looked as though she might be sick any second.

"I'd sit down if I were you, dear," Miss Delafield offered calmly.

Arianwyn placed Estar near the stove and busied herself laying a small fire. He felt worryingly cold; his breathing was shallow and there were the longest gaps when his chest didn't move at all. "Hang on, Estar," she muttered in his ear. She couldn't lose him when she had only just gotten him back. Her hands trembled as she lit the stove.

"What should I do, dear?" Miss Delafield asked, standing over her, her raincoat dripping on the floor. Arianwyn reached out a trembling hand and held it against Estar's forehead, which felt cold and clammy. Then she checked his wrist for a pulse—she couldn't feel anything, but then she wasn't even sure feylings had a pulse. She had no idea what she was doing!

"I think we need the doctor," Arianwyn said. Though she wasn't sure the doctor would be able to help either.

The door opened. "Hello, all! We thought we'd just come to see how you got on this evening. My word, what on earth is going on here?" Mayor Belcher's voice cut through the anxious quiet in the Spellorium.

Arianwyn twisted around to see him, Miss Newam, and Colin at the door. The mayor looked at Gimma and Salle hovering nearby, then at Miss Delafield, and finally at Arianwyn and Estar on the floor. She imagined they were a strange sight indeed, soaked through and muddy, surrounding the still form of the little blue feyling.

"Estar was attacked by a skalk in the wood, Arianwyn and Gimma rescued him, and Gimma managed to dispatch the skalk. But Estar has been badly hurt," Miss Delafield explained quickly.

Mayor Belcher gazed more carefully at Estar and gave a dismissive sniff. "Oh!" He pulled out his little black notebook.

"Are you telling me *that* creature has come from the Great Wood?" Miss Newam asked, taking a step back.

"Yes, that's what I just said," Miss Delafield sighed.

"Well, you can't bring him in here, then. He could be crawling with hex!" Miss Newam said, her voice shrill and panicked.

"Miss Newam, this is *Estar*!" Arianwyn said, hoping she would catch on and realize this was who they had been looking for in the Great Wood, that Estar held the key to the *Book of Quiet Glyphs*.

"I don't care if he's the emperor of Dannis, Miss Gribble. Look at him, he's covered in hex"—she backed away, her eyes widening—"and by bringing him here you are putting us all at risk!"

"That's *mud*!" Arianwyn replied, wiping away at Estar's thin arm.

Miss Newam stared hard at Arianwyn, her eyes unblinking like a lizard's behind her thick spectacles.

Colin looked as though he was about to respond, but Miss Newam shot him a cold hard look and he stopped dead.

"He needs help, Miss Newam," Arianwyn said. "We have to—"

"We have to do nothing but get him outside the town walls," Miss Newam said levelly.

Salle was suddenly at Arianwyn's side with a pile of blankets. She knelt down and handed one to Arianwyn, who wrapped it carefully around Estar. He looked so ill. She couldn't possibly leave him outside the town! He would die, she was certain of it!

"I'm fetching the doctor," Arianwyn said, getting to her feet.

"As a representative of the CWA, I am telling you that you're not allowed!" Miss Newam said, her voice rising ever so slightly. "Until we're certain he is free of the hex, he will have to stay outside the town walls. Your duty is to the people of this town, and at present you are putting everyone at risk, Miss Gribble."

The mayor coughed. "It seems to me that Hortensia . . . I mean Miss Newam, is right, Miss Gribble. I can't have you risking everyone's lives for the sake of this . . . creature."

Arianwyn felt tears of frustration in her eyes. Why didn't they understand? "But he doesn't have any hex on him, Miss Newam. Estar might die! Is that what you want? Will you be happy then? He might die and then everything we've been doing will be for nothing." Surely she would catch on? Arianwyn looked at Colin, who seemed totally lost.

"You're just being dramatic now—"

"And you're just being difficult!" Arianwyn snapped.

"I am following *policy and protocol*, set down by the Civil Witchcraft Authority," Miss Newam said coldly.

Salle suddenly stood up. "Wait here, I'll only be a few minutes," she said.

"And just where do you think you're going?" Miss Newam barked.

"I'm going to see Dr. Cadbury!" Salle said, standing and lifting her head a little higher. She pushed her way past Miss Newam. "And if you don't like it . . . then you can boggin well arrest me!"

CHAPTER THIRTY-TWO

MORE POWERFUL THAN A SPELL

I t felt like hours before Salle returned to the Spellorium. Arianwyn turned at the sound of the door charm's bright notes and Salle was suddenly at her side, clutching a small tin in her shaking hands.

"Where's Dr. Cadbury?" Arianwyn hissed.

"You don't need the doctor," Salle said crossly, fiddling with the tin. "Besides, I knew old grumpy knickers probably wouldn't let him in anyway."

"So what are we going to do?" Arianwyn asked.

The tin clattered to the floor and Salle knelt there gazing at Estar, holding a syringe. The glass cylinder glinted in her hand. "What . . . what is *that*?" Miss Newam asked, moving forward quickly from the counter.

But as fast as lightning Salle grabbed the feyling's thin arm in her hand and pressed the slender needle into the muscle of Estar's blue flesh. The milky liquid in the syringe vanished.

"What was that?" Everyone seemed to ask the question at once.

"Salle, what have you done?" Arianwyn asked, fear bubbling inside her. She pushed Salle to one side and grasped

Estar's arm. A small bruise was blossoming under the blue skin.

"It's medicine from Dr. Cadbury," Salle snapped, picking up the tin. "An antibiotic." She packed the syringe away carefully. "I described his symptoms to Dr. Cadbury, and he said Estar probably has an infection."

"I said there was to be—" Miss Newam started to hiss.

"No DOCTOR!" Salle interrupted, her head whipping around, her eyes locking with Miss Newam's. "And I didn't bring the doctor here. Just the medicine that we thought might help."

The Spellorium fell silent and everyone looked at Salle.

"We?" Arianwyn asked.

Salle looked ahead, avoiding Arianwyn's eyes. "I'm Dr. Cadbury's new assistant," she said, lifting her head a little higher.

"Oh, Salle—that's wonderful!" Arianwyn said, her heart swelling with pride for her friend.

But Salle didn't reply. She got to her feet and disappeared upstairs, returning moments later carrying a small bowl of water. She pulled out a clean collection of white cloths from her pocket and busied herself cleaning Estar's cuts and scratches. He was streaked with mud and moss and dirt.

"You are to move that creature out of town at once!" Miss Newam commanded.

Arianwyn's vision blurred with tears, the day of emotions suddenly too much to contain. "Oh, Miss Newam, don't you see? He might have the BOOK!" she roared.

Everyone in the room jumped, clearly shocked by Arianwyn's outburst. And in a moment that seemed to stretch on forever, she realized her huge error.

She looked at Colin, Salle, Miss Delafield, Gimma, the mayor, and Miss Newam. They all stared at her, faces dressed in equal measures of shock.

"What book? What is Miss Gribble talking about?" Mayor Belcher asked at last. She heard him step away from his perch by the door. "Miss Delafield, do you know what's going on?"

Miss Delafield shook her head. "No, Mayor Belcher, though I suspect Miss Newam might be able to enlighten us." She sounded angry.

Oh, snotlings, Arianwyn thought. *What have I done now?!*

"Josiah, I can explain," Miss Newam said, her voice trembling. She reached toward the mayor.

"Wait!" Colin said, stepping in front of Miss Newam, as though he was shielding her from attack. "We promised to keep the mission a secret."

"Mission?" Miss Delafield asked. "Arianwyn, what is going on here?"

Arianwyn's eyes flicked around the Spellorium. She could feel herself shaking. She looked at Salle, who just glanced away quickly, as if confused. She looked at Miss Newam, who simply glared at her for the hundredth time. She looked at Colin. His hair had flopped over into his eyes, but he only smiled gently, as if to say "go on, you might as well."

Arianwyn took a calming breath and she looked over at Miss Delafield.

"The High Elder asked us to try to find the *Book of Quiet Glyphs*. That's why we went into the Great Wood. To find the book—or Estar, because he knows where it is. So we can't turn him away, Miss Newam. We *need* him."

"What is this book?" the mayor asked.

"It's the book that contains more of the powerful quiet glyphs, like the shadow glyph that Arianwyn can see," Miss Delafield explained. Her voice sounded a bit far away, as though she was recalling a dream. "Like the ones my sister saw . . ."

The Spellorium fell silent.

It was Gimma who eventually spoke. "So Estar has the book?" She sounded expectant, curious. She stepped forward, eyeing the still feyling cautiously. But there was only the small pouch at his waist, too small for any book, and the stone blade at his side.

Arianwyn looked down at Estar. "Perhaps he's hidden it somewhere," she said hopefully, suddenly feeling helpless again. So near and yet so far.

"Well, you'd better hope he has, Miss Gribble, or the High Elder will not be pleased," Miss Newam said quickly.

Arianwyn's eyes fell on her copy of *A Witch Alone*. The slip of paper that held the glyph of silence was safe between its pages. She should just tell everyone now and get it over with. "Miss Newam—"

"And you cannot tell anyone about this mission. Any of you!" Miss Newam interrupted. "We have to keep what has been discussed here between us—it can't go any further."

"I doubt anyone would believe us anyway." Gimma smiled.

"That's neither here nor there, Miss Alverston," Miss Newam said quickly. She gave everyone one final sour look. "Well, it has been an eventful day and I'm tired, so I will be returning to the inn. Are you coming, Colin?"

Colin looked quickly at Arianwyn and shrugged his shoulders in agreement. "Good night, Arianwyn. Let me know if Estar wakes up?"

"Of course," Arianwyn replied.

"I should be getting Gimma home," said the mayor, laying a hand on his niece's forehead. "You look quite peaky again."

"Stop fussing!" Gimma snapped, storming out of the Spellorium ahead of him.

Miss Delafield yawned. "What a muddle!"

"I'm sorry, Miss Delafield. I couldn't . . ." She trailed off, noticing that Salle was moving toward the door. "Salle, wait," Arianwyn called, hurrying over to her friend. "Thank you for your help," she said simply.

"It's nothing, I wanted to help," Salle said. A look of uncertainty rushed over her face, like clouds gathering for a storm. She made to move but Arianwyn caught her arm. She desperately wanted to pull her friend into a tight hug. But something was different now; something had shut down between them, and she didn't know how to make it go back to how it had been before. "Well, you were great," Arianwyn said softly.

"I had to help, Wyn. Don't you see? *You* taught me that . . ."

"Well, just don't get yourself into any more trouble with Miss Newam," she said. Salle looked hurt. Arianwyn had meant it to sound lighthearted. But suddenly she realized it sounded like she was scolding Salle. "Wait, I didn't mean—"

"Why don't you just spit it out, Wyn—you don't think I can manage this, do you?" Salle said, her voice rising. Her eyes shone.

"No—it's not that!" Arianwyn said quickly.

"I think you're annoyed that for once you're not the only one who can help and everyone isn't depending on you. You've tried to hold me back, admit it, Wyn. You liked having me as a hanger-on until I had something of my own to do and now you're trying to . . . stop me."

"No, Salle, I wouldn't—"

"You're just *jealous!*" As Salle spat out the words, a look of surprise flashed across her face. "You're jealous and you can't stand it. And now you feel guilty as well because of forgetting my interview."

"Well, I am sorry about that . . . ," Arianwyn started to explain. She could feel tears welling behind her eyes. Her nose itched and all she wanted to do was run away. She was horribly aware of Miss Delafield trying to stand discreetly on the far side of the Spellorium, desperately pretending she couldn't hear every single word.

"Well? Spit it out, then." Salle glared, her eyes burning with anger, frustration, and something else.

Arianwyn tried to speak but her words caught in her throat and all that came out was a small rough squeak.

"I knew it," Salle said, turning away. "I think I'd better go."

The words cut Arianwyn like a knife. She watched Salle leave the Spellorium without looking back. She barged past Colin and Miss Newam, who had stopped a little way along Kettle Lane. It felt as though someone had shoved Arianwyn hard against a wall, knocking the wind from her.

Miss Delafield crossed over and pulled the door of the Spellorium closed. "I think I'll stay here tonight, dear. Bit too far to drive home so late."

"Where will you sleep?" Arianwyn asked, though she was suddenly grateful that she wasn't going to be all on her own.

"I'll be fine in the chair. Perhaps you could lend me a blanket and a pillow, though?"

"Thank you, Miss Delafield. I'm sorry about not being able to tell you about the book."

"Don't worry about it, dear. I know how these things work. And I think you've got enough to be worrying about for now."

Arianwyn felt a moment of relief. She smiled weakly at Miss Delafield and then crossed slowly to where Estar lay. She sat on the floor, taking her friend's blue hand in her own.

He really was their only hope now.

"Oh, Estar, please, *please* wake up."

CHAPTER THIRTY-THREE

A DAY OFF

Early the next morning, Arianwyn padded downstairs with a mug of hot tea. She crossed quietly to Miss Delafield and gave her a gentle shake where she slept in the chair beside the stove. Estar was lying on a bundle of blankets beside her.

"I brought you some tea." Arianwyn smiled as Miss Delafield blinked and yawned.

"Wonderful. Thank you, dear." She took a huge gulp of tea and then looked down at Estar. "At least he looks peaceful and he's here now. We just have to wait for him to wake up." Her face suddenly became grave. "Young Colin told me about your father, dear. I am so sorry—if I'd known I wouldn't have made you go out yesterday evening. If you want to take some time off . . ."

Arianwyn shook her head, even as the tears fell down her cheeks. "No, it's fine. I just wish I . . . I just want to speak to my grandmother," she said. She had a sudden longing for her grandmother that she hadn't known had been there until she had said it. Arianwyn missed her voice, the smell of her hair. The safe feeling of her arms around her.

Miss Delafield sat forward, her red hair all bunched up and flyaway, not its usual sleek bob. She reached out a hand to Arianwyn. "And what would you say to her, if she were here now?"

Arianwyn gulped back a sob, remembering how helpless she'd felt the previous night, when she hadn't been able to defend herself against the skalk. "I'd ask her if it was possible for a witch to lose their powers, or the ability to control magic?"

Miss Delafield sighed. "That's what's been worrying you?"

Arianwyn nodded. "Among other things, of course."

Miss Delafield looked at her square on. "Every witch has a rough patch when spells don't go right, dear. You're probably just tired. You've been working so hard since you came back from Kingsport with the workload here doubling and your"—she lowered her voice—"*secret mission*! It's no wonder your spells have been a bit off. Happens to the best of us, dear." She smiled. "My mother used to say it's all about confidence, like chopping wood. If you don't swing the ax with enough confidence you'll never get it to split, dear. So, don't you be worrying about that anymore."

"Thank you, Miss Delafield," Arianwyn said. Her supervisor's words had cheered her a little. Perhaps that was it; she was tired. But still a feeling niggled in the back of her mind that there was something else at work. But what?

Miss Delafield stretched in her seat. "And now I am ordering you to take today off. We'll keep the Spellorium closed and I can stay here to mind Estar. Go on, out you go and enjoy the day."

A day off? She hadn't had a day off in weeks. Arianwyn looked at the feyling. He did look comfortable and peaceful. She smiled at Miss Delafield. "Thank you."

"Not at all, dear. My pleasure—but perhaps before you go you could rustle up some breakfast?"

Arianwyn left the Spellorium a while later after a breakfast of thick buttery toast and strawberry jam . . . and a visit from Dr. Cadbury, who administered another injection and made hopeful mumbling sounds. "I am sure he'll be back on his feet in no time," the doctor had said, peering over the top of his spectacles and smiling.

Arianwyn had taken some writing paper, a pen, and a book and headed for the meadow. Now she sat against the walls of Lull, where the sun felt almost as warm as it did on a summer's day, though she had on her coat and scarf. The new charms glowed at the edge of the wood and the qered grazed the grass, which was touched here and there with patches of frost.

She wrote to her grandmother, though she knew she wouldn't receive the letter until she returned to the bookshop in Kingsport, whenever that might be.

She read her book and tried not to think about her father and the telegram. "Don't you dare come back until after six o'clock. Or I'll have you relocated to somewhere really boring!" Miss Delafield had warned her.

For a while she considered going into Flaxsham to the movie theater, but that wouldn't be any fun on her own and she was certain neither Colin nor Salle would want to go with her at the moment. *How did it all go so wrong?*

She heard the church clock strike midday and decided to treat herself to some Grunnean potato dumplings at Bandolli's; they were almost as good as the ones her grandmother made.

"How did you enjoy that, my flower?" Mrs. Bandolli asked, clearing away Arianwyn's empty bowl.

"Delicious, thank you." Arianwyn smiled and glanced out the window just as Colin and Salle walked past the café, arm in arm and deep in conversation.

Salle spotted Arianwyn through the window and the pair pulled to a halt. They both looked at her. Arianwyn took a deep breath and smiled quickly, then studied the menu intently. She tried not to think about what they might have been talking about. She knew she wasn't the center of the universe, but something told her they had been talking about her.

The café door bells jangled as the door opened. *It could be anyone*, she thought. Bandolli's was very popular. She wasn't going to embarrass herself and turn around.

"Salle! Colin!" Mrs. Bandolli called out cheerily. "Arianwyn's in the corner there."

Terrific!

"Hi, Arianwyn."

She looked up to see Colin and Salle standing beside her table. "Hello," she said uncertainly. "Miss Delafield gave me the day off," she added quickly, as though she had to explain.

The air was thick with awkwardness.

"Can we join you?" Colin asked, at last.

What is going on?

Arianwyn could feel her cheeks burning as they lowered themselves into the seats opposite. She smiled quickly at Salle, who said rather formally, "How is Estar?"

"Still asleep, but otherwise he seems okay. Dr. Cadbury visited this morning before I left, thanks to you."

Salle shot her a curious glance, her brow wrinkled, lips pursed. She looked as though she was about to say something but Colin quickly interrupted with: "Shall I get us some cake? Yes, that's what we need. Cake!" He leapt from his seat and crossed over to the counter, where Mrs. Bandolli was waiting.

Arianwyn and Salle sat looking at each other in silence until Salle said, "Boys are so odd sometimes, don't you think?"

Arianwyn felt a small laugh bubble up in her chest. She couldn't remember the last time she had laughed. It felt like medicine.

"I'm sorry about your dad—and don't be mad at Colin. I made him tell me," Salle said quickly. "And I'm sorry I was horrid to you."

There was so much to say and yet so much had shifted and changed between them that Arianwyn didn't even know where to begin. "You were never a hanger-on," she started. "You're my best friend, Salle. The best friend I think I've ever had."

Salle reached out and grasped Arianwyn's shaking hands in her own. "I know. It was just what you said that day about people never really changing. I thought you meant me. I thought you doubted me."

"I never doubted you, Salle. I only ever doubted myself. Everyone expects so much, and I expected too much of myself as well. Everyone thinks I've changed just because I'm not an apprentice anymore. But some days I feel like I still don't have a clue what I'm supposed to be doing really."

"I know how you feel!"

"Do you think that feeling ever goes away?" Arianwyn asked.

"Maybe . . . maybe not. But does it matter—as long as you've got people to look out for you?" Salle reached into the pocket of her apron and pulled out a slightly crumpled envelope, her name and address neatly typed on its front. She held it up, a huge toothy grin stretched across her shining face.

"What's that?" Arianwyn asked, reaching for the envelope.

"The Ethel Claymore Theater have called me back for a second audition."

"What? Oh, Salle, that's wonderful! In fact, that's the best news I have heard . . . forever!"

"But I don't know if I should stay here instead, helping Dr. Cadbury. What do you think I should do, Wyn?"

They leaned over the table, pulling each other into a tight hug. Arianwyn felt warm tears on her cheeks, but she wasn't sure if they were her own or Salle's.

"Girls can be very odd sometimes," Colin said as he returned, setting three plates of lemon sponge cake onto the table.

"Thank you, Colin." Arianwyn smiled, and she and Salle pulled him into the hug as well.

They dug into their cake, and a few minutes later Mrs. Bandolli brought over three mugs of steaming hot chocolate with whipped cream on top. They sipped their drinks and ate their cake, talking about everything and nothing. Arianwyn sighed contentedly; she hadn't felt this relaxed in weeks. She felt a warmth spreading inside her, and it wasn't just the hot chocolate.

After they'd eaten, she found herself reaching into her bag and pulling out her copies of *A Witch Alone* and *The Apprentice Witch's Handbook*. She'd wanted to tell Colin and Salle about the new page for weeks, but it hadn't felt right until now.

"If I tell you something you have to keep it a secret," Arianwyn said quietly.

Colin and Salle glanced at the handbook, eyes alight. "What is it?" Salle asked.

Arianwyn retrieved the two pages, hidden for safety in the two books, and placed them carefully on the table in front of her friends. Of course, neither Colin nor Salle could see anything more than the two empty sheets of paper, but she could tell by their faces that they both knew what they were.

"Another page?" Colin asked. "But how, when?"

"Tas gave it to me." She felt a flush of shame for having kept this from them, and worried this might set their friendship back again.

They were both quiet for ages. Arianwyn's heart galloped in her chest until finally Colin said, "You did the right thing not telling Miss Newam."

"What? Really?" Arianwyn couldn't believe what she was hearing.

"She would have only interfered and upset things further, you know she would. And anyway, Estar will have the rest of the book with him. Or know where it is."

Arianwyn hoped that was true.

"He's right," Salle agreed. "Have you tried the spell? What does it do?"

Arianwyn pushed the piece of paper closer so they could read her handwriting on the bottom of the page: *The Glyph of Silence.*

Miss Delafield smiled as she pulled open the Spellorium door. "Good day, Arianwyn?" she asked. Something in her eyes told Arianwyn that she knew exactly what sort of day she'd had, and that Miss Delafield most likely had been involved in setting it all up.

"An excellent day, thank you. How is Estar?"

"Still no change. I've moved him upstairs so he's more comfortable. Mat brought an old cot by for you to use."

It felt good to have her friends back, for everything to be on a more even keel. The whole world had felt out of sorts when she had fallen out with them, and she had felt so alone.

But that was done now. They just needed Estar to wake up and tell them where the book was.

CHAPTER THIRTY-FOUR

RESULTS

It was a couple of days later when Arianwyn found herself knocking on the door of Miss Newam's office in the town hall and waiting. She fidgeted. It felt as though she had done one shoe up too tight, and her skirt was twisted. As she started to straighten it the door flew open and Miss Newam glared up at her. She was swathed in her usual gray suit, but with an oversized white lab coat flung over the top. "Ah, Miss Gribble. It's you."

"I got your note, Miss Newam. You said it was urgent?"

Miss Newam's face was pale and she looked a little disheveled, as though she hadn't had enough sleep. She nodded and stepped aside, admitting Arianwyn into her domain. The blinds were pulled down, casting the office in a permanent twilight. The desks had been pushed back against the wall and were covered in networks of glass containers. Tubes were clamped to funnels that joined to strangely shaped glass vessels holding various colored liquids. Here and there, burners were lit beneath bubbling glass beakers.

Colin waited beside the table of equipment facing Arianwyn at the opposite end of the room. He looked uncomfortable as he came forward, as though he was about to take a very hard and unexpected exam or had an appointment with the headmaster. He smiled at Arianwyn, but it wasn't convincing.

They were in trouble. That was it. Miss Newam had been biding her time and now she was going to tell them both off—maybe even hand them an official warning or some sort of punishment from the High Elder. Colin came to Arianwyn's side as Miss Newam shut and locked the door of the office. Then she turned slowly to face them both.

"I have made a discovery that I need to share with you both. I . . ." She sniffed. "I think I may have made an error of judgment."

Was she apologizing for something? Arianwyn suddenly felt more nervous than she had a moment ago.

Miss Newam beckoned for Arianwyn and Colin to join her at the long table that stood at the center of the room. It was laid with a clean white cloth and held several containers of different shapes and sizes. Even from here Arianwyn could see that they all held samples of hex. She could smell it, could feel the prickle of its dark magic in the air and against her skin. She tried not to breathe through her nose as she stood beside Miss Newam and peered at the containers. Small slips of paper were tucked under or taped to each one.

"Now, you both have to promise that what I am about to tell you goes no further than this room . . ."

"Oh, Miss Newam, I'm not sure—"

"Promise me!" she said again, gripping Arianwyn's hand with such force that she almost cried out in shock. She was clearly worried or frightened about something.

"Okay! I promise, of course." Arianwyn placed her free hand on top of Miss Newam's and patted it twice.

Miss Newam looked at Colin. "And what about you?"

"Oh yes, course. Scout's honor," he squeaked, looking rather puzzled.

Miss Newam took a deep breath and released Arianwyn's hand, smoothing back her hair—her braids, usually so perfect, were all flyaway today. She gestured to the table again.

"These samples are all from the CWA science archives." Miss Newam pointed to the collection of small containers on the left-hand side of the table. "They represent the known types of hex prevalent in Hylund and the Four Kingdoms." She straightened her glasses and looked at Arianwyn as though she should have made some wonderful exclamation.

Arianwyn nodded.

"*These* samples are what we gathered in the Great Wood." The containers on the right were marked with red and green labels. There was another container that seemed to hold just broken pieces of glass. It was also labeled with a red tag.

"The green tags all match up with the samples from the CWA, but the red ones . . . do not!" She looked at Arianwyn.

"What does that mean? How can they *not* match?"

"Exactly. When we were in the wood I found these shards of glass near to the sites where all the red-labeled hex was located." Miss Newam lifted the container full of broken glass and turned it this way and that for a moment. "The glass shards all have traces of hex on them as well, and while

I can't be certain, I think the glass must have come from some sort of container." Miss Newam said the last words deliberately slowly and then stepped back from the table.

Arianwyn let her words sink in, her mind working it all out slowly. "So do you think that the hex was brought to the Great Wood in glass containers and released on purpose?" she asked—but even as she said the words, she thought there was no way they could be true. *Who on earth would do such a thing, and why?*

"The hex hasn't spread naturally?" Colin added, his voice hardly louder than a whisper.

Miss Newam nodded. "That would seem to be correct." She straightened stiffly, lifting her chin and not looking either Arianwyn or Colin in the eye. She took a deep breath that made her shoulders shake. Then she said in a rush, "I'm sorry. I was wrong to blame the feylings, Arianwyn. Very wrong indeed." She looked straight at the wall.

Miss Newam sounded as if she'd choked on her words, but had she actually apologized to Arianwyn . . . ? She couldn't quite believe it! Arianwyn glanced quickly at Colin, who stood slightly openmouthed and gazed at her in disbelief.

"But wait, who would plant hex in the wood in the first place?" Arianwyn asked. "Who would put themselves in that sort of danger?"

"Someone who didn't want anyone to go in the wood?" Colin asked.

Arianwyn chewed her fingernail for a moment. "But why?" she sighed.

"And who?" Colin asked, his voice a nervous squeak. He looked at Miss Newam.

"Well, we need to tell the mayor at once," Arianwyn said, heading for the door.

"No wait, Miss Gribble. Arianwyn, stop!" Miss Newam called, her voice urgent, full of fear. "You can't tell anyone about this—you promised, remember? We can't be certain who it was that released the hex into the wood in the first place." Arianwyn froze, her hand hovering over the door handle.

Miss Newam was right—it could have been anyone. "So, what do we do?" Arianwyn asked, turning back to face Colin and Miss Newam.

Miss Newam looked at Colin and then at Arianwyn. She tucked her hands behind her back and looked at the floor. "We do nothing, for now. I'll report my findings as inconclusive to the council until we can find out more."

"You're going to keep this from the High Elder too?" Arianwyn asked.

Miss Newam nodded. "We cannot trust this news with *anyone* outside of this room." She looked at Colin. "Agreed?"

He nodded.

"Arianwyn?"

"Yes. Of course, if you think it's for the best."

"For our own safety, it must remain a secret," Miss Newam said, her voice heavy with dread.

There was a sharp knock on the door that startled them all.

"Miss Newam? Mr. Twine?" It was Miss Prynce. "Are you there?"

Miss Newam pulled her lab coat straight and walked slowly to the door. "Yes?" she snapped in her usual manner, as she pulled the door open.

Miss Prynce peered into the room. "It's the mayor, he says you're to—oh, Miss Gribble, you're here as well, that's good. The mayor wants to see you at once in the town square. It seems a delegation from the Council of Elders has just arrived, including the High Elder herself!"

Every witch's abilities are as unique as his or her fingerprints. Often a witch inherits her abilities from her family; most commonly skills and indeed level of magical ability are passed from mother or grandmother to child. On occasion abilities will skip generations entirely. Elder Paslow was the only witch in his family for eight generations and yet possessed significant skills from an early age.

There are some theories that suggest all witches can be traced back to the founding witches of the Four Kingdoms, those who received the original gift of magic from the great spirits.

CHAPTER THIRTY-FIVE

A DELEGATION

Arianwyn walked slowly out of the town hall, Miss Newam and Colin close behind her. Across the town square, parked in front of the Blue Ox, was Beryl, gleaming in the late afternoon light. Four smartly dressed women stood beside the bus. They could have been another group of tourists come to gaze at the Great Wood from afar, but Arianwyn knew from their stiff postures that they were certainly not tourists. She glanced back at Miss Newam, who kept her eyes fixed ahead. As they drew nearer she could hear the mayor's welcoming words: ". . . huge honor to welcome you all here to Lull, and especially you, High Elder."

He bent forward in a dramatic bow, almost tumbling into the High Elder, who was dressed in a brown tweed suit and sturdy walking boots, a green scarf wrapped tight around her neck against the chill. She looked entirely embarrassed by the whole performance. And then she saw Arianwyn. Her steely eyes gleamed and she half smiled, an expression Arianwyn remembered from their first meeting back in Kingsport. "Ah, Miss Gribble, it's good to see you."

She turned away from the mayor, who appeared to now be stuck in his bow. He clutched at his lower back.

"It's a surprise to see you, High Elder. Welcome to Lull." Arianwyn inclined her head and scanned the other three witches by the bus. She recognized the blonde-haired witch who had helped her during the royal parade, but the other two elders were complete strangers. She'd briefly hoped her grandmother might appear from Beryl, but there were no other passengers on the bus.

"I've heard wonderful things about these new charms you're using against the hex in the wood and, as I hadn't heard from you, I thought a trip to Lull was in order." The High Elder grasped her hands before her and fixed her unblinking stare on Arianwyn. "We're also under pressure to provide answers about the increased threat posed by all these dark spirit creatures. I'm hoping you might be able to help."

Did she expect a report there and then? "That's partly the reason I've not been in touch, High Elder. With the spread of hex, all manner of magical creatures and other things have come out of the wood, I'm afraid."

Suddenly the High Elder took Arianwyn by the arm and led her away from the others. "Any developments with the book, though, Miss Gribble?"

"Well, yes and no . . ."

"Oh?" The High Elder's grip tightened on her arm.

"Estar is here; we rescued him—well, actually, Gimma rescued him and me from a skalk in the wood a few days ago." She felt a cold dread thinking about that horrible creature—she could almost hear the click of its bony beak.

"And does he know where the book is?" The High Elder kept her voice low.

"He was wounded and he's been unconscious since then." Arianwyn glanced over at the elders, who were all watching carefully. "Although we're hoping he'll make a full recovery in time."

"And you say Miss Alverston recued *you*?" The High Elder chuckled as she moved Arianwyn back toward the bus again, arm in arm. "Well, that is a turn-up for the books; obviously sending her back to Lull was the right decision. And how's she been, other than seeing off skalks?"

Arianwyn studied the High Elder carefully, trying to read her face. *Why the sudden concern for Gimma?*

"She's fine," Arianwyn lied, thinking of Gimma's recent erratic behavior. Despite their differences, she didn't want to make trouble for Gimma.

"And where is she this afternoon? I'd be intrigued to hear how she dispatched that skalk." The High Elder glanced around as though Gimma might suddenly appear from nowhere.

"I haven't seen her today," Arianwyn answered.

The High Elder looked at the mayor, who was busy fiddling with his sash and medal.

"Gimma?" Mayor Belcher said, glancing around the square. "Oh, she must have gone home. She did say she was feeling unwell."

"Well, tell her that I'd like to see her tomorrow, bright and early. And, Miss Newam, how goes your research?"

The High Elder moved Miss Newam away from the group in the same way she had just done with Arianwyn.

"What are they doing here?" Colin whispered quickly.

"She said something about the hex charms, and wanting answers about the problems with dark spirits . . ." Arianwyn whispered back. Even as she spoke, it didn't seem particularly convincing—it didn't really make sense for the High Elder to suddenly descend on Lull for a research trip. "Really, I have no idea."

"It's a bit suspicious, don't you think?" Colin hissed.

Arianwyn could feel her heart racing in her chest. She couldn't shake the feeling that they were all in huge trouble, or danger, or both.

Once she'd finished talking to Miss Newam, the High Elder returned to the group. "Miss Gribble, I'll come and see you tomorrow for a full update. Shall we say ten o'clock at the Spellorium?"

"Of course, High Elder," Arianwyn replied, her fingers twisting into nervous knots.

"Very good." The High Elder turned and led the group of elders across the town square and through the open doors of the Blue Ox, leaving Colin and Miss Newam staring at Arianwyn.

"What do we do?" Colin asked, his voice coming out in an anxious squeak.

"We stick to our plan," Miss Newam hissed. "What we've discovered stays between us for now. Any one of those witches from the High Elder's inner circle could be the one who planted the hex in the wood. If they know that we know, it could put us in a far more perilous position."

They watched one another carefully, silently, for a few moments. "Okay," Arianwyn said, though she was feeling more uneasy as the moments passed. The whole thing felt dangerous and wrong.

"Miss Gribble, I suggest you go home and get the ledger ready to show the High Elder what has been happening in Lull since your return, anything that can keep them distracted from asking too much about the hex or the book," Miss Newam said. She turned to Colin. "In the meantime, we'll go and prepare the samples to show the High Elder."

"But I thought . . . ," Colin started.

"Well, of course not the *actual* samples," she snapped.

Just then, Cyril Myddleton came running toward them across the town square. "Miss, Salle says you're to come to the Spellorium at once."

"What is it?" Arianwyn hurried toward him.

"She says . . . Estar is awake!" Cyril said, clearly with no idea what the message meant.

"What?" Arianwyn gasped. She looked back at Colin and Miss Newam and smiled. "It's Estar. He's—"

Miss Newam strode to her and pulled her around, their backs to the Blue Ox. "Yes, I heard what he said. Now go back to the Spellorium quickly, but don't make it look as though you're hurrying off." Miss Newam's eyes flicked back to the Blue Ox. "Better that we know before they do."

Arianwyn turned and walked at her normal speed toward Kettle Lane, her heart thundering in her chest. She cast one quick look at the Blue Ox and was certain she saw a curtain move in one of the upstairs windows. Someone was watching.

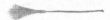

As soon as she had turned off the town square, Arianwyn broke into a run, her feet pounding against the cobbles of Kettle Lane. She burst through the door of the Spellorium and flew up the staircase. At the top, though, she stuttered to a halt. The bed was empty, and there at the small table sat Salle and Estar, sipping cups of tea and chatting as though nothing at all was unusual about the scene.

"Oh, Estar!" Arianwyn cried, clearing the last few feet in one giant leap. She caught Estar in her arms, pulling him tight, frightened to let go in case he vanished.

"Careful!" Salle cautioned, her hand on Arianwyn's back. "He's still recovering."

"Oh my goodness. Estar, what happened to you? Where had you been?" she asked, then looked at Salle. "Is he okay?"

Estar's slender blue hand wrapped around Arianwyn's cool trembling one. "I am quite well, my dear friends. All the better for being back here in Lull with you both."

Arianwyn quickly brushed at her tears and looked at Estar properly. He was thin, his skin still bruised here and there. But his eyes sparkled just as she remembered. *Perhaps things will be okay now at last?*

"Estar, I'm sorry but you have to tell us now. Where is the book?"

He looked at Arianwyn and then at Salle. Finally, he looked at the floor. "That is a long and strange story, my dear friend."

CHAPTER THIRTY-SIX

ESTAR'S STORY

E star climbed into the armchair, pulling a flowery blanket around himself like a robe. He gave a deep, weary sigh and looked off past Salle and Arianwyn, as though he was looking back through time, back into the Great Wood and Erraldur.

"When I returned to my home, all was not well. The magic of the Great Wood has always been strange and far more powerful than anything in the human lands. But the darkness had crept there as well. There were night ghasts at large in the woods that surrounded our home and we were powerless against them. We made the decision to abandon Erraldur and to flee to other feyling outposts throughout the Great Wood."

"We met some," said Arianwyn, "led by a feyling called . . . Virean—she mentioned that you'd stayed behind. They were going to a place called Edda." Arianwyn thought back to the kindness the feylings had shown them when they were lost in the wood, her fingers seeking out the little stone charm under her sweater.

"She survived?" Estar asked. He smiled at Arianwyn. "That's good. I stayed to help as many feylings as I could, but it grew more and more dangerous and in the end we all had to leave. Those of us that protected the demon library were forced to burn it to the ground, for fear it might fall into the wrong hands."

Arianwyn felt cold wash across her back. The room seemed to spin for a moment. "But the book. Tas gave me the page you sent," Arianwyn continued slowly. "But, Estar, the rest . . ."

Estar smiled. "Tas did well," he said. "But that was mostly just a message so you would know I was coming—that it came from me. I didn't . . ." An expression of sadness and confusion clouded Estar's face. "It all went so wrong so quickly. There was little we could do. Erraldur, and our beloved library . . ." He looked away, sad again.

"What happened to it?" Arianwyn's voice was flat and frightened. The *Book of Quiet Glyphs* was their only hope against the hex and the night ghasts and skalks and who knew what else. *It couldn't possibly be . . .* She shook her head, unable to finish the thought.

Estar glanced away, his eyes fluttering, and then pitched forward a little, nearly falling out of the seat. Salle reached forward to hold him steady. "He's tired, Wyn. We should let him rest."

"But the book . . ."

"It's of little consequence now, Arianwyn," Estar said calmly.

"What do you mean, Estar? Do you have it?" Arianwyn looked at the meager possessions on the floor beside the armchair.

"Pass me the pouch, please, Salle," Estar said.

Salle handed him the small leather bag. Estar opened the mouth of the pouch and then turned it inside out. Finally, he pulled the drawstring tight before opening it once again.

The air in the apartment fizzed with magic. *A magic compartment!* Arianwyn realized, hope fluttering in her chest.

Estar reached inside the pouch and slowly pulled out a small object. It may once have been a book. But now it was blackened, ruined, and barely intact. A flaking ebony fragment of paper fluttered to the floor.

Arianwyn gasped.

Estar relinquished the burnt remains and handed them to Arianwyn. "I tried to get it, but I was too late," he said, slumping against the arm of the chair, his eyelids fluttering.

"We really need to let him rest, Wyn," Salle said firmly, getting to her feet.

"But Salle, the High Elder has just arrived with some of the council . . ."

"What does that mean?" Salle asked.

"She's going to want the book."

Salle looked at the blackened mess in Arianwyn's hand. "Well, there it is," she said quietly. "I'm sorry—I know it was important to you."

"Important? Oh, Salle, this was . . . everything!" Arianwyn groaned. "And not just to me. To everyone." Her mind couldn't work its way around just what this all meant. Everything suddenly seemed pointless.

Estar coughed rather theatrically and smiled up at Arianwyn and Salle. "But what I've been trying to tell you is that the book isn't what contains the glyphs!"

"What does that mean? Is it some sort of riddle?" Salle asked, looking at Arianwyn.

"Estar, I'm not in the mood for games."

"The book was indeed magical," Estar said. "But just not in the way I thought it was. Magic isn't words and shapes: We feylings have always known this to be true. Magic is part of the natural world, like air, like laughter—not something that one can capture and pin to a page." His slender blue hands fluttered around him as he explained, his luminous eyes glowing brighter. "The book contains magic certainly, but it acts like a *mirror*," Estar went on, "showing whoever holds it the magic that resides within them, if only they look hard enough for it." He sat back in his chair and looked directly at Arianwyn.

"What does that mean, 'within them'? Are you saying that the glyphs are—" She stuttered to a halt as her mind whirled with possibilities. "*Inside* of me?"

A broad smile spread across Estar's face, his eyebrows raised high. He nodded. "Yes. And when you looked at the pages from the book, you saw the magic inside yourself, Arianwyn Gribble. The glyphs reside within you. You *are* the book."

"Oh, wow!" Salle said after a long silence. She turned to Arianwyn, her mouth hanging open in shock.

Arianwyn reached out to steady herself against the kitchen table, her legs suddenly feeling as though they were made of jelly.

"I think I'd better make us some hot chocolate," Salle said quickly as she crossed to the stove. "And you'd better sit down before you fall over."

Estar's revelation still hadn't sunk in. Even after two mugs of hot chocolate and a slice and a half of Aunt Grace's fruit loaf, Arianwyn still felt wobbly. Estar had fallen asleep as Salle and Arianwyn had chatted over the drinks and cake.

"It's quite huge to take in, though, isn't it?" Salle asked as she pulled on her coat by the Spellorium door, the frosty night air rushing inside.

Arianwyn nodded. "Please don't tell anyone, Salle. Not until we can figure it all out. The High Elder arriving just makes this all the more complicated. I wish Grandma were here." She looked across Kettle Lane to the dark houses and shops opposite. She heard the church bells sound midnight; she really should get to bed.

"You're not alone, though, Wyn. I'm here. I'll help you." Salle took her hand and squeezed. "Come and see me tomorrow as soon as you've seen the High Elder. What will you say to her?"

"I have no idea." Arianwyn shook her head. "I guess I'll think of something, though."

Salle waved as she dashed off along Kettle Lane, swallowed up by the night. Arianwyn shivered against the chill as she closed the door, locking it and pulling down the blind.

She yawned as she crossed to the stairs, finally heading for bed, though her mind whirled so much she didn't think she would ever sleep. She should feel different, Arianwyn thought; instead she felt just the same as she had before—but even more confused. The glyphs were somehow inside her, but what did that mean? Had they always been there? Or had something happened to make this come about? Did her mother or grandmother know? And why couldn't she just summon the quiet glyphs as needed?

She was halfway up the stairs when something caught her eye, a movement in the darkness of the Spellorium. She stopped and peered downstairs—nothing. Maybe she'd imagined it.

She was about to continue when she saw a shadow move quickly across the Spellorium floor. Arianwyn gasped, quickly clamping her hand over her mouth. The shadow had been quite distinct: a person wrapped in a long coat with a heavy hood pulled over their face.

The intruder stopped and started to pull at a small collection of books on the shelf behind the counter, clearly unaware they were not alone. Were they looking for the book?

Arianwyn's heart started to pump, fear fueling its rhythm. She rushed downstairs and stood in the center of the Spellorium floor. "Get out!" she shouted, a small stunning orb already crackling between the fingers of her right hand.

The intruder paused, but didn't turn around. "Where is it?" The voice was muffled and dry, like autumn leaves rustling across the street; it sounded familiar and strange at the same time. Then the figure turned and moved toward her—a fluid movement, like a scarf sliding to the floor, or water pouring silently into a glass. The intruder's steps made no sound against the floorboards, and their face was still hidden by the shadows under the hood.

"You have no right to be in here. Get out," Arianwyn said calmly, though she could feel herself trembling. "Or I'll stun you and summon the constable."

"Give. Me. The. Book!" said the intruder.

The voice rose in volume with every word, the last spat out like cannon fire. Arianwyn felt as though she had been punched. *Magic?* Then the doors and windows in the Spellorium began to shake, as if they were being blown in a gale. The next thing Arianwyn knew, she was propelled back against the hard iron staircase, her stunning orb flying uselessly to one side and fizzing to nothing. She fell hard on the floor. Pain ran across her back and she struggled to sit upright, her breath knocked from her. She saw her feyling charm stone now lay on the floor beside the counter—it must have snapped off when she fell.

So the intruder was a witch! Strange—she hadn't seen her sketch any glyphs . . .

"What's going on here?"

Arianwyn glanced up to see Estar wobbling halfway down the stairs, his yellow eyes bleary and blinking.

"YOU! *You* have the book!" The witch pointed a dark-gloved hand at Estar and surged forward, long dark coat billowing, hands reaching out toward Estar. Arianwyn struggled to her feet . . . but she was too slow, and Estar was too weak to fight back. The intruder grabbed the feyling, pulling him from the stairs and pinning him against the boards of the Spellorium floor.

"Unhand me at once!" Estar demanded. "I am Estar Sha-Vam—"

"Shut up!" the intruder rasped.

"Let him go!" Arianwyn shouted.

There was a bright flash of white light and something slammed into the stranger's side.

Bob!

The moon hare snarled and swiped with its long white legs, throwing the intruder off balance, and Arianwyn leapt up and kicked the witch away from Estar.

"Erte!" Arianwyn shouted instinctively. She felt the surge of power as the glyph and a nearby seam of magic connected. She glanced about the Spellorium for something to use and focused the energy on a small, spindly potted plant near the counter. Before the intruder could regain her balance, two thick vinelike tendrils shot out across the Spellorium and gripped her by the arms. Estar rose slowly to his feet and limped across to Arianwyn.

But no sooner had the vines snaked around the intruder's arms than they turned brown, and then gray, and finally fell to the floor in a dusty, ashy pile.

Arianwyn went cold. What kind of magic was this?

The intruder stood straighter, brushing the gray dust from her coat. Bob moved forward again, like a brilliant white light flashing across the dark Spellorium. But the intruder was ready and a swift foot flew out of the coat, hitting Bob squarely in the side. The moon hare skittered toward Arianwyn, whimpering in shock and pain.

"Bob!" Arianwyn crouched and gathered the moon hare in her arms. It buried its face against her cardigan, shaking.

"Where is the book?" the intruder demanded again, her voice rasping. "Next time I won't be so gentle with that wretched moon *rat*!"

Arianwyn had her back against the end wall of the Spellorium now, Estar behind her, Bob in her arms.

They were trapped.

Except . . . the small storeroom door was to her left. But that was just another dead end full of snotlings.

Snotlings!

She still hadn't dealt with the wretched nest. They might just provide the perfect distraction. She took two small steps toward the storeroom door, shuffling slowly, her back against the wall as the intruder moved forward again.

"If you don't give me the book, you'll be sorry!" the voice snapped.

The door handle was just a few inches out of Arianwyn's reach.

"Ready, Bob?" she whispered. The moon hare's eyes flashed brilliant blue and it was suddenly arcing through the air once more, beyond the intruder this time, causing the perfect distraction. Arianwyn wrenched the door of the storeroom open and without another thought summoned Årdra and hurled a crackling fiery spell orb into the store-room, straight at the snotling nest.

Which appeared to have gotten a little bigger.

Excellent!

The spell orb exploded into sparks and smoke just before it hit the nest, splitting it apart. A gaggle of incredibly agitated snotlings scrambled out of the nest and into the small storeroom, shrouded by a haze of smoke.

Arianwyn pushed herself and Estar back against the wall as the intruder surged angrily toward the storeroom door.

"Where are you?" the intruder demanded, coughing. "Enough of these stupid distractions—just give me the book!"

The snotlings, assuming they'd found the person responsible for their smashed, smoking nest, leapt straight at the hooded figure.

"Argh!"

The small green creatures were soon crawling all over the intruder, dangling from the long coat and hood, biting with needle-sharp teeth. "Ow!" the intruder yelped, jumping into the air. Two of the snotlings scrambled inside the hood. "Get off me!" they screeched, thrashing about to try and throw the snotlings off.

Suddenly the hood was thrown back and long pale hair cascaded over the dark coat. A bleached face snapped around, locking eyes with Arianwyn as the smoke cleared.

"Gimma?" Arianwyn gasped, dodging to one side just as a snotling flew into the wall beside her, bursting with a squelching splat on impact.

CHAPTER THIRTY-SEVEN

TWO MAGICS

Gimma glared at Arianwyn as she fell to her knees, weighed down by a dozen snotlings. "Get these wretched things off me!" she moaned, tears glistening around her eyes and running down her pale cheeks. She collapsed to the floor in a heap of dark coat and pale hair.

A few minutes and several stunning spells later, Arianwyn was kneeling on the floor of the Spellorium as she summoned up the banishing spell. The chill of the void whispered around her as the snotlings' bodies faded and vanished. Gimma glanced away, wincing, as Arianwyn completed the spell, closing the void.

Arianwyn swallowed hard. "So, are you going to tell me what's going on?" She dusted her hands on her skirt and stood up. Bob had taken up a position on the stairs and kept eyeing Gimma with great caution, tufts of white hair in a thick ridge along its back. Estar was sitting in the seat beside the empty stove, clearly exhausted.

Arianwyn studied Gimma carefully. She had changed so dramatically in the last few months that Arianwyn couldn't believe she hadn't noticed it before: her hair, always light and golden, was lifeless gray. Her skin was powdery and ashen, though her eyes still flamed brightly.

She was sitting on the floor, and now pulled the long coat tightly around herself, glowering at Arianwyn. "Don't look at me like that."

"Gimma?" Arianwyn said. Not knowing what else to do, she reached out toward Gimma. "Let me help."

"Help?" Gimma's eyes flickered, a blackness clouding across them briefly, like ink in water. "I'm beyond help now, Arianwyn. Can't you see that?"

Arianwyn took a deep breath and edged closer. "What's happening?" she asked, trying to help Gimma stand.

"Don't touch me!" she snapped.

She scuttled away from Arianwyn on all fours, backing herself up against the wall like a wounded animal and pulling the long coat around herself as though it were a shield. They watched each other in silence for a long moment, tears falling down Gimma's face. Whatever she had done, whatever she was trying to do now, this didn't seem to Arianwyn to be Gimma at all.

Arianwyn glanced uncertainly at Estar, who looked as bemused as Arianwyn felt. Then slowly, carefully, Arianwyn stepped across the Spellorium, as if negotiating a perilous footpath, to Gimma. Her face was illuminated by the street-light outside in Kettle Lane. Her eyes were wide in fear, her breathing quick and shallow.

"Come and sit by the stove," Arianwyn said calmly. She reached out to Gimma again, whose shaking hands slowly clasped her own. She let herself be led closer to the empty stove as Arianwyn laid a few logs, and conjured the fire glyph. The stove burst into life, warm light and heat slowly filling the quiet Spellorium. "Why don't you take your coat off?" Arianwyn asked, helping Gimma out of the long black coat.

As it slipped from her shoulders, Arianwyn gave a small gasp of shock. Gimma's bare arms under the coat were traced with black marks that swirled and swept across her skin in fine feathery, ferny patterns. Beautiful, somehow, and yet . . . at the same time there was something very dangerous and dark in the markings. Arianwyn felt a wave of nausea hit her.

Dark magic danced through those markings.

"What is that? Who's done this to you?" Arianwyn asked. She glanced at Estar, who raised one bushy black eyebrow.

Gimma pulled away a black leather glove on her right hand, revealing a thick, angry patch of hex that seemed to be growing around and into her flesh in heavy ridges. The sight was horrifying and yet Arianwyn couldn't tear her eyes away from it. It was so strange and so familiar, as though she'd seen the shapes before . . . in a dream, perhaps?

"Oh, Gimma . . . I'm so sorry." The Spellorium was silent except for the crackle of the fire. "It was the hex in the meadow, wasn't it?" Arianwyn asked, creeping dread spreading along her spine like icy fingers. "When we fought the night ghast."

She remembered Gimma lying in that patch of hex on the edge of the Great Wood. She remembered how she'd become paler and paler, as though she might disappear like a wisp of fog or mist. She had witnessed it all, and yet somehow missed it at the same time. A cold hard lump filled her stomach.

"The Kingsport doctors my parents paid knew nothing about how to help." Gimma sniffed. "And soon it spread from the small patch on my hand . . ." She scratched at it, wincing in pain, her skin cracked and red around the hex.

Arianwyn bit down on her lip and looked away briefly.

"And then *she* said she would help, said she'd find a way to cure the hex if . . . if I got her the book."

"What?" Arianwyn asked. "Who?"

"A witch. Some elder. She sent notes at first and then she came to our house in Kingsport when my parents were away, said she would help if I made sure she got the *Book of Quiet Glyphs*."

"Someone from the council?" Arianwyn asked, confused. Another wave of nausea hit her, but not from the dark magic marking Gimma's waxen skin. "Are you sure?"

"Maybe. She looked different each time she came . . ."

"Different?" Arianwyn asked.

"Her *face* was different, somehow—I don't know!" Gimma shouted.

It sounded to Arianwyn very much like a glamour spell or charm had been used. They were dangerous spells, the magic unstable and unreliable. They had all but been banned.

"I think she's here, in Lull," Gimma continued, "with those other witches. What if she's come for the book? I don't know what she'll do if I don't give it to her—perhaps she'll just wait until the hex takes over me completely." Her eyes filled with tears. "I'm begging you to help me, Arianwyn. Please give me the book."

Fear drove Arianwyn to her feet; she paced back and forth across the Spellorium. What could she do? What could she say? The room felt suddenly chillier, despite the fire flickering away in the stove. Arianwyn swallowed and looked at Estar, who bowed his head.

"We should tell her," he said softly.

"Tell me what?" Gimma asked.

Arianwyn was about to speak but Estar coughed, disturbing the heavy silence. "The book has been . . . damaged."

Gimma's head snapped around and she stared at the blue feyling. "What?" she asked quickly, and then added, "You're lying."

Estar bowed his head. "I assure you, I am not. I am truly sorry. Fetch it, Arianwyn."

Arianwyn took a deep shuddering breath and got to her feet, then went quickly up into the apartment and retrieved the black ashy remains of the *Book of Quiet Glyphs*.

She handed the book to Gimma, who took it in her shaking hands.

"No," Gimma said sadly.

They were quiet for a while. Arianwyn stared at Gimma's hand and the hex marking her arms. Now she remembered what it had made her think of: the letter from her father about the Urisian witch marked with "black tattoos."

"Oh, this is so boggin bad," Arianwyn breathed. "The hex is affecting your spells, isn't it? That's why your magic seems so much stronger than before?"

Gimma nodded her head and looked away. "I liked it at first," she said quietly. "I thought, this is what proper witches feel like. Strong and powerful. Like you could do anything."

"You *are* a proper witch," Arianwyn said.

"Hardly . . . it was always a struggle for me. I've felt so alone, nobody to talk to. No one I could tell about what was happening." Her eyes flicked up to meet Arianwyn's.

"You should have told me or Miss Delafield, or your uncle, at least—somebody." And yet Arianwyn had kept all *her* own worries to herself as usual, hiding her fears and insecurities from the world.

Perhaps she and Gimma were not so different after all.

"I thought the hex's magic would make me stronger, and no one needed to know the power wasn't exactly my own. But after a while, things changed . . . the hex, it's . . ." Gimma stared off into space.

"What?" Arianwyn asked, her skin prickling, her mind flashing to the sight of the stagget, the hex laced through its antlers, struggling against itself.

"It's like I can feel it. Like it's waiting in the back of my mind," Gimma continued.

She's making no sense, Arianwyn thought. "What do you mean, Gimma?"

Gimma's eyes locked with Arianwyn's, watery and wide with unspeakable terror. "The hex, it can feel. It can sense things."

"What? No. It's just—" Arianwyn's mind flashed back to the stagget again, its too-dark eyes and heartrending cry.

"The hex is *alive*," Gimma said slowly. "It can see. It can hear. And it can feel . . . everything."

Cold dread crashed against Arianwyn. "But that's not possible!" she breathed, stepping away from Gimma.

"It's as real as you and me," Gimma said, tears falling down her dry gray cheeks. "And I can feel it twisting around me, tighter and tighter and tighter. Like it's wrapped around my soul. There are moments when I can barely remember who I am. I don't even remember coming here this evening." She coughed back a sob.

Could Gimma have somehow been responsible for spreading the hex through the Great Wood? Arianwyn suddenly wondered. But something in Gimma's terrified eyes told her that wasn't possible.

"I'll help you stop it, of course I will," Arianwyn said quickly, though she hadn't a clue where to even begin. She looked at Estar, who only shrugged. "I could get Miss Delafield . . ."

"No, Arianwyn, please."

"Well, who, then? Perhaps the High Elder can—"

Arianwyn was suddenly flying back across the Spellorium as Gimma shoved her hard in the chest.

"NO!" Gimma roared, suddenly on her feet, an orb of dark crackling energy tumbling over and over in her palm. She cried out in frustration and fear, shaking the dark spell away. A dark film swirled across her eyes as they widened in terror.

Arianwyn understood. The hex was gaining control again. What could she do?

"Gimma, fight it," Arianwyn said, gripping Gimma's hands in her own, ignoring the rough ridges of hex. A flash of inspiration burst into her mind. "Gimma, remember the pangorbak. Remember what Miss Delafield said. Turn away from it, ignore it. The more attention you offer it the more it will grow."

She saw confusion rush over Gimma's face before she nodded in agreement.

"Will that actually work?" Estar asked, leaning forward in his chair and watching Gimma carefully as her breathing started to slow, the effort clear on her face.

"It's all I can think of . . . unless you have another idea that might help?" Arianwyn said. And then something caught her eye: Glinting on the floor near the counter lay the feyling stone charm that Virean had given her.

She remembered the hex charms hanging in the trees at the edge of the Great Wood. Arianwyn thought back to that night, and how happy Gimma had been. She had even laughed. Had the charms helped her?

"A charm . . . ," she breathed.

"I don't think this is the time—" Estar began, but Arianwyn ignored him.

"Hang on, Gimma!" she shouted, scrabbling quickly to her feet. She moved behind the counter and started to pull open drawer after drawer, searching in the dark for the hex charm components. She pulled out a small glass sphere, placing it carefully on the countertop with trembling hands. Next, she reached into the drawer of small silver beads—and after that, a sliver of kartz stone that gave off the faintest glimmer of light. Her supplies of padora flower petals was low, but she added those next. "Estar, pass me the charm stone." Arianwyn pointed to the stone charm on the floor and Estar handed it over, his face lighting as he caught onto her plan.

She glanced up to check on Gimma. Her eyes were shut and she seemed to be mumbling something to herself.

Arianwyn secured the lid on the charm and lifted it, the kartz stone emitting a soft glow.

"Will it work?" Estar asked.

"I hope so."

Arianwyn moved carefully toward Gimma and reached out to touch her gently on the shoulder. She jumped, her eyes opening quickly, the inky film still swirling across her irises. "I need to put this around your neck, Gimma." Arianwyn reached around her, fastening the charm. "Årdra," she said gently as she tried to activate the charm with the protective fire glyph, just as they had done for the charms around the Great Wood. She could feel magic flowing nearby, but she could also feel the hex, blocking it. She focused, held the glyph in her mind as the magic flowed around the dark energy of the hex and at last connected. There was a small flash of light and Arianwyn pressed the warm glowing glyph toward the new charm around Gimma's neck.

There was a crackle of magic, sharp and sudden. Sparks flew in the air around the two girls as the charm worked against the dark magic of the hex. Arianwyn could feel the wild pulse of the spell beating in the air like the urgent wings of a sparrow.

And then all was still.

There were a few long minutes of near-silence, broken only by Gimma's fast breathing and the quiet fizz of magic in the air. At last, her eyes fluttered open, and Arianwyn saw that the inky swirls had disappeared. Instead, Gimma's cool, tear-filled eyes met her own. She gave a gasp, like someone who had emerged from deep underwater.

"Well?" Arianwyn asked.

Gimma's breathing slowed and she felt for the charm around her neck with shaking hands. "I can still feel it, the hex. But it's contained, trapped almost." Her lips formed the faintest smile. "You did it, Arianwyn."

"We have to tell the High Elder," Arianwyn said quickly.

"No, Arianwyn, I can't," Gimma said, rising unsteadily to her feet.

But Arianwyn was quicker. She grasped Gimma's arms, gently, firmly, and stared into her red-rimmed eyes. "We have to, Gimma. She is the only one who can help us."

Gimma shook her head, like an uncooperative child. "No. We can tell Miss Delafield, or your grandmother . . ." Her voice was pleading, frightened.

"Miss Delafield would just have to tell the High Elder herself, and my grandmother is still away traveling. I don't know when she'll be back. We can't wait. I'm not entirely sure the charm will last that long."

"But you'll make another one, won't you?" Gimma asked, clutching again at the charm.

"Yes, Gimma. Of course," Arianwyn said calmly. "But we still need to speak to the High Elder. This is too big now.

Too dangerous. And she needs to know one of the council threatened you. Who knows what else they might be planning, or doing?" Arianwyn thought of the hex samples and Miss Newam's test results.

Gimma was trembling as she gripped tightly to Arianwyn's arms. "You'll go with me?" she asked.

"Of course I will," Arianwyn replied.

CHAPTER THIRTY-EIGHT

MEETING THE HIGH ELDER

Fifteen minutes later, Arianwyn, Estar, and Gimma waited near the huge empty fireplace in the main room of the Blue Ox. The clock on the mantelpiece read two o'clock—Arianwyn had had to hammer on the door for ages to wake Uncle Mat, who'd quickly left to summon the High Elder.

After a few moments, Salle appeared—Arianwyn was sure Uncle Mat would have woken her. "Oh my goodness, what's happened? Are you all right, Gimma? Estar? Arianwyn? What's going on?"

Before Arianwyn could answer, the High Elder appeared in the doorway, followed by Uncle Mat and Aunt Grace. The High Elder was wrapped in a thick dressing gown with bright blue bed socks peeking from underneath. Her hair lay in two thick braids over her broad shoulders.

"Miss Gribble?" she said, yawning. "What is the meaning of this?" She spotted Gimma. "Miss Alverston? What on earth has happened?"

Arianwyn was about to speak when Gimma, her hands shaking, slowly pulled off her gloves, revealing the thick ridges of hex.

Everyone gasped, knowing full well what they saw and how dangerous it was. Salle took a step backward, but the High Elder did not. She stayed calm, stepped forward, and bent down to look at the hex before peering up at Gimma. "This will have been having some interesting effects on your spells, no doubt?"

Gimma nodded cautiously as tears streamed down her face again. "I'm sorry."

"I'd best fetch the mayor," Uncle Mat mumbled quickly from the doorway before disappearing back through the corridor.

"And I think we could all use some nice hot tea," said Aunt Grace brightly, walking through to the kitchen. Several lamps flickered on in the hallway, and Arianwyn heard the distant clatter of the kettle.

"I used a charm," Arianwyn offered quickly, once the room was quiet. "Similar to the ones we used at the edge of the wood to try and stop the hex. Or at least slow it."

Gimma pulled the charm free from under her long black coat, the glass catching the light.

The High Elder took the glass sphere in her fingers and moved it this way and that, examining the individual components inside. "My word," she breathed. "Is it working?"

Gimma nodded. "I can still feel the hex, but it's not . . . in control anymore."

"This is strong work, Miss Gribble," the High Elder said as she continued to study the charm. "It's no mean feat to counteract the hex in this way." Then her attention turned to Estar. "You are the feyling who assisted Miss Gribble?"

"I am Estar Sha-Vamirian, Alemar of the third Jalloon." Estar bowed low.

"Does he have the book?" the High Elder asked, ignoring Estar and looking at Arianwyn.

Arianwyn blushed indignantly—annoyed at the High Elder for her rudeness to Estar—but she pulled the charred remains of the book from her pocket and handed them over. Her eyes flicked to Salle, and prayed some silent unspoken message would pass between them so Salle would know not to mention what Estar had said about the true nature of the *Book of Quiet Glyphs*.

"All destroyed?" the High Elder asked quietly as she tried to look at the few remaining pages that clung to the binding of the book. They were blackened and useless. "Nothing was salvaged?" Her voice trembled. "Nothing at all?" The High Elder's voice rose sharply now. She swore and slammed the book down onto one of the nearby tables, smashing it against the wood with her large hand. Everyone jumped. Then she sank into a seat and stared at Arianwyn and Gimma. "Is it really all gone?" she said more calmly.

"We still have the original page that has the shadow glyph on it, but that's it." Arianwyn hadn't known that she would lie until she did, keeping the glyph of silence a secret. Miss Newam's warnings sang in her mind. She wanted to help Gimma, but she couldn't bring herself to tell the High Elder more than was completely necessary.

But the High Elder didn't seem to be listening to her now, anyway; she was entirely distracted by Gimma, unable to look away from the markings of the hex on her hands and forearms.

"I will need to return to Kingsport at once and discuss this with the full council," the High Elder said quickly. "You will have to return as well, Miss Alverston."

Gimma looked at Arianwyn, her face carved with a look of terror. She shook her head and looked pleadingly at Arianwyn. "I can't . . ."

"What's that?" the High Elder asked.

Arianwyn took a deep breath and looked at the floor. "Gimma was . . . threatened."

"Threatened? By whom?" The High Elder didn't sound as though she entirely believed this.

"By . . . an elder, she thinks," Arianwyn said quietly. "Possibly someone on the council." Arianwyn fixed her gaze on the High Elder. "We think they used a glamour spell to disguise themselves."

Gimma looked away, and Arianwyn knew she was crying again.

"What? Is this true, Miss Alverston?"

Gimma nodded.

"And when did this all begin?" The High Elder had folded her arms over her chest, standing a little straighter.

"When I first went to Kingsport, after the summer."

"That is a very serious allegation, you do understand that?"

"I think that's why she hasn't told anybody until now. The elder who threatened Gimma wanted her to try and steal the book," Arianwyn explained. "She said if she found it, she would cure Gimma of the hex."

The High Elder looked away, off through the dark windows of the Blue Ox. "This is incredibly serious," she said. "If you are correct, then we have an enemy among us." She looked around at Estar, Gimma, Arianwyn, and Salle. "That remains classified until I can investigate further and figure out what my next move should be. You are to share it with no one at all, do you all understand?" Her voice was a low growl.

Everyone nodded.

"Miss Alverston, you had better remain here in Lull for your own safety for now, until I can discover what is going on and who can be trusted. I shall return to Kingsport first thing tomorrow."

Mayor Belcher arrived soon afterward. He was pale as he followed Uncle Mat into the room. Gimma rushed toward him at once and he caught her up in a tight hug. "My dear, whatever is the matter?" he asked, looking around at the odd gathering in the Blue Ox. "What is going on here?"

Aunt Grace bustled in carrying a tray full of mugs of tea and, after a few minutes, the mayor was brought up to date with the worrying news about Gimma's condition. His face had grown paler and paler, especially as he saw the thick ridges of hex on her hands. Arianwyn feared he might shove Gimma aside and run away. But he only clung to her tighter, and after the story was told he said bravely, "I won't let anyone harm you, don't you fear."

In the midst of that dark night, it made Arianwyn think that everything might be all right.

CHAPTER THIRTY-NINE

REUNION

I t was more than a week later, an icy-cold morning. Life in Lull seemed to have returned to something like normality.

Arianwyn had just opened the Spellorium, waving to Millicent Caruthers as she hurried along Kettle Lane to open her boutique. She had a mug of tea on the counter and was enjoying a few moments of peace and quiet before the day got busy.

The High Elder had returned to Kingsport and there had been no further news on her search for the traitor in the council. In fact, there had been no news at all.

Gimma was recovering slowly—after a few days' rest her skin had started to regain its color. The charm seemed to be working, halting the further spread of hex, though the thick black ridges still ravaged her hands, and the strange swirling patterns still marked her arms. She had not left the mayor's house since that night.

"We should go and see Gimma later," Arianwyn said to Estar as he came down the stairs, Bob close behind. "I want to replace her charm before the spell degrades too much."

"A wise precaution." Estar smiled.

Arianwyn took a sip of her tea and turned to retrieve something from the shelf behind the counter. As she did she heard the bell charm sing out as the door opened. "I'll be right with you," she called brightly, lifting down a small box of charm components that had been delivered the day before but she hadn't yet gotten around to unpacking.

As she turned back to the counter she saw a tall woman with long silver hair standing in the doorway, two suitcases at her side and a bright yellow scarf thrown over her shoulder.

"Grandma?" Arianwyn gasped, unsure for a moment that she wasn't actually seeing things.

Grandmother smiled. "Hello there. I thought I'd surprise you!"

It felt as though it took an age, but it must have only been seconds before Arianwyn threw herself into her grandmother's arms, squeezing her as tight as she could.

"Oh, now then," Grandmother chuckled. "That's a welcome and a half!"

She smelled of lemon soap and books and warm sunshine. It took Arianwyn back to a thousand happy memories. "Oh, Grandma," she sobbed, unable to hold it in. "I've missed you so much. I didn't think you were going to be back for another few weeks."

"The High Elder asked me to come back," Grandmother said calmly. "She told me about the book, and all about poor Gimma. It's just awful. I hear she's already launched a full investigation. Oh, hello there, Estar." Grandmother bowed gracefully to the blue feyling and then bent to scratch the moon hare's too-long ears. "Yes, I've missed you too, Bob!"

"Who do you think would do something like that?" Arianwyn asked as she lifted her grandmother's suitcases over the doorstep and carried them to the counter.

"I really don't know. There are several newer members of the council who I don't know so well, but that doesn't necessarily mean it would be one of them. I think everyone is under suspicion." She pulled off her jacket and scarf.

"But not you, surely?" Arianwyn asked.

"Everyone is a suspect. Unless Gimma can identify the witch in question, which if they are using a glamour charm or spell will be nearly impossible."

"And Gimma is terrified," Arianwyn said quietly.

"Well, I'm not surprised." Grandmother settled herself in the seat next to the small potbellied stove, which was lit, warm flames dancing inside. "Now, I have something for you, but I want you to remain calm," she said, her voice suddenly very serious again. Arianwyn didn't like it. "This arrived just before I set sail for Hylund. I wanted to deliver it to you myself." Grandmother pulled a small square of paper from her jacket pocket and handed it to Arianwyn. "I gather the High Elder herself pulled some strings on our behalf."

Arianwyn recognized the shape of the telegram. Her heart paused for a second, fear gripping it in tight hands.

She took the slip of paper and gazed down at the boldly typed letters:

```
(PRIORITY COMMUNICATION)
MADAM MARIA STRONELLI,
  C/O HOTEL GALLOZI, 39 VIA ROSA, SAN
SERENO
  GRUNNEA
  VERIFIED-SGT. OLIVER E. GRIBBLE
S/KD6911779 LOCATED AND ALIVE FURTHER
DETAILS TO FOLLOW
  T. S. MORTIMER-GREAVE, SECRETARY OF WAR
```

It felt as though her heart was about to burst from her chest. The room seemed to spin and pitch for a second.

Her father was alive. They had found him and he was alive!

She looked up at her grandmother, who was beaming from ear to ear, her own eyes wet with tears. A small sob, followed by a laugh, escaped Arianwyn's mouth. "He's alive!" she called.

"And will soon be on his way back home, I believe. I need to make more inquiries."

"Oh, Grandma." Arianwyn buried her face into her grandmother's jacket and sobbed. She cried with happiness for the news of her father coming home, she cried for poor Gimma, she cried thinking about the new riddle of the glyphs and how on earth she was ever going to figure out how she could discover the truth of them. She cried for all that and a dozen small and big things besides. There, in her Spellorium with her grandmother's arms wrapped tightly around her, she felt safe enough to let go.

"So did you find any other witches . . . ?"

"Like you?" Grandmother asked as she sipped on her tea. She watched Arianwyn carefully over her mug, then sighed. "There were rumors, but I only managed to go around in circles. Not that I suppose it really matters now anyway, without the book."

Arianwyn glanced quickly away, unable to meet her grandmother's eyes. "Oh, I should show you these new charm globes I've started using," she said quickly.

"What is it, Arianwyn? I know well enough by now when you're keeping something from me."

Arianwyn looked at Estar, who smiled and bowed his head.

Then she smiled at her grandmother, took a few steadying breaths, and eventually said, "What if the book wasn't lost? What if it was never even a book we should have been looking for in the first place?"

CHAPTER FORTY

A NEW SPELL

E arly the next morning Arianwyn stood at the edge of the Great Wood. The trees were white with frost. The qered herd moved around the meadow, calling happily back and forth with their long low song. Grandmother, Colin, Salle, and Estar stood behind her, all bundled up in coats, hats, and scarves. Arianwyn glanced over her shoulder. "I'm not sure this is a good idea . . . what about the hex?"

"It's safer to try this out here than in town," Grandmother cautioned.

"But we don't even know if this is going to work. I might not be able to find the glyphs without the book."

"Perhaps," Estar said quietly, peering at Arianwyn down his long blue nose. "But you won't know until you try." He smiled.

He was right, of course. Even though the book had gone, there was still a way to discover the quiet glyphs. And Arianwyn was the key to that. She had the glyphs within her, somehow, buried in her mind or soul. She still didn't quite understand it, and if she tried to think about it too much, it gave her a headache.

But it didn't matter. Every day there were more sightings of dark spirit creatures at large across Hylund—and Arianwyn had to find new ways of protecting people.

"Well . . . maybe we should go back to town and leave you and Estar alone for your discoveries?" Grandmother smiled gently. She gave Arianwyn the briefest of hugs. "It may be safer for everyone else . . ."

Arianwyn took a deep breath. She felt suddenly unprepared and horribly nervous, like a nest of worms was writhing in the pit of her stomach.

"Do you want us to stay?" Colin asked.

"Yes, let us stay?" Salle pestered.

She really did want them to. She was nervous, even with Estar to help her. But it really wouldn't be safe for them to be anywhere near, just in case the first new glyph she summoned, assuming she could do it, turned out to be something worse than the shadow glyph.

She shook her head. "I don't think that's a very good idea."

"Understood." Colin smiled, his hair flopping across his eyes as it so often did. "We'll see you later then, at Bandolli's for lunch?"

Arianwyn nodded.

"Oh, potato dumplings?" Grandmother called, getting another nod in reply.

"Good luck, then," Salle said, squeezing her friend into a tight hug. As she drew back, she pressed a small item into Arianwyn's hand.

Arianwyn gazed down to see it was the luck charm she had made for Salle for her audition in Flaxsham over the summer, the thyme leaves all dried and curled up, the veren stone still glistening. The magic had long since faded, but it didn't really matter. "Thank you, Salle," she replied.

"Oh, and we got you this." Colin blushed as he handed her a small parcel wrapped in bright tissue paper. "We know we missed your birthday, Wyn . . . sorry."

Arianwyn pulled the tissue paper away and stared down at the small leather notebook that nestled in her hands. The glyph of silence was embossed on the front.

"We thought you could use it to record the new spells," Salle offered with a broad smile.

"Thank you," Arianwyn said. "It's beautiful."

She watched as Grandmother, Salle, and Colin made their way back toward Lull, leaving her alone with Estar at the edge of the Great Wood. The nearby hex charms still emitted a faint glow, but how long would they work for, she wondered?

"Come along, then," Estar said gently.

They walked on into the wood, soon reaching a small clearing. The high walls of Lull were still just visible through icy branches.

There was no sign of hex nearby.

"Are you ready?" Estar asked.

"Yes, I think so." She felt her pulse quicken and her throat tighten.

"Close your eyes," Estar said softly.

Arianwyn's other senses suddenly took over, and she felt as though the quiet woodland was suddenly alive with the sounds of hundreds of animals and birds all scrabbling around, calling to one another, and generally making a distracting racket.

"Somewhere in your mind, the glyphs *are* waiting," Estar said.

Her mind suddenly conjured all the cardinal, secondary, and quiet glyphs at once—they seemed to swoop and zoom behind her eyes. She could feel their individual powers brush her consciousness, and she felt the air around her crackle and spark.

But there were no other new glyphs waiting there. A sudden squawk from a nearby bird distracted her. Her eyes flew open and she looked down at Estar. "I can't do it here, there are too many distractions. I can't . . . clear my mind enough for this."

"Well, who on earth said anything about *clearing your mind*? What a preposterous notion." Estar sniffed. "You humans do have the strangest ideas when it comes to magic, you know."

"But I thought—"

"Clearing your mind is all well and good when you want it empty for something else, but you need to find something *buried* in your mind, in your soul! Quite a different process, believe me. Embrace the chaos, Arianwyn!"

She angrily brushed her hair out of her face. She stretched and yawned, frustration bubbling inside her. Then she closed her eyes again, and this time she let all her thoughts rush at her at once. Gimma, the book, the High Elder, and the darkness that appeared to have crept into the Council of Elders. Then she was thinking about what she would have for her lunch, then she thought about Colin and his dark floppy hair. She could hear Salle laughing. She saw her grandmother framed in the doorway of the Spellorium. She saw her father wounded but coming home. She saw her mother smiling down at her as she tucked her into bed. A memory, or maybe a dream—she wasn't sure anymore. In among all of this, the glyphs swarmed and drifted like bright flakes of snow.

But she hadn't seen a new glyph. Not one. Not yet.

"Open your eyes!" Estar said quietly in her ear.

Her eyes fluttered open. She hadn't realized she had raised her arm, and quite unconsciously in the air before herself she had drawn a shape.

No, not a shape. A glyph!

A new glyph!

The shape was pale blue and it curled and twisted in a way that was both familiar and so very strange. Arianwyn could feel its power already, though what it could do she had no idea.

"Is it . . . ?" she asked Estar, scared that by speaking she would somehow chase it away. She stared hard at the new glyph, tracing the shape with her eyes. Something was missing. She didn't know how she knew, but she did.

She raised her hand and in the air before her she carefully completed the new shimmering glyph.

With the last curl of its shape, it flashed brilliant pale blue in the air before them.

From somewhere nearby, Arianwyn detected the pull from a seam of magic. It flowed speedily, easily toward the glyph, like water rushing around rocks and stones. For a moment nothing happened. And she thought she had surely made a mistake.

But then the glyph burst into light, a light so brilliant and bright that Arianwyn had to shield her eyes.

The new spell was formed.

SPIRIT CREATURE GLOSSARY

Extracts from *A WITCH ALONE: A MANUAL FOR THE NEWLY QUALIFIED WITCH*

Feylings
These rare magical creatures feature heavily in the mythology of the Four Kingdoms and beyond, but no two descriptions ever match. Some believe they are a crossbreeding of spirit and dark spirit creatures—others believe they are something altogether different.

Gant
Standing at over twenty feet tall, gants are gentle spirit creatures that live primarily along coastal regions. They use their two long trunks to communicate and find food, mostly crustaceans and seaweed. Their dung can be utilized for various magical purposes.

Harvest Bogglin
The skin of these dark spirit creatures, which have not been seen for seventy-five years, is toadlike and camouflaged, though their bright red eyes will often give them away. Extremely territorial, they are known to claim whole fields, preventing crops from being harvested.

Moon Hare
These rare spirit creatures were once a common sight across the Four Kingdoms and beyond. They are neither male nor

female and are believed to be born from eggs. Partly scaled and partly covered in pure white fur, they are naturally shy but incredibly intelligent.

Night Ghast
No recorded sightings for nearly a thousand years. These extinct dark spirits stood at over nine feet tall, with a single orifice serving as eye, mouth, and nose. They were extremely violent and hungry for living creatures, possessing a distinctive insectlike call.

Pangorbak
Pangorbaks are dark parasitic spirits that thrive on attention. When they attach themselves to a host, they resemble a slug. Over the course of a few hours they will grow tentacles and expand rapidly. If they are not removed quickly, they can cause serious damage or death.

Qered
Standing at over nine feet tall, these horselike spirit creatures are scaled, with long flowing manes and tails. Gentle herbivores, their call is similar to that of whales and can carry for over seventy miles. They live in large herds and mate for life.

Razlor
These rarely seen dark spirit creatures are winged, doglike beasts, with oily black skin and bony but strong bodies. They are expert hunters and usually do so in small packs of three to five creatures. They were once hunted for sport.

Skalk

No recorded sightings for seven hundred years. Adaptable to most conditions, these dark spirit creatures were easily identified by their large bony beaks, dark matted hair, and scuttling movements. They were fast and incredibly dangerous.

Snotlings

Common and pesky dark spirit creatures that build hibernation nests in shadowy, sheltered places. She-snotlings have thick crests of spines, are generally larger than the males, and can deliver a sharp and painful bite. If you spot signs of a nest, it is best to deal with it at once.

Stagget

These sacred spirit creatures guard forests and moorland and generally live in large herds. They resemble deer and are often mistaken for them, but they are much larger and their antlers are usually gold or silver.

Velastamuri, commonly referred to as "shrieking ritts"

These spirit creatures have small birdlike bodies, but a massive ten-foot wingspan. They emit a high-pitched shrieking noise while in flight, which is often mistaken for their call, but is actually a result of the air passing through their wings.

Wild Brunkun

These gentle spirit creatures grow to no larger than four inches in height and nest in thistle patches. Wild brunkun are entirely covered in thick brown hair, which they shed and regrow every month. They have a fondness for sugar.

Winged Grippets
These dark spirit creatures stand around fifteen inches tall, and have hoglike faces and tusked mouths. Each of their four legs end in many-fingered, dextrous hands. They are not terribly dangerous unless they swarm, when they can cause considerable damage and disruption.

= Acknowledgments =

So now we are two!

Now let me tell you, second books are just a little bit tricksy, I'm not going to lie—tricksier than I thought they would be, in fact. But, as ever, I am so thankful to numerous wonderful people who gave their kind love and support whilst I was writing *A Witch Alone*.

My thanks, as ever, to Imogen Cooper and the Golden Egg Academy family for continuing to offer support post-hatching and my transformation into a chicken!

Lorraine Gregory and Vashti Hardy, the best writing friends you could ever ask for. Thank you for always being there for every little triumph and occasional tragedy, for wisdom, laughs, and for helping to come up with the title! And sorry for getting the giggles during the zombie apocalypse! Much love.

Karen Minto and Sian Schwar—thank you for helping to uncover Gimma's rather dark side at the Golden Egg workshop. I pray I'm never interrogated by either of you ever again.

To the most brilliant agent ever, the incomparable Kate Shaw (total legend!) for doing all the business stuff so I don't have to, for thoughtful input on all levels, and for always making time and telling it like it is. I love working with you.

Thanks to my wonderful colleagues at Cambridgeshire Libraries for all the support, especially Brenda, Rosie, Anne, Lou, Sue, Yueh-Wen, and Marjorie, who have ensured I didn't get too "authory" on them and coping with *everything!* I've had three wonderful bosses whilst writing my second book; huge thanks to Lynda, Elaine, and Sue for being so flexible, supportive, and excited—especially Elaine—who didn't mind when I totally fluffed up my calendar . . . once or twice!

Lots of love to the splendiferous Chicken House team, Rachel H, Jazz, Laura S, Laura M, Esther, and Sarah, for all the little and massive things they do behind the scenes, for making everything fun, for making me feel like part of the family, and just being total stars! Extra big hugs to Elinor for helping my little witch find new homes around the world—something I never even dreamt of happening!

And to my fellow Chicken House authors especially Ally, Maya, Kiran, Maz, Kate, Emma, Sarah, Natasha, Laurel, Lucy, and Chris. You are all inspiring and brilliant.

Also all my love and thanks to the Scholastic US team for all their support and encouragement from across the wide, wide oceans. Especially to Sam Palazzi, my editor, Lauren Donovan (my stage mom!), and everyone who has helped bring Arianwyn and all her friends and foes to America and Canada. And my grateful love and thanks to the brilliantly talented Elizabeth Knowelden for her beautiful reading of the audio for *The Apprentice Witch*. You made it far more magical than I ever hoped it could be.

Special thank yous to Dea, Buffy, Nikki, Chris, and Roz for all being champions of the book and for your friendship. A magical and surprising bonus to being published in different countries are the people you connect with as a result and you are the very best of the bunch!

To all the many brilliant reviewers and wonderful bloggers who took time to read and share lovely words about *The Apprentice Witch*—thank you a squillion times over!

To all the wonderful booksellers who have taken *The Apprentice Witch* to their hearts and pressed it into the hands of readers across the US and Canada and been excited for the second book—here it is!

Thank you to my wonderful family and gorgeous friends for being the very best fans the books could have, for being twice as excited as I am all the time, and for all buying copies of *The Apprentice Witch* like they were going out of fashion.

And the most thanks of all to the most superb UK editors, Barry, Rachel L, and Kesia for their patience whilst we got everything right, for keeping me on track, and reminding me of the important stuff, for letting me go a bit wrong and helping me find my way back again and for staying calm all the way through. Extra special thanks to Kesia for her most fantastic idea, which gave *A Witch Alone* a wonderful ending, for cheering me on, and for loving all the characters and taking as much care of them as I do and for making sure Arianwyn maintains a balanced diet and doesn't just eat chocolate cake for lunch . . .

And last, but never least—dear reader, you've done it again, read this far—aren't you super! Thank you for coming on another adventure with us, and I hope you join us for many more. You are the book's most vital ingredient, completing the story with your own amazing imagination. So, thank YOU! You are the very best.